EXPOSURE

EXPOSURE

Kathryn Harrison

RANDOM HOUSE
NEW YORK

This is a work of fiction. The characters and plot are products of the author's imagination. Some scenes take place in famous department stores whose actual names are mentioned. However, the characters, incidents, and dialogue in these scenes are wholly fictional. The author possesses no knowledge regarding the security systems of the stores or the stores' policies and practices regarding theft.

Copyright © 1993 by Kathryn Harrison

All rights reserved under International and Pan-American Copyright Conventions. Published in the United States by Random House, Inc., New York and simultaneously in Canada by Random House of Canada Limited, Toronto.

Library of Congress Cataloging-in-Publication Data

Harrison, Kathryn.
Exposure/Kathryn Harrison.—1st ed.
   p.   cm.
ISBN 0-679-40942-4
I. Title.
PS3558.A67136D37   1993   813'.54—dc20   92-22130

Manufactured in the United States of America

98765432

FIRST EDITION

Book design by Carole Lowenstein

for Joan

A photograph is a secret about a secret. The more
it tells you, the less you know.

DIANE ARBUS

The author wishes to thank all those who helped with the research for this novel, including Pamela Harrison Chizkov, Holly R. Gotcher, A. M. Homes, Al Kulik, M.D., Anmy Le, Katherine Lonergan, J. Brad McCampbell, Katharine McCaw, Kevin Roman, Mindy Ross, Jill Simonsen, Sidney Stein, M.D., and especially Robert Younger.

Thank you to Kate Medina and to Binky Urban for their support, which transcends the completion of a single book.

And, of course, thank you to my coach.

EXPOSURE

New York
June 27, 1992

As the taxi cuts through the rain, Ann struggles out of her black skirt, keeping her eyes on the driver as she hurries to free the heel of her black satin pump. She kicks the crumpled garment under the front seat as he lunges out his window to yell at a street vendor. He mutters obscenities, weaves in and out of the heavy traffic; sweat runs down the back of his hairy neck and rings his collar. She hopes he isn't going to be a problem.

Sitting in her blouse and slip, Ann examines the spot where she inadvertently nicked the dark green suede of the new skirt when she pried off the alarm device. She rubs the nap with her finger, and satisfied that the offending mark is nothing a stiff brush won't remove, struggles into the narrow skirt, lurching back and forth awkwardly in the seat as she pulls it up over her hips. It's snug—a perfect fit that leaves no room for lingerie—and Ann discards first her short slip and then her underpants, arranging them flirtatiously, like dropped handkerchiefs, over the hump in the middle of the car's floor. She'll remember to keep her legs crossed. Besides, everyone will be looking at the bride, not at her. Even now, she thinks, the world is still mesmerized by a woman in a white dress.

The steaming summer storm obscures the facades of buildings, rendering them blank and flat and erased, like the expressions on the faces of the people they pass. Caught unprepared for a downpour, they twist newspapers or shopping bags into makeshift rain gear. Watching them, Ann buttons the skirt's tight waistband and settles back against the vinyl seat. The driver makes a sudden illegal turn, and Ann is thrown against the door, interrupting her fantasy about the next passenger: she envisions a stolid banker in pinstripes, his surprise as he notices the crumpled slip washing up over the toes of his wingtipped shoes. Will he retrieve her underpants from the car's floor and press them to his mouth? Will he keep them, snapping them into his attaché?

Ann has turned her clothes loose over the city in the past month.

Blouses, dresses, trousers, lingerie. Silk camisoles and brassieres, leggings still musky and moist-crotched, smelling of sex. She leaves her slacks like firemen's dungarees, legs neatly accordioned as if to receive a new occupant, their posture conveying a sense of urgency. Once she left a pair of beige linen walking shorts with a surprising flower of blood between the legs, red and rank—a woman's little emergency.

Traffic jam; Ann is alerted by the car's sudden deceleration. She looks up to see the eyes of the driver in the rearview mirror. Perhaps he saw her, perhaps he was watching as she removed cuticle clippers from her camera bag and cut the tags from the skirt's satin lining. Did he see that the garment didn't come from a shopping bag?

He turns around and peers with frank curiosity through a ragged orifice in the dull Plexiglas separating the front and rear seats. "Whatdja do, steal it?" he asks.

Ann returns his gaze levelly. "Yes," she says.

The driver nods, says nothing.

Ann adjusts the skirt over her legs, smooths it down and looks away, out the wet window. When she looks back the driver's dark eyes are trained on her reflection in his mirror. He nods again, and when there's an opening, guns the cab into the left lane.

She picks up the crumpled price tags from the seat and tears them into little pieces, drops them, along with the little envelope that contains spare buttons for the skirt, out the window. She's late, as usual. The wedding is scheduled to start in less than half an hour; she's paid to record the occasion and still has to stop at her loft and grab the backup videocamera and battery pack.

Maybe her assistant is already there, maybe the rain will have slowed everyone else down. Maybe someday her life will be in order.

Texas, 1975

F orget it. It isn't right." The muscle in her father's jaw clenched and unclenched in anger, frustration.

"What isn't right?" Ann sat up and pulled a shirt around her. One of his work shirts, it was too big, and the cuffs dropped to her knees as she stood. "What?"

"*It. It.* God damn it. Nothing. Nothing is working."

Ann followed him out of the studio, ten paces behind him, not daring to draw closer, her bare feet cold on the cement floor. She walked into the glow of the red safelights over the darkroom sink, where he sat on the black metal stool, elbow on the counter, cheek on hand, eyes closed, wearing a familiar exasperated expression.

"Papi. Papi? Come back. I'll do it better. I wasn't concentrating."

He opened his eyes, looked at her as if without recognition, eyes betraying nothing. "No," he said slowly. "It won't work, Ann. You're too old. I can't use someone with, with—" He stopped, put out his hands in a gesture of helpless dismay, palms up and empty. Dropped them into his lap. "Breasts," he said.

"Papi!" Her laugh was too loud in the cool, quiet room, falsely lighthearted. "They're not new! I'm sixteen! Besides, I'm so skinny they hardly show. You said before it didn't matter."

"Yes. Well, now I'm saying it does. And other things show."

Ann put her arms into the shirt's sleeves, looked down. There were only two buttons left, and she held it closed over her chest.

"There's the razor for other things," she said finally.

"Put your clothes on, Ann," her father said, and he stood and held out his arm almost formally, showing her the door.

On the Monday following the wedding Ann drags into the office at a quarter to two, video cartridges in hand. Just thinking of the editing that will be required to transform tapes of the tearful bride and nervous groom into the quintessential happy couple makes her tired; the image of the distraught father standing amidst trays of canapés under the sodden reception tent wondering how, on the day that he spent thirty thousand dollars for a party, it could rain. It's up to Ann to render what she has recorded into a happy, if inexact, memory.

June is like this. Celebrations are booked as much as a year in advance, and every employee of Visage Video is overextended and irritable, everyone except their unflappable, black receptionist. Ann leans over the little wall around Theo's desk, interrupting his reading of an unsavory-looking novel, a battered paperback with a lurid cover. Theo is twirling one of his many braids with one hand and turning the pages of the book with the other.

"Hi," she says, and he slowly looks up from the book, his manner betraying no embarrassment over his choice of reading material.

"I need a jump," she says.

"How much?" he asks. "A gram? Two?"

Theo is the only receptionist that Visage has managed to keep for more than a month. He chews bubble gum compulsively, manicures his nails on his typing table, uses the company's incoming lines to keep up with his complex social life, watches his Watchman, stares out the window, and incidentally answers calls and greets visitors. He also deals crystal meth—speed—between eleven and two on Mondays.

"Not good for you, honey," Theo says to Ann. "I never knew your sugar was fucked. Benny told me." Benny is one of Ann's partners, one of the four who own Visage Video.

Ann pulls her wallet from her camera bag. "I want three," she says. "Still thirty each?"

"Yeah," Theo nods. "I guess you didn't hear me," he says. He looks innocently around the empty reception area as Ann counts off five twenties, crisp from the bank machine, and hands them to him. Despite Theo's pornographic novels and myriad dissipations, he looks genuinely incapable of sin, like a huge child in costume. No one would suspect that he deals.

"No change, sweetie," he says.

"That's okay, I'll take credit." From Theo's large, smooth hand Ann accepts a particularly embarrassing magazine featuring gay sex; the drug, in three tiny Ziploc bags, will be folded into the "personals" pages. Though Ann and Theo have been acquaintances for five years, the transaction of even a small-change drug deal demands protocol, and the magazine and money switch hands at the same instant.

"Thanks," Ann says.

"I'm serious, sweetheart." Theo shakes his large head at her, braids wagging. "I'm not in the preaching business, God knows, but you seem like exactly the girl who shouldn't be messing around with this kind of temptation. I'm a strapping boy, but look at you, you're just a slip of a thing." He lowers his voice into a Truman Capote drawl, mimicking the infamous lisp with uncanny accuracy. "It's *nasty*, you know. You heard what happened to that Carolyn girl, that little hole she scratched in her neck. You haven't seen her around lately, have you?"

Office gossip, more gruesome with each retelling, has it that one of the assistants succumbed one night to the sensation of bugs crawling on her skin, an unfortunate side effect of meth addiction. The most promising of their apprentices, she made the mistake of equating a disordered life with an artistic one, and her parents took her back to Hoboken.

Ann smiles and shrugs. "You know what they say—I can quit anytime I want." She tucks the magazine into her bag.

"Yeah, right." Theo cracks his gum and blows a big pink bubble which he bursts and sucks back into his mouth. His lips have an unsettling, childlike beauty, and Ann finds it challenging to picture them in acts such as those undoubtedly featured in the novel he holds.

"Your funeral," he says. Two calls come in at once, and rather than choose between the blinking buttons, Theo disconnects both of them. "Tie goes to the receptionist," he smiles.

Ann goes into the bathroom. She is Theo's boss, but the fact that he is her dealer disrupts the power hierarchy, and Theo can afford to look unindustrious, even cavalier. Benny wants to fire him, but Ann figures Visage has too much business anyway. They can hardly keep up; whoever called will call back.

Sitting on the closed lid of the toilet, Ann takes the magazine from her bag and flips to the folded page. A series of diagonal creases transforms the columns of personal ads into a clever envelope which she unfolds to reveal three little bags of sparkling white powder held fast to the page with tape. Ann carefully unsticks the bags and crams the magazine into the metal sanitary container. She uses the tip of the smallest blade of her army knife to lift just one-tenth of the powder from one of the bags, and with a steady hand she puts the knife's dull point under her tongue. She salivates in response to the powder's bitterness, involuntarily making a face. The crystal will be absorbed by capillaries in her mouth, taking just a little longer to hit than it would if she inhaled it. Drugs may not be cool anymore, but according to what she read in May's "Addiction" column in *Lear's* magazine, she's succumbed to what is fast becoming *the* nineties drug. She's a trendsetter. Ha.

Impatient for the kick, still she cannot bring herself to snort the powder: her sinuses are too close to her eyes, and she worries that the amphetamine, which constricts blood vessels and raises blood pressure, could attack her retinas more easily from the proximity of her nose. Ann's retinas have deteriorated in the past year, a secondary symptom of diabetes. "Early BDR," as Dr. Ettinger called it, frowning meaningfully. *Background diabetic retinopathy.*

Aware that she is rotten to her body, Ann tries to be conscientious about her eyes. She wears UV-filter sunglasses whenever she's outside, even in winter; she doesn't miss any of her frequent checkups. She knows Theo is right — speed is one of the worst addictions a diabetic could have. Not that the disease leaves much room for dissipation, and Ann doesn't take speed every day. In fact, until last month, she hadn't taken any for years.

Still, like her camera—hidden in a camera, actually—her crystal is with her at all times, a safeguard against bad moods. Every once in a while, lately, Ann feels desperate enough that she thinks of walking off the roof. She tells herself that crystal is a kind of crisis intervention.

The three little bags fit easily into the space behind one of the mirrors in her Rolleiflex, which broke a number of years ago and which she has never bothered to have repaired; she had already switched her allegiance to the Leica. Ann isn't doing any still photography these days, but she always carries her bag, and an intruder would never think to look in her clever cache: she even leaves it lying open under Carl's scrutiny, in close quarters with his wheat grass and lentils, his jars of brewer's yeast. It's foolproof.

Since crystal excites and confuses her sugar metabolism, Ann skips her insulin when she knows she's going to do a hit. Her blood sugar plummets even without the correction of the shot, so she carries candy with her and tries to remember to eat it. The drug makes her irritable, impatient, gives her diarrhea, and though she cannot think of food, it causes a strange ravenousness that ends in a stomachache. On several occasions lately, Carl has found her curled, cramped and unhappy, on the couch, the diversion of a magazine or television ignored, even the stereo, which she plays almost nonstop, off. He'll push some holistic cure on her like catnip tea. In that he thinks he's treating indigestion, rather than the side effects of speed, his cures only make matters worse, adding nausea to her woes, but she says nothing. A few hours of euphoric energy are worth it, all of it.

There. *There.* She feels it: fingers tingling, heart fluttering, mood lifting. Now, she thinks, it's time for Bergdorf Goodman and Company. She smears some makeup over the circles under her eyes and runs a brush through her long, red hair before she quits the bathroom. Hurrying past Theo's desk, she winks at his knowing smirk and runs upstairs to get business over with. She should edit tape while the wedding is fresh in her memory, but it's already after two and she needs at least an hour at Bergdorf's.

There are a number of messages on the spindle next to the empty flower vase on her desk, and she shuffles through and discards them, returning only the call from her husband.

"Listen, Carl," she says to the machine at his office, "I can't get home by seven tonight, I've got a christening at five-thirty and—" Carl's voice comes on the line, the machine uttering an electronic squeal of protest at the interruption, and she says, "Oh, you're there."

"Why are you going to be late again?" Carl's voice sounds thick, as if she woke him from a nap.

"What are you doing in the office?" Ann says. "I thought you were looking for a mantel for the place on Ninety-third."

"Found what I wanted at the first stop." He yawns audibly.

Carl renovates buildings, mostly nineteenth century brownstones and limestones of heroic proportions—the rich expansiveness of a long-ago New York. He buys houses in disrepair, fixes them, and sells them: always in love with a new find, he can part with the old ones without too much grief. This summer he's working on a mansion, an old consulate building on the east side of the park, one whole floor given over to a ballroom. It's been six months and still the job is not done, but Carl is so exacting that he's fired, to date, seventeen subcontractors. In the current bottom market he's not in a hurry to sell, but, like Ann's work, Carl's isn't really affected by the general economy. His potential buyer is someone too rich to notice the misery of a recession, either that or an opportunist whose fortunes are multiplied by the collapse of others'. In any case, Carl is involved with the house itself, not its potential value. He always says that a buyer will turn up. In his faith he is happy to work slowly, and by himself for the time being, on the thirty-seven room edifice. For the past few weeks he's been stripping baseboards in the hallways with a heat gun. Lying on his side with his head on a pillow, a mask over his nose and mouth, he's removing coats of institutional latex paint from the burled walnut, remains of the building's long tenure as a Montessori school. When his hands cramp, he goes out in search of fixtures and architectural details plundered from other old buildings. Generally, Carl oversees the work of hired craftsmen, but it's hard to find people as meticulous as himself.

"Why can't you edit some other time?" he asks now, sounding grumpy. "I haven't seen you for days."

Ann sits on her desk while she talks, swinging her leg, fidgeting. She can picture Carl in his storefront office on lower Broadway, two Corinthian columns from a condemned church framing the doorway and reaching up to the building's third floor. He's got the receiver caught between chin and shoulder while he picks paint and varnish out from under his fingernails. Over his desk are his degrees, a masters in American history, another in English. "So why do you fix up houses?" she had asked on first meeting him, and he laughed. "To make money," he said. "I planned to be a history professor, but after five years I realized I wasn't going to finish my dissertation." A man who takes satisfaction in using his hands, Carl is at peace with his compromise. He would tell anyone who asked that instead of talking about history, he preserves it.

"I'll get away after the christening," Ann says to him. "I'll call you later from the church." She raises her eyebrows at Benny, who's flapping a little piece of paper at her from the other side of the office they share. "Carl," she says, "I have to go. Benny's giving me the evil eye. Love you." She hangs up and stands.

Tomorrow is Carl's thirty-sixth birthday, one they agreed to celebrate quietly since last year Ann threw him a surprise party from which their loft never completely recovered. Still, nothing is simple, and she has three stops to make after the christening. They're leaving early tomorrow for a summer picnic in the Berkshires and the rental car is reserved, but she needs to pick up the new wallet she bought him and left to have monogrammed; she has to get to the bakery by six-thirty for the carrot cake, also inscribed; and she wants to stop at Kwik Kopy.

A wallet was what Carl said he wanted, but she hates giving gifts that aren't a surprise, so she's created her own currency to enclose. Written on each of three little cards, in an arc above a perfect imprint of Ann's lipsticked, puckered mouth, are the words *Good For One Blow Job;* under the lips, her best guess at the Latin translation: *Fellatio Gratis.* She knows the offering will amuse Carl—bed is one place they've always been light-hearted and enthusiastic—and the phrases are rendered prettily in calligraphy. To prevent smudges she'll run each card through the self-service laminating machine at the Xerox shop, out of the sight of any other customer.

Meanwhile, Benny. "Hey," she says to him as he walks over and hands her a car service voucher with the address of Riverside Church scrawled in the blank. Ann looks at it and hands the voucher back.

"I don't know why you won't just take the contracted cars," he says. "I'm sick of processing all these cab rides. Besides, you lose half the receipts you claim. No one else does this, everyone hates cabs. What's it with you? Take a car service to the jobs, it's cheaper, it makes for more profit. Profit for *you.*"

"Look," Ann says. "The cabs are always there. You go when you want instead of waiting. And I don't like having some guy sitting there while I'm working, it makes me nervous. I hate looking out the window and seeing him slouched in one of those black sedans, his elbow out the window, donut wrappers on the dashboard." She talks fast and says too much, as she tends to when she's hopped.

Benny rolls his eyes. "So why don't you take the subway like you always used to?" he says. "Not that I approve of your running around under-ground with expensive equipment.

"Remember?" he goes on when she doesn't respond. "You used to love the subway. It was such a bargain, you said, it was faster than surface streets. It was the great stage upon which the drama of life was played. It was this; it was that." He turns back to his own desk, a polished, slate-topped expanse.

"I'll tell you why," Ann says, following him. "I can't take the pressure, the drama. There's always someone acting out, and last time I took the subway I was groped by a guy who handed me what looked like a business card but on it was written 'If you are what you eat, then tomorrow you'll be me." Ann cracks the bubble gum she cadged from Theo. "I attrack these *weirdos.*"

She is, of course, unable to disclose the real reason she's been taking cabs—that she changes into stolen clothes en route to appointments—and she seems to be having this transportation argument with Benny almost once a week now. "So, tell me, what would you do?" she asks.

"I would take the car service," he says slowly, enunciating each syllable with hostile precision. He looks at Ann as she stands before him, cracking her gum, chewing fast, and his face betrays some inner debate, thick blond eyebrows meeting in concentration. Finally he says simply, "Are you okay?"

"Of course. Why not? You asked why I don't take the subway anymore, I answered. Perfectly normal human interaction, right?"

"Sure," Benny says, sighing. "Right. Suit yourself. You will anyway." He consults the Visage calendar, a huge book bound in red leather. "You've got Andy tonight," he says, rubbing fiercely at his perenially bloodshot blue eyes.

"Have him meet me there," she says. "I've got to do an errand on the way."

"Sure you do," he says, and he looks up at her again, his eyes searching behind her sunglasses, his freckled arms folded over his chest.

Ann knows Benny feels sorry for her, and she has intentionally cultivated his pity, a response she generally abhors, because his sympathy is useful. Courting his indulgence—her moodiness, tardiness, her demands for special considerations—Ann has implied that her diabetes is far worse than it is; that, in fact, her days are numbered. She paints an affecting picture of metabolic crashes and attendant ravages of mental and physical well-being. Consequently, Benny's response to her varies between anger and a sort of confused, irritated tolerance. She's sorry about the friction; in fact, she likes Benny, prefers him to her other partners.

Visage Video is booming. Booming, even in a recession. Founded in 1985 after an excited, late-night plan concocted by four out-of-work photographers, alumni of the same fine arts program, the company has doubled and then tripled in size, outgrowing office space and booking calendars. The partners still work, but only on exclusive assignments—society functions, parties given for movie stars. It's a curious service they provide, the recording of weddings and christenings, other people's celebrations. The consummation of such rites once rested in the kiss between a bride and groom, the light rain of holy water on a baby's face. Now it's the nearly silent whir of tape through a camcorder that ensures the experience is real: the presence of a hired acolyte with his eye to the viewfinder of a magic device. And the resulting ability to play the experience back, to guard against some future famine of love or hope.

The birthday parties and anniversaries, the awards dinners and christenings, Ann can do without. She loves recording weddings. It's as if she is the only one who actually sees what happens, who really experiences the rite. The people involved are too nervous to know what's going on, and the one performing the ceremony—the pastor, the rabbi, the justice of the peace—has usually done so many of them that he says the words by rote, lips moving, eyes focused inward.

Ann never gets tired of weddings. She sees that kiss, watches the bride's face, the groom's hands as he lifts the veil: the instant described by the church as a sacrament, flesh bound to flesh, as mysterious as bread becoming the body of Christ. Not that Ann actually believes in it all. Ann loves Carl, but their flesh is not one. Carl would have a nervous breakdown at the very thought that Ann's self-polluting appetites might be attached to his body.

Still, even if Ann isn't a romantic, she enjoys what she can make of a wedding. She edits hours of tape down to a perfectly choreographed ninety minutes that reveal each participant at his or her best. She's the only one of Visage's videographers who finishes her own work, dubbing and redubbing until the ceremony is a seamless success. Even a disappointing wedding like last Saturday's drenched fiasco is transformed by Ann into a happy memory. She makes of a wedding what she imagines the bride fantasized it would be, what the bride's parents paid a fortune to realize, what the groom expected, the attendants looked forward to; she weaves a fairy tale for the tiny ring bearer and flower girl.

Ann leaves Visage in her usual flurry, hoping her assistant, Andy, is up to speed today. He's often too lazy to be of much use to her, almost an impediment to accomplishing anything. It takes him so long to do the simplest chore, to load a cassette, to plug in a light; she is ten times faster. He's been known to bring batteries that aren't charged; he screws up the log of the participants, which she needs to use later for the titles. He's not like the peppy Carolyn. Visage employs nine "associates," four tape editors, and twelve assistants who caddy for the videographers—about thirty people plus the hippest receptionist in town.

Thinking about Theo's tart comment, *your funeral,* Ann hopes he hasn't traded confidences with Benny. Her partner's compassion might be adversely affected by the notion of her being . . . well, not an addict—not exactly.

————

She takes a cab down Broadway to Columbus Circle, bails out in a traffic jam, runs three blocks along Central Park South, heading east to Bergdorf's on Fifth. If she's not going to be late, she has about half an hour before she has to head back uptown for the christening. Running in the heat, her heart pounding anxiously from the crystal, one day she'll drop from a coronary in Grand Army Plaza, right under the gilded nose of General Sherman's equestrian statue: dead before she even gets to Bergdorf's.

She dodges between a bus and a limousine, bounds over the sidewalk, bursts through the store's northeast door, pulls her Walkman off and stuffs it into her bag so she can concentrate.

Of all the stores she loves, Ann loves this store best: everything about the place, the pilasters with their whimsical capitals of winged nudes, the plaster beadwork and chandeliers, the thickly padded, pearly gray carpet. Built on the original site of the Vanderbilts' one hundred and forty-four room mansion, Bergdorf Goodman and Company's first floor is high-ceilinged and well-appointed, more like a grand residence than a store.

When she isn't actually involved in a criminal pursuit, Ann fantasizes about stealing, and she always imagines herself in Bergdorf's. Sometimes she even dreams about it, and in the dreams most of the action takes place on the ground floor. Last night, she realizes, she was slipping through this very department, running down the aisles of belts and jewelry, heading, even as she is now, for the escalator.

Every time Ann does drugs, she ends up shoplifting.

She does a quick survey from the vantage of the six flights of moving stairs en route to the ladies' lounge on the top floor. Usually, half the reason for going to the bathroom is to look in the mirror, but since the store offers hundreds of reflections along the nacreous, frosted glass walls of the moving staircase, that's not her immediate motive. Crystal makes Ann have to pee about every half hour. Between that and what it does to her stomach, she really has got to cut back; she can't afford to take it as often as she has lately. She's thin anyway, but she sees that she's getting a little gaunt, even for her. Her gray eyes look too big, her chin too sharp.

The rest room has real furnishings, not the usual ladies' room vinyl chair and couch that looks like it belongs in a shrink's office. There's a tasteful trio of antique ballroom chairs, a divan of chintz and cherry wood and a marble and mahogany vanity at which a woman is busily applying foundation. Spread before her is a battery of cosmetics; she looks as if she has just washed her face in preparation to start from scratch.

Ann passes by in a wind of motion and latches a stall door behind her. She can hear the lounge attendant humming as she scrounges in the bottom of her camera bag for her nasal spray, her fingers groping through all the pseudoephedrine tablets she has rolling around in the bottom of the bag. Last week she recorded the fiftieth birthday party of the bouffant-haired star of a sixties sitcom, multiple face-lifts disharmonizing the famous rerun face; and on a trip to the bathroom Ann discovered a veritable stockpile of over-the-counter drugs. No one has sinus problems so pernicious that she'd keep over five hundred doses of Sudafed on hand. Ann recognized the cache of an addict and lifted the contents of two bottles, dumping the little red pills into her camera bag and leaving the empty vessels as a message of her discovery. Pseudoephedrine isn't bad, a sort of thready, nervous, industrious high, but it's a weak sister to crystal, and she stole it more for fun than from the desire for a chemical she can buy at any drugstore.

She finds the nose spray and, when she finishes peeing, inhales two long squirts. After a bad cold last month, she's also addicted to whatever's in nose spray, oxymetazoline something, and can't stand not being able to breathe out of her nostrils. She doesn't want to know how the stuff does what it does; like crystal, it works too well to be good for you.

"Damn," she says, a little too loudly in the quiet rest room. What about the curse? It's really late, and she's been careless about birth control this month, using her diaphragm without the Ortho goop because she keeps forgetting to buy a tube. Maybe she'll find a bathroom at the church and check again before the christening.

Ann's period is irregular, she never knows when it's coming. Last time she happened to be in Bergdorf's, where most of the ladies' lounge attendants now recognize her. She needed a tampon, and the woman opened the door to the big mahogany wardrobe opposite the clean row of sinks and retrieved one from a little bag. "Here, honey," she said, her expression that of an indulgent governess. Ann offered change in return, but the woman refused. This time she's two weeks late. Still, she reminds herself, it's not a crisis. Why would she be on time for that and nothing else?

Ann zips up, her pants, her bag. She bursts out of the stall, glances in the mirror, and then she's out of the lounge and into the store, where all the women seem to have a look of studied fatigue. No one else in Bergdorf's ever seems in a hurry, and Ann checks her accelerated passage through the departments; she must not call attention to herself. By the time she has ridden down the escalators a few floors to the designer boutiques, she has forced herself to slow down to a languid stroll.

Ann's stealing depends on her photographic memory. She can recreate in her mind any store's floor plan, knows just where every corner and corridor and display case lies. She can lift something and outwit the detectives as she swiftly navigates the maze of the store.

Now she drifts through the designer collections, which are always underpopulated, at least from the perspective of a thief. Figuring the employee-to-patron ratio at about one to one, both equally well-dressed and unhurried, Ann must concentrate to tell the two apart.

Everyone wanders among the racks of opulent garments, placed among club chairs and coffee tables, the occasional sofa glutted with brocade cushions, all resting on an immaculate expanse of thick carpet. Bergdorf's is a country of women. The few men in evidence appear as envoys from without, and look either like movie producers or homosexuals in fancy dress. The occasional bored spouse slumps in an armchair; a gigolo leans admiringly on his patron's arm.

After figuring the options and lingering over an entirely too-well-guarded silk skirt in the Ungaro boutique, Ann wanders through the Christian Lacroix clothes, feigning interest in a playfully patterned chemise. She begins to plan her attack.

Next to her, a faded blond woman is fingering the sleeve of a hot-pink bolero. The woman looks put-upon, furious with life, but the merchandise seems to mollify her. With its red collar, appliquéd flowers, and whimsical insect buttons, the cropped pink jacket is a garment Ann wouldn't usually choose, but perhaps it would be fun to wear this evening. In less than two hours she'll be recording the christening of a Wall Street trader's firstborn, and the man has invited half the city to the event. The jacket will be perfect in the richly dressed crowd.

She cases the other boutiques on the fourth floor and returns to Lacroix. Watches the blond woman make eye contact with a saleslady who's hovering.

"I'd like to see this in a six," the woman says, and the saleslady takes a key dangling from a long, violet ribbon around her neck. She unlocks the tiny padlock at the end of a slender, plastic-sheathed cable that connects the jackets to the rack. Checking inside the collars for the right size, she hands a jacket to the woman. The exacting customer tries it on, looks at herself in the triple mirrors, turning slowly to the right and to the left. She buttons it, unbuttons it, and takes it off. "It isn't right," she says.

As the blond woman wanders away, idly stroking the sleeves of other jackets as she leaves the department, the saleslady rehangs the garment. Ann rehearses the line she's thought of and approaches. "I'm sure I saw this same jacket in *Vogue*, exactly this same one, but in green. Can you check for me? With red hair I really can't wear bright pink."

The saleslady frowns in thought. "I don't think it comes in any other color," she says, shaking her head. The enameled Bergdorf Goodman employee brooch glints on her lapel, an obscure heraldic crest.

"I think it does," Ann insists. "Could you just check?" She smiles and lets her hand rest on the older woman's cuff for a moment, a daughter begging a mother's kindness.

The saleslady shrugs. "I'll see," she says, and she goes around one of the pale green columns to the desk between Lacroix and Mizrahi. She picks up a telephone receiver.

Ann severs the security cable with her wirecutters, jams the tool back into her camera bag, looks to make sure the saleswoman isn't returning, and tugs the size six jacket off the hanger. The cable slithers through its sleeve and drops to the floor. She crams the jacket in her bag and is off.

Everywhere she looks there are mirrors, and it's hard to judge whether the thief or the store is better served by so many multiplying reflections. Ann can see someone's approach from around a corner and can watch herself stealing; but then, so could someone else. And what if the mirrors are one-way, security guards sitting like fat, sly spiders behind them?

Ann runs. She slips through two long racks of faux fur coats left temporarily in the aisle, diving through the strangely slick and smooth corridor to the escalator, where she cuts in front of two dowagers weighed down by shopping bags. She streaks down the empty flights of moving stairs, jumping three at a time with her heart in her mouth. Escalators frighten Ann, but she never has time to wait for an elevator. On the second floor she hides in a wigwam of evening gowns to pry the alarm device off the red velvet collar, and then she slips casually down the last flight of the escalator, through cosmetics to the southeast exit.

Out. In less than two minutes from the time she cut the steel cable—one two-handed maneuver of the imported tungsten shears—Ann is standing on the corner of Fifth and Fifty-seventh, just across from Tiffany's. She's not even breathing hard. A well-dressed man in his fifties smiles at her hopefully; she ignores him. Her hand is inside her camera bag, touching the new jacket, feeling the buttons. It gets easier and easier.

Woman Sets Self on Fire at Museum

By ADRIAN SMARTT

NEW YORK, *July 10.* Contributing to the controversy surrounding next fall's scheduled opening of a retrospective of the photographs of Edgar Rogers at the Museum of Modern Art, a young woman set herself on fire today in the museum's sculpture garden. Flames were extinguished by security personnel, but not before the unidentified woman suffered severe burns, police said.

The incident was the latest in a series of occurrences that have clouded plans for the retrospective. "We were prepared for protests from feminists and various interest groups," said museum spokesperson Holly Solomon, "but no one expected an event like this." She added that she interpreted the early protest as evidence of the upcoming show's cultural significance.

All this month, following an op-ed column in this paper by the publisher of *Ms.* magazine, crowds have gathered outside the museum to protest the exhibition of, in the words of one demonstrator, "work of an offensive and misogynist nature."

Doused Hair with Kerosene

Until yesterday, the situation remained "deeply unpleasant but basically nonviolent and nondestructive," Solomon said. Museum property was not damaged, although an enameled steel sculpture by Alexander Calder suffered scorches and will have to be cleaned.

The woman, clad only in underpants and a tee-shirt bearing the name "Ann Rogers," the late photographer's daughter and longtime model, was reported to have doused her hair with kerosene before setting it on fire at the east end of the museum's sculpture garden. In front of those eating in the museum's crowded café and hundreds who flocked to the nearly 18,000 square feet of windows overlooking the garden, the young woman's act was, in the words of museum patron Betsy Feinstein, "unforgivably sad, and very ugly."

Museum security put out the flames with a hand-held fire extinguisher, but the woman suffered third-degree burns over 45 percent of her body, including her face. A bundle of clothes found in the first-floor women's room included no money or identification.

The woman, approximately nineteen and of medium build, remains unidentified and is listed in critical condition at New York Hospital. Hospital spokesperson David Brockman said that the prognosis for such serious burns was poor. "We're talking about a level of shock that the body may not be able to withstand," he said. The patient, blinded by the damage to her optic nerves, remains unconscious.

Controversial Works in Show

Edgar Rogers, who committed suicide in 1978, left a body of work that has long been the focus of debate over the definitions of art and obscenity. Of his previously exhibited photographs, the more graphic include nudes of his daughter, Ann Rogers, some documenting self-mutilation and sexual play.

In a much publicized Milwaukee hearing in September of 1987, it was ruled that eleven of Rogers's photographs featured in a show at that city's Contemporary Arts Center were in fact works of art. The Arts Center was found not guilty of charges of lewd exhibition.

Given the controversial nature of the Rogers photographs already seen by the public, rumors that the coming retrospective will feature work that the Rogers estate had not previously released have provoked conjecture over what these never-before-exhibited works might portray. Museum spokesperson Solomon would say only, "This exhibit will be the most comprehensive and compelling show of Rogers's work to date."

Each day of the past week protesters have gathered outside the Museum of Modern Art. Some lay in the street halting traffic. Others harassed gallery-goers and distributed pamphlets outlining the criteria of pornography, obscenity, sexual harassment, rape, and other "crimes against society," as one leaflet was titled.

Show to Open Early

Solomon confirmed that the unidentified woman was neither Ann Rogers, nor any known relation or associate of the late photographer.

The tee-shirt the woman wore was identical to those worn by other protesters outside the museum, but police said they could not determine whether the woman's act was that of a single individual or part of an organized protest.

Expressing deep regret for what she called a "terrible, terrible thing to have happened," Solomon went on to say that the exhibition will open as much as a month earlier than its original opening date of September 24. Like the earlier protests, the self-immolation was judged by museum officials to be further testimony to Rogers's power as an artist. They hope that the earlier opening will avert other planned demonstrations.

Ann Rogers was unavailable for comment, and her attorney, Doris Ashton, said only that as a representative of Ms. Rogers and the estate of the late photographer, she was deeply troubled by the incident.

Texas, 1967

Jessup wasn't a large or populous town, and Edgar Rogers accepted any work he could find as a photographer: weddings, of course, and civic events such as the yearly Cattlemen's Dinner and the anniversaries of the local Rotary chapter. By the time Ann was five, he was teaching a weekly class at the high school and was the photographer for the local paper, an occupation that demanded his attendance at football games, swim meets, county fairs. Ann often accompanied her father to these gatherings, where he was not a participant but a peripheral figure who watched from the edge, his Leica hanging from his neck. Like a name tag, his camera defined his presence: it gave him a function and the means of saying so. As he rarely spoke, Edgar Rogers depended on such identification.

His reputation as a teacher of photography was of a stern and distant man. Not unkind, exactly, but intolerant of ignorance, scornful of laziness—both common qualities in the classrooms in which he found himself. He wore his camera to class, and into the school darkroom. He told his students that a real photographer did not consider that there was a difference between his organic eyes and his mechanical one.

In the last years of his life, Edgar Rogers wore the Leica all the time, taking it off only at night, when he put it on the little table by his bed; he put it back around his neck as soon as he woke up, over his pajama top. It was always loaded with film, even though he rarely used a 35mm by then, shot most pictures with a view camera. Still, he looked through it, constantly framing his vision. At breakfast, he'd pick the Leica up, still chewing; he'd look through the dark lens, change the aperture, the focus, put it down, take another bite of toast.

After school, on afternoons when her aunt Mariette worked as a receptionist for the dentist in town, Ann had to stay with her father until he finished work. At the games, the interminable swim meets, Ann usually played under the bleachers with other bored little children, younger brothers and sisters of the students on the team.

The bleachers on the high school football field were old and in need of a coat of paint. Under the tiered benches the sparse grass gave way to dirt, sticky with spilled pop and littered with candy wrappers. It smelled under the bleachers, rank and damp, a little like sweat and sugar, a smell not quite of decay, but almost. Overhead the spreading thighs of mothers, the rumpled pant legs of fathers were neatly spaced along the wooden slats, an occasional sweater falling through, along with the constant rain of popcorn kernels, Popsicle sticks, scraps of notebook paper, a purple mimeographed algebra assignment. It all floated down around the little brothers and sisters who appropriated useful items in their games.

One September day, though, no other children were under the benches; none slid down through the slats overhead, leaving a sudden emptiness beside their mothers' warm hips. Ann sat alone in the gray dirt and began to trace drawings. She cleared a space in the litter, brushed the ground smooth, uprooted the few tenacious blades of grass, and made herself a drawing board which she neatly outlined with a deep scratch in the dirt. On this slate she drew pictures with a popsicle stick and then brushed them off and started again.

She looked up once or twice, stood and peered through an unoccupied space in the bleachers, and located her father. He was a tall man, handsome if you saw him beyond the camera, the frown. He was leaning against the far fence waiting for a shot, a graceful leap to catch the spiraling ball, two players colliding, a pileup of boys diving for the ball. Finally, she curled up on her side in the dirt and went to sleep.

It was a windy day, and trash, wrappers and papers, cellophane, an empty paper cup, eddied around her still form. She slept the way children sleep, deeply, and with a surrender never observed in adult rest. She slept through touchdowns and injuries, through cheers and whistles and screams.

That was the day her father took the first great photograph, his first real photograph, the one that freed him from small-town obscurity, from recording ribbon-cuttings and weddings, the plump hands of the bride and groom around the knife as it slipped into the cake. He found his daughter lying under the bleachers, stood watching her as she slept, so still. He squatted by the opening at the side of the bleachers, put the camera to his eye, and composed a shot. Her slender legs, magically this once without their usual bruises and scrapes, their fair skin set off by torn sneakers and dirty, rumpled shorts. Her blond hair in the dirt. One hand to her mouth, the thumb just grazing her bottom lip. Ann sucked her thumb as she fell asleep, an unbroken habit, a childish comfort.

Everyone else had gone by the time Ann's father came looking for her. There was no one to see as he photographed his daughter, the still, small S of her body threaded through the dying grass. It looked as if she were unconscious, or dead, abandoned on the periphery of the playing field. The late afternoon sun, just sinking, sent a beam through the benches, and the knives of shadow cut across her throat, severing head from torso. The peculiar light made a halo of her fair hair, and evoked a certain anxiety. Surely, any viewer of the picture hoped, death could not effect so perfect a balance, the curve of the child's slightly bent legs echoed in the disposition of her slender neck.

The film was Tri-X, nothing special, but there was the magic of a Zeiss lens, and Edgar Rogers was skilled in his darkroom, an artist. He used quality paper and summoned up every available detail from the negative. Submitted to a contest sponsored by *American Photographer*, the photograph took first prize and was published. Edgar Rogers made ten gelatin silver prints and sold them each for one hundred dollars, and with that modest step into professionalism his career as an art photographer was launched. It wasn't long before a dealer called him.

Five years later, galleries in Dallas, Houston, then New York displayed his photographs. Ten years later, original copies of the local paper that featured his prediscovery photographs were collector's items.

Still, Edgar Rogers's fame depended on his daughter; every photograph of note was of Ann. Cautious, he stuck with a successful theme— Ann posed as if dead—and over the years, as she grew and changed, there was something increasingly fascinating and seductive in the fact that it was the same child, the same girl, teenager, woman, who died a thousand deaths for the camera. Perhaps it implied the immortality in which everyone wanted to believe. That all the drowned children, leukemic children, children hit by cars—that their deaths could be captured, controlled, recorded, and then over with like one more unfortunate stage of development.

He took other photographs as well, but it was this eccentric series of Ann that first won acclaim, the fiction of Ann's death that gave them power, a lie more interesting and marketable than truth. And the other famous photographs, his secret work, were not released until after his death.

Ann shuddered sometimes as her father arranged her into the position he wanted. Sometimes as she lay quietly waiting for him to finish, she felt as if she were truly dying. His will seemed to paralyze her; she was good at posing dead because she found herself actually unable to move when he told her to be still. Posing for her father was like being hypnotized by the man who came to the school's science fair and demonstrated the hidden "power of the mind." Ann intended not to raise her arm; she told her arm to remain frozen at her side; but up it floated at her father's command. Although she fantasized about disobedience, rebellion, when her father laid her out before his camera, when he closed her eyes, his fingers heavy on her lids, she could almost feel her heart slow, her breathing become shallow. For an impossible two minutes she did not blink. A thousand little deaths. Was it because she loved to see herself in the eye of his camera? Because that was how she knew she was there? Or was it simply the overwhelming desire she felt to please him?

At first, the formula of the photographs was one with which both Ann and her father felt uncomfortable, but as with any aberration, with repetition it became usual and normal; they forgot to find it odd. Ann was something of a loner anyway; it seemed to her that other little girls were initiated into complicated rites she didn't care to know. Their games of house and supermarket, nurse and ballerina, seemed passwords to a club she didn't want to join.

In the evenings after school, Ann ignored the television which fascinated her aunt Mariette, and watched her father work in his darkroom. She had her own place there, off to the side and out of the way of the chemicals, and it was peaceful in the red glow of the safelights, the constant lulling sound of running water: a womb in which a thousand variations of herself, her face, her body, gestated in the clean trays under her father's beautiful hands. He was silent while he worked.

Ann sat on an upturned box by the developer bath. Sometimes she dozed, her narrow back against the wall, her legs held knees tight together by the circle of her arms. Her father looked at her—she could have told you this even without seeing it. He shook the chemicals from his hands, rinsed and dried them. Sometimes he touched her chin, her cheek, brushed the hair back over her shoulders. Once she started awake with his fingers on her neck, the smell of fixer in her nostrils.

"Time for you to go to bed," he said.

"Can't I stay up?" She put her arms around his waist, but he untwined her fingers at his back.

"Bed," he said.

"Please, Papi."

"No."

But once in a great while he said yes, talking as he rocked the prints back and forth in the plastic developing trays, watching images take shape. The photographs emerged as he called back other pictures from the past. He might, in a rare expansive mood, tell Ann about her mother. Virginia

Crane Rogers died in childbirth, unusual in 1959. She hemorrhaged in the kitchen of their house. But Ann's father never talked about that, and what he did say was less in response to her careful questions than a sort of broadcast reminiscing, during which he actually seemed to forget she was listening or even present.

———————

Virginia Crane had been nineteen when Edgar Rogers met her. She was, probably in truth, but certainly as embellished by time and longing, beautiful. Beautiful in the blooming flush of youth and energy. Forever beautiful because she died young and, as they say, stayed pretty. She was a wild preacher's daughter; her own mother long dead and the second youngest of four girls, she and her little sister Mariette were brought up by the older two. When she died, Mariette came to stay with Edgar and care for his infant daughter, her niece; came to stay for a month that grew into a year and then a lifetime. Ann's father said, one Easter dinner, water glass lifted in toast, that when gifts were divided among the sisters, Virginia had been given beauty, Mariette, charity. "Ah," said Mariette, "but Virginia had hope as well."

Whether or not she could claim one of the cardinal virtues, and despite her growing up in a parsonage, religion had made little impression on Virginia, and after the death of her mother when she was twelve, she believed fervently in spirits but little else. It was spirits who told her she was pregnant. They whispered in her ear the night that Ann was conceived, her ear which was a little large for a girl's and pink-lobed from the clasp of a too-tight earring. Of the twenty or so pictures Ann had of her mother, three documented that passage to Virginia's brain, the same that spirits called into, close-ups rendered exotic by their lack of context—no neck or ringlet of hair, no cheek to proclaim the identity of its neighbor—just that small terrain of the body made large and mysterious, a cave, a spiral, a downward slide, an entrance to another world. Ann had pictures of parts of her mother's body, hands, knees, shoulders, spine, and not one picture of the whole woman.

When Virginia's father, a stern and rigid man who used religion as a vise, learned she was pregnant, he threw her out. And so she married Edgar, packed her two bags and moved into the only place they could afford—a struggling photographer and a secretary with marginal skills—a three-room shotgun house quite literally on the wrong side of the tracks, and so close to those tracks that the rumble of freight trains cracked the plaster patches that Edgar had painstakingly laid on the big bedroom's ceiling.

Edgar brought Virginia flowers. The white clapboard house had few furnishings—a table for eating that fell down on a hinge from the kitchen wall, a soft feather bed leaking goosedown onto the floor—but it was brightened by bouquets of anemones, red and yellow and orange and pink. He tried to photograph them, brought the lens right up to the flowers' black eyes, but the pictures were failures and he tore them up.

The first good photographs Edgar took were of Virginia. He apprenticed himself to his new camera, a twin-lens reflex into whose top he peered, learning to compose a picture upside down. Virginia on a topsy-turvy wooden stool, her milky white legs in the air, her heels over her dark head. He got the camera in trade for a 1939 Chevrolet that he found junked in a gulch; he had worked on the car until it ran, barely, but enough for him to drive it to the Ten Cities Swap in Midland. He came home and took a picture of Virginia nude and pregnant, from just below her breasts to just above her mons, her belly swollen taut and planetary.

The smallest of the three rooms in the house he used as a darkroom, piping in water from the kitchen's bathtub tap, sealing the shuttered window against light with rolls and rolls of duct tape. Virginia watched while he printed from the film he carefully exposed. He printed and re-printed from the same negative, never satisfied; he turned off the water and the developing light only when he was too exhausted to remain standing, never because he thought he had what he wanted. Virginia sat on the stool and even learned to sleep on the stool, her back against the door, her ankles, during pregnancy, no longer slender, but swelling in the summer heat.

Whether Ann's father had always been a cold man—thawed briefly by Virginia's passion, only to return to that state after she died—or whether it was her death that froze and embittered him, Ann never knew. But on those few occasions that memory bewitched him, Edgar Rogers was a different person, voluble, sentimental, the set lines around his mouth disappearing in the soft glow of the red safelights. Ann waited for such moods, and tried to learn all she could during them.

But there were questions she knew better than to ask her father, and for those answers she went to Mariette. She interrupted her aunt as she studied for a test, note cards spread on the kitchen table, her eyes rolled up to the ceiling as she struggled with her poor memory. Mariette went to college in Odessa at night, taking one class per semester. She wouldn't finish her degree until she was twenty-five at least, but she was reverent in her studies. When she finally had her bachelor's in biology, she planned to get a teaching certificate. By then, she'd laugh, Ann would be in college herself.

"Was she very pretty?" Ann asked Mariette, her elbows among the note cards.

"Very."

"Did she have gold hair?"

"No, dark, you know that."

"Was she tall?"

"Taller than me."

"Were her eyes blue?"

"Gray, like yours."

"And she died because of me?"

"She died because she bled to death, Ann."

On the wall in the corridor between the doors to the bedrooms, the bathroom, the linen closet, were pictures of Virginia: her feet, her arm from wrist to just above the elbow, her navel, her thigh, her neck, her lovely face tipped back in laughter—disorganized fragments from which, with concentration, it was possible to reconstruct a whole woman. When her father was safely in his darkroom for an evening, Ann would take the pictures down, arrange them on the floor in their proper places. Bigger than life, her mother stretched from the living room to the bedroom. Captured on film, she looked like a person incapable of death, incapable of such stillness, such quiet.

Sometimes, in the fall after school, Mariette would pick Ann up by the gate near the gymnasium and they would walk together to the reservoir by the feedlot. Ducks, migrating south, rested on the still water, huddled and cold-looking in the waning light. Mariette had a bag of white bread in her satchel, fresh bread from the market, a one and a half pound loaf.

"Why shouldn't the ducks have good food?" she'd say, pointing to the label: "Enriched with Vitamins and Iron!"

Slice by slice, they fed the bread to the greedy birds, Edgar's disapproval of such waste heightening their enjoyment. They tore it into pieces and dropped it slowly into the birds' open bills or sent it in whole slices like spinning saucers over the reservoir, the birds, frantic with hunger, lifting in a mass and falling on the sodden square. Ann ate pieces of the bread as they walked around the water's periphery. Crushed it into balls and chewed it as she watched pieces disappear down the ducks' gullets. Invariably, she came home too full to eat any supper.

"What was her nose like, Mariette?"

"It was straight and long, just as it is in the pictures."

"But I don't always look like myself in pictures. She might not either. Were her cheeks red?"

"Yes."

"So she looked like Snow White?"

Mariette laughed, paused in feeding the ducks. "A little, yes." She crouched on the slimy bank of the reservoir, tempting ducks out of the water to snatch bread from her hand.

"And what happened to her?" Ann persisted.

"You know the story. I've told you, and your father has told you."

"Tell me again."

"Oh, Ann. She was alone in the house, that little place I've showed you on our walks. Your father was working at the paper. It was time to have you and something went wrong. A rupture . . . a—a something. It wasn't your fault. It happened very quickly. We were lucky to save you."

Snow White. Lips as red as blood. The drop of red blood upon the ground. The drop that spread, became a puddle, an ocean. Red.

"And Papi found her?"

"Yes. It must have been horrible for him. He loved your mother so. He was a different person with Virginia." Mariette stopped, turned the empty bread bag upside down so that the last crumbs would fall to the ducks. "He was, well, he was lighthearted then."

Papi with a light heart. A red heart with wings, soaring.

The ducks plunged after the last crumbs as they sank. Ann watched the water run off their heads, drops bright like tears. Their eyes were black beads, the water black glass, impenetrable surfaces. It was getting dark.

"She died before I was born?"

"The same morning. I'm not sure exactly when. You know this story better than I do, Ann. Don't make me tell it again."

"I like to hear about how it was."

"It was sad, Ann, too sad to talk about. It's something we have to forget, not remember."

As soon as it happened, I rehearsed the sound of it as if it were something long ago in the past: painful, yes, but so long ago now — "Oh, I was nineteen when my father died, I was a grown-up." "Well, you know I was almost twenty when he died." As if it didn't bother me anymore. I started saying these things to myself over and over, as if to a stranger I was meeting and telling him about my life: "You know, nineteen is old enough to be out in the world alone."

For a long time, I haven't thought about the years that preceded your death. I didn't remember them, I put them away. Oh, I knew I was the daughter of Edgar Evans Rogers, I recognized myself in pictures on gallery walls. But anything that didn't confront me with material evidence, I forgot. As for the things that did, I changed their stories, without meaning to exactly. Or, if the first lies were intentional, the later ones were helpless.

In the weeks after you died, I dreamed about you every night. Often the dreams were realistic, almost factual. Events I could no longer recall while waking, I relived in my sleep.

Now I never dream of you. I dream about stealing and running. Or about that girl at the museum: I got to the hospital to see her. Who is she, and how is it that she succeeded in immolating herself for you? Who is she—or perhaps, who was she—wearing my name, that she knew me so well?

I tried to please you before myself, but I was young, Papi, and I wanted my life, it seemed only fair—I asked myself sometimes if I was being fair in wanting myself for myself. I knew I had to get away, but even about that I was ambivalent: I went to college far from home, but came back at every opportunity, just to check—maybe I was wrong, maybe you had missed me.

The way you'd shout if I knocked into anything in that room. I broke a lens once, that was bad. You could yell so loud it was frightening, as if you could kill me. I would hear the sound of your voice and everything would go blank, I wouldn't see or hear anything, just wonder dully, what comes next? A fist? But you never hit me, you never dared touch me outside the demands of your craft.

Because you hated me, perhaps. People are very careful around those they hate, they have to make sure their hands don't betray them.

How black your hair was and I liked to take a bath in your bathroom. Suddenly I see you sitting on the edge of the tub, I was little then. Once or twice when Mariette was away, you washed my hair. Afterward, as you combed the tangles out, I could feel your impatience travel through the comb. Feel your hands resist pulling and hurting me.

Sometimes on a Saturday in the summer, we would get up before five to take pictures in the gulch behind the cattle ranch. The light at that hour was perfect, you said.

On the night before you were cremated, Mariette asked if I refused to bury you with Mother because then the two of you would have excluded me forever, there in the dark under the quiet dirt. She was right, of course, I didn't want you in that double grave, under the epitaph you chose for her: "Why did my love outlive you?" And since your will made no provisions for your remains, I abolished them, had you burned up, expected you to disappear. And for a while you did. But now you're back.

I was walking home last week and the name Diane Castleton came into my head. I was walking on Sixth Avenue. Diane Castleton, Diane Castleton, I kept saying as I saw myself pass in shop windows. Who is Diane Castleton? I thought. I tried to find her in my life: had I done her wedding? Was she someone from some party: an introduction, ignored at the time, that resurfaced? Then suddenly I knew.

You were mysterious, sleeping with Diane for all those years. When I found out I wondered at what I thought was a betrayal, but Mother was dead for a long time, and I see now that life isn't simple. Still, Diane was old, her hair was gray, she was fat. When I shook her hand in the lawyer's office, I felt the fleshiness of her fingers, and I looked for a ring, something you might have given her over the years. It wasn't that I begrudged her anything, God knows—I didn't want what I'd inherited—just that thinking of Mother, that girl who was so beautiful, and your misery—for what else could explain your life other than despair?— Diane was just the last person. Maybe that's the answer, though, maybe it could only have been someone so different from my mother.

Suddenly, without trying, without wanting to, I can smell your hands, the way they always smelled of the darkroom chemicals, even when you washed and washed them before meals. Hear you saying at the dinner table, out of the blue, well at least we know you aren't a lesbian, Ann. Mariette's little smothered gasp. I must have known then that you followed me. But I was so careful. So secretive. Still, you knew all along that I wasn't just the good girl I tried so hard to be, that the straight A's, the quiet studying in my room, the forty-seven Girl Scout badges—it was only part of the story. And my good-girl life wasn't the one that you found useful.

No, there were two Anns, and that was how it started with the speed: the only way I could study all night, the only way I could keep two selves going, the only way I knew how to smile and say, believing it, I'm fine. And the fact that for those brief excited hours I did feel well.

I never really learned to manage the diabetes; that was another thing, I resisted learning how. Looked to my insulin shots as a simple cure to my otherness, a reversal of fate. Without the injections, I was a diabetic, but the needle restored me to my rightful place, among normal people. I know it must be possible to do better—how many times have I been told about athletes who are diabetic and all those other healthy achievers?

I never feel well anymore. After a hit, I feel ecstatic for a few hours and it's like an antidote to all those years of insulin reactions. But then I have to pay.

Trying. Trying. Always trying. After that first time in college, I knew I had an answer. Even in all those years when I was fine, when it wasn't necessary to be more than one Ann, the possibility of two has always existed. Like a bad habit only temporarily conquered.

And what about you? What were you like? Obsessed with your work, you rarely spoke, and when you did you were not kind. The things you said when I was little, just to be mean—saying if I made faces the wind would change and the face would stick and I'd look like that forever and you'd never take another picture of me. And that was all I had, wasn't it? Me on one side of the camera, you on the other. I didn't have any value apart from that. Not for you. Not for me.

You were a handsome man, I always thought so, your eyes were the kind of brown that burned, warm isn't the right word for them. And your mouth, the top lip so defined and controlled, the bottom one thicker, improvident. Greedy.

Your back was very broad for a man who never cared for any "physical culture," as you so quaintly called it; when you died I saw what a big man you were, like I never did when you were alive. You looked bigger lying down, bigger in death. And you still are big, so big—monolithic. In that particular way of dead American celebrities, you've continued to grow. I wonder if perhaps your fame—some would say infamy—would have made you happy. If anything would have.

New York
July 15, 1992

When Ann comes in, it's quarter to five. The shower is running, so Carl is home, too. She drops her bags by the bar and hurries into the bedroom. She'll have to get rid of this blouse, hide it before he comes out of the bathroom—just this morning she saw him looking into her closet, his expression thoughtful. Guilt makes her paranoid, of course, and she's alluded to shopping trips, but they don't explain returning home in clothes different from those in which she left.

It is hard to get the fabric-covered buttons through the small holes, and it seems forever before she manages to struggle out of the shirt. She's just crammed it into the zippered lining of her trench coat when she hears the water being turned off. "Hello," she calls brightly, too brightly. "I didn't expect to find you home so early."

"Uh huh," Carl says through the door, offering no explanation. His voice sounds odd, distant, and Ann feels another twinge of anxiety. She waits a minute, then says, "Are you ever coming out of there?"

"Do you need the bathroom?" he says.

"Not immediately."

"I'm just getting a splinter out."

Ann goes back to the closet and quickly shuffles a few of the more familiar garments into prominence. Then, thinking better of the subterfuge, she reshuffles: it should look as it did this morning when he was staring into it. But how was that? She can't remember, she's too nervous to think clearly. She forces herself to close the door.

She paces the loft, stops in front of the stacked stereo components, punches a few buttons to start a sequence of previously selected CDs, then forces herself to deal with the phone's blinking answering machine. One message from Benny at work, complaining about something; she's worked too hard all day to care what, fast forwards over his voice. One from Doris, saying there's a problem with one of the art handlers transporting prints for the retrospective; also that a Laura someone wants to profile her in the

September issue of *Vanity Fair*, a little extra hype for the show. As if it needed any. Since the thing with the girl at the museum, Doris has been deluged with calls from journalists; she will have assumed, correctly, that Ann will refuse the interview, but she passes along all requests.

The last message is from Bellevue pediatrics, where Ann works as a volunteer each Tuesday from two until five. Three hours a week Ann holds babies born to mothers who didn't want or couldn't keep them and left their infants in the crowded arms of the city, where affection is always in short supply. "Please call Mrs. Hunt at Bellevue Volunteer Services," a voice says.

When she calls, she's informed that next Tuesday the hospital will be relocating its pediatric patients temporarily, while some of the sixth floor's plumbing is being replaced. "But," she says to the volunteer coordinator, "don't they still need help? Just tell me where to go."

The coordinator sighs. "We don't even know where we're putting the kids," she says. "Just show up the following Tuesday." She says goodbye firmly, hangs up.

Ann looks forward to Tuesdays. Because of her diabetes, she is someone whose health cannot take the strain of bearing a child herself; pregnancy might damage her kidneys too severely for them to recover. Her disappointment over this peaked a few years ago when Ann was consumed with longing for a child; she looked covetously at other women's babies, found herself crying during diaper ads. She and Carl talked about adoption; they went as far as the initial interview with an agency. But then Ann backed out, frightened, saying she wasn't ready. Still, on Tuesdays, holding the babies, she finds herself pretending they are hers. Fantasizing about taking a child home. Silly, really, because she can't see herself as a good mother for more than a few hours a week.

After Ann hangs up, she finds herself standing again at the door to her closet. Why is Carl taking so long? She makes herself leave the bedroom. At the bar she gets a syringe from the black lacquer ice bucket where she keeps them, her insulin from the little refrigerator under the stainless steel counter. She's been on so many regimes for better management of her blood sugar that the refrigerator holds all the available types of insulin: regular, fast-acting, slow, ultraslow, and she has to rummage among the little stoppered vials for the one she's currently using. They're all jumbled in the door, along with fake screw-top lemons and limes of varying vintage.

Ann prepares her shot without bothering to check her blood glucose or even to think about the day, what she's eaten and when, what she's likely to eat for dinner, whenever that might be. She should eat within a half hour of her injection, but her blood sugar is probably high enough to keep the insulin busy for a while. Working while cranked, she supplemented the crystal with enough candy to prevent a hypoglycemic crash. With such an inexact science, she tries to err in the direction of high rather than low blood sugar, but either way she ends up feeling like shit.

Ann knows just how much speed she's used today, and how much she has hoarded for the coming weeks when Theo will be on vacation, but she can't remember if she took an insulin shot this morning. It's all getting too complicated, the choreography of her chemical imbalances, both intentional and accidental. Not that she doesn't realize she's being irresponsible, but recent research—one study, anyway—indicates that people who try too hard to control their diabetes, counting everything and exercising and generally living like clock and calorie watchers, don't live that much longer anyway. Since it wasn't by some sort of mismanagement that she'd gotten the disease in the first place—just some rogue gene from her mother's mother's mother—Ann prefers to think of it as a crapshoot, and her attempts to responsibly control her blood sugar are short-lived.

She drops the used syringe into the big studio trash can, watches it disappear into the litter of torn Polaroid backs, crumpled, failed photographs, film boxes, old batteries, empty plastic jugs that once held fixer, all the usual photography trash generated by her infrequent black and white work. She's good, actually; she knows she is very good—a free ride through Yale graduate school on the basis of her portfolio in 1980, and she's gotten better since then. But the work depresses her, standing in the dark depresses her, the smell of the chemicals depresses her; and once she started videotaping, she let what she used to consider her real work slip away. Still, she never empties her big trash can; she likes the illusion of industry. When they moved into the loft, she insisted on a workable studio space, but she hasn't used it except to make a few portraits of Carl.

Ann and Carl's loft is divided by temporary walls into their bedroom, her studio and darkroom, a living space with entertainment center, a kitchen-bar-dining area, two bathrooms, and a dressing room adjacent to Ann's walk-in closet. None of the divisions have any ceiling, and so the brightly lit loft is like a stage: the illusion of their living there ends about ten feet above the oak floor. Carl designed and built the spaces; every once in a while they rearrange the walls, satisfying a restlessness they share.

When Ann met Carl, she was a veteran house sitter, someone who didn't have a place of her own but who moved her suitcases and camera equipment from one furnished apartment to another. There was always some Vintage client who needed a warm body in a temporarily empty home, someone to walk the dog and water the ficus. One spring she was taking care of a place on East Sixty-third next door to a brownstone Carl was renovating; she stepped over the foyer's broken marble floor and called hello. Carl emerged from a room off the entry hall, his dark hair gray with dust. He lifted plastic goggles to reveal blue eyes, a little too close together, but still handsome, very handsome. He looked at her. "Can I help you?" he said.

"I just, uh, hi," she said. "I'm sort of your neighbor. I see the door open every day, so, since I had a minute, I thought I'd look inside." The walls of the once beautiful parlor behind him were badly scarred, original horsehair plaster falling away from the lathes in chunks, the marble mantel scarred and paint-splotched.

"I guess you're tearing it down," she said, looking up at what must have been the house's original chandelier, crystal swags hanging down like broken necklaces.

"Not at all."

"Condos?" she asked.

He stiffened, handing her a business card from his pocket. *Carl Graves. Renovation and Historical Restoration.* "I revive buildings," he said. "I don't put them out of their misery." He turned and looked up into the pink wash of dusk coming from a stained glass skylight over the staircase. "This place was, and will be again, a palace."

"This place is a wreck," Ann said.

"Well now, maybe."

Ann raised her eyebrows.

"You just don't see what I see," Carl said. "People don't. It's all here, under the paint and dirt and broken plaster."

Ann looked at his business card. "What's historical restoration?" she asked.

"It means I spend a lot of time going to salvage companies," he said. He pointed at the newel post at the bottom of the staircase. It was sawed off halfway, making a level surface. "Previous owner used it as a pedestal." He shook his head. "Even if you could get a piece of mahogany like that today, you couldn't find a craftsman to carve it." He smiled. "But I'll find a replacement." He stopped, suddenly self-conscious, and folded his arms over his chest. His left middle finger was missing the last two joints, and he smiled as he saw Ann notice the imperfection. "I guess you haven't been around many woodworkers," he said, waggling the remaining joint. "Sort of a badge of the trade. Just can't flip anyone off with this hand."

Ann returned once before she moved on to the next empty apartment, and then a week after that, when proximity couldn't excuse her visit. She bantered with Carl, betraying her infatuation like a high school girl, pretending not to be impressed as the miracle he had promised took shape before her eyes. In seven years, he told her, he had given up on only one project, a structure whose staircase had collapsed under the weight of the equipment necessary for its repair. "That was a house with a serious design flaw, beautiful but hopeless. It had *twelve* Tiffany windows. Now they're in the Metropolitan Museum." He sighed, clearly disappointed, and unhappy to admit defeat.

A month later they met by chance at a party in Bridgehampton, at an estate owned by a mutual acquaintance. Ann knew their hostess from graduate school, a woman who took pictures of food for *Redbook*, ice cream that wasn't ice cream but whipped lard mixed with food coloring, ice cream that didn't melt under the lights. Raw chickens painted with coat after coat of Liquid Smoke, so that they looked roasted yet juicy. There were huge pictures of food on all the walls of the house.

At the party, sucking hard candies and avoiding the bar, Ann bumped into Carl in the hallway that lead to the powder room. "What are *you* doing here?" she said.

"Rosemary is an old friend of my brother's," he said, gesturing behind him at the hostess. "That's him standing next to her." Ann looked at the tall man, an older edition of Carl, same high forehead. Carl had told her about him; a specialist in pulmonary medicine, he had recently taken over their father's practice.

"What about you?" Carl asked. "How do you know Rosemary?" His face was flushed, and he put his hand out as if to touch her cheek. She reached up to block it.

"If you'll excuse me," she said, "I'll be right back." Once in the safety of the bathroom, Ann didn't want to return. She looked in the mirror, fussed with her hair, reapplied makeup. Suddenly, she decided she couldn't go back.

A drunk girl sitting on the closed lid of the toilet with her chin in her hands, her elbows on her knees, watched with a stupefied interest as Ann bent and removed her shoes. She stripped off her stockings, threaded them through the black straps of the shoes, and then tied them around her waist. The girl, blond, pale, and wearing a beautiful cocktail dress of deep blue moiré silk, sat up and watched as Ann stood on the étagère and opened the high window. She undid the latches that held the screen in place, pulled it into the bathroom, and dropped it on the floor near the bathtub. Then she climbed through the window and jumped into the garden below.

"Hey," the girl called.

Ann was out of condition, barefoot, and it was a warm night, but she started to run as soon as she stood up from the jump. As she sprinted over the humid, summer-salty lawn, the smell of someone's kitchen garden filled her lungs, basil thick and pungent mingling with something sharper, mustard perhaps. She felt her short skirt riding up her thighs. The longer her stride, the higher it forced the skirt. Her feet were getting cut, and she was dimly aware of her heel coming down hard on a small, sharp stone, not pain exactly, just a cataloging of experience.

Ann ran in the street, it was past midnight, quiet. She ran down the white line that divided the two directions of traffic. A distant car honked in irritation. She had already run a mile at least, two, three. Oddly, she wasn't tired, or even winded; she was running, not jogging, but moving fast. And since she had had no dinner, there was that pleasant emptiness as she ran; she was light, free, and she ran and ran, her shoes banging against her hip, her skirt high, her shirt ruined.

Her hair slipped out of its barrette. The night was warm and the road felt hot; she ran further, further. She stopped finally at the ocean, and sat down in the damp sand. She could still feel the heat of his hand as he reached to touch her face. The heat of anxiety, of love. What if she loved him, too?

When she returned to the city, there were two messages from him on the machine.

Ann avoided Carl for a month, and then she moved in with him. What was supposed to be a couple of nights between house-sitting jobs turned into a long-term arrangement. On the morning she was to show up at a place on Gramercy Park, Ann called the tenants, whose own suitcases were probably packed and waiting in the lobby. "I'm sorry," she said, "I think I'm getting married."

Maybe Carl doesn't realize it, but he proposed to her in a health food store; the formal question, weeks later, was just a confirmation. They had been meandering through an aisle of vitamins and esoteric supplements—echinacea, goldenseal, yarrow—all herbs with which Carl was familiar. Ann was carrying a bottle of health-crank root beer in her hand, something probably made from actual roots, when Carl turned around and looked at her.

"Are you taking calcium?" he asked.

"What?" she said, her eyes on the label of some box, the contents of which claimed to cleanse your liver.

"There can't be enough calcium in your diet," he said. "No dairy products and you hardly ever eat greens. Do you take a calcium supplement?"

"Why should I?" she asked.

"Because fifteen years from now you might start getting osteoporosis. Especially since you don't get enough exercise." He looked at her appraisingly.

"Fifteen years from now?" Ann asked with genuine incredulity, incapable of planning for the next week, of getting her shot right so that her sugar didn't spike from day to day.

Back then, she shrugged off his concern, refused to pick out a calcium tablet and put the one he chose back on the shelf. But the question stayed with her, repeating itself in her head. She couldn't imagine any reason that he would ask other than a sincere concern for her health. Even her father, who hoarded thousands of doses of aspirin, enough to ensure against a headache or fever into the next millennium, never suggested she take a vitamin. No one, Ann included, had ever expressed interest in her durability. That question, "Are you taking calcium?" was for her Carl's proposal.

Their wedding was private, because a big ceremony would have been like one more assignment for Ann. Carl's brother came with them to the courthouse but left when his beeper went off; his parents were in Tanzania, and he didn't want to wait for their return.

When Carl's father retired, his parents began traveling six months of every year, usually to exotic places with tour groups of people like them: athletic couples in their sixties who seem determined to have been everywhere and seen everything before they die. When his parents aren't out of the country, they are either preparing for or recovering from a trip, and Ann has never seen Carl's mother without a Band-Aid on her arm covering the site of a recent inoculation against some tropical fever. For Christmas, the family convenes in the Central Park West apartment where Carl grew up. His parents give them souvenirs: scrimshaw and tribal masks, unwearable jewelry. With each other they exchange backpacks and colorful, lightweight windbreakers, compact camera equipment, snake-bite kits. Carl is not close to his parents: ten years of boarding school, followed by out-of-state universities—Berkeley, UCLA—effectively disconnected them. His brother lives less than a mile away, and they never see him either.

The five years Ann has been with Carl have been the happiest in her life. Around the time of Mariette's death in a car accident two years ago, there was a bad patch when Ann briefly rediscovered the chemical solace of amphetamines; but mostly things have been good. It's just that, so far, this summer has been a season of backsliding. She has to get herself in hand.

The only time Carl and Ann have ever talked about drugs was after he discovered a tiny envelope of crystal in her address book. The ensuing fight, to which they now refer as "the big drug bust," ended with Ann's sobbing and flushing the speed down the toilet as Carl watched. In the heat of confession she somehow told him about stealing a pair of earrings and a few magazines—"It just, I don't know, made me feel better about Mariette"—and if Carl's shocked disgust had not scared her into any ultimate reformation, it did end in making her more secretive about her sins this time around. And, she reminds herself now, it had been *years*, two of them, since she'd taken anything, drugs or clothes.

Ann doesn't feel as reckless as her behavior implies—she worries that Carl would leave her if he knew what she's been up to, and she is always saying goodbye to her vices, always in the midst of what she would call a final indulgence. She knows Carl is right in his complaint that she hasn't been home much lately. Scared he might sense her guilt, she's been avoiding her husband and has begun to think of their loft as a pit stop, a place to bathe, change her clothes, eat, sleep. The rest of the time, she's on the run.

When Carl emerges from the bathroom and walks into the bedroom, Ann is sitting in the rocking chair. He towels off while, undressed, she slumps in the chair. She's suddenly tired: the crystal, the candy, it's all gone. When the insulin kicks in, she's really going to crash.

He looks at her. "So," he says, "where are you?"

"I'm here," she says.

"In body, you are."

"I'm just tired."

He sits down on their bed. He's not a prude, but some innate modesty insists that, naked, he drop his towel into his lap. "Is it the show?" he asks.

"Is what the show?"

"Is it the idea of your father's photographs being looked at and talked about that's making you more anxious and, well, weirder than usual?"

"How do you mean *weird*?" Ann carefully avoids glancing at her closet. She has an absurd vision of the clothes becoming suddenly animate and bursting forth to announce their presence. Shaking empty sleeves at her in condemnation.

Carl sighs. "You're distracted, you're irritable, you're always either dead tired or charging around the place like a maniac." He counts the accusations off on his fingers. "I talked to Doris yesterday and she said you haven't returned her calls in a week, and that you cancelled your last lunch date with her. I mean, come on, Ann. Doris is your best friend."

"His . . . well it's nothing to do with Doris, anyway."

"Well, what then?"

Ann sits forward in her chair. "I'm a little preoccupied, I know. It's like . . . This sounds odd but I suddenly am remembering all sorts of things that I haven't thought of for years."

Carl looks at her. "What things?" he says.

"Like—" Ann stops. "I'm not sure," she says. "Just things, things that happened that I forgot."

"Like what?"

She opens her mouth, closes it. "Nothing," she says.

Carl looks at her; neither of them speak. "Nothing?" he says finally. "You suddenly remember 'nothing'?"

Ann gets up, starts toward her closet for a shirt, stops. "I don't want to talk about this right now," she says. "Can we not talk about it right now?"

He shakes his head, reaches for his glasses on the bedside table. "Sure. Sure," he says after a moment. "We can not talk about it right now." He gets up to pull on a pair of jockey shorts. "Come on, I'll make dinner."

Ann smiles, as grateful for the reprieve as for a meal she doesn't have to cook. She'll talk later, but for now, whatever she remembers threatens to recede, evaporate, when she contemplates articulating it for someone else. Even as she tried just now to tell Carl about posing for her father's camera, it was as if she were trying to recount a dream: what she remembered seemed absurd, and parts of what she had thought was a coherent story were suddenly missing. Her mouth open to speak, she was left with nothing more than the idea of herself at the grade school science fair. Chosen from the audience of children to come stand on the stage, putting her hands over her head at the hypnotist's command—as she said to Carl: nothing.

———

After dinner, they stretch out on the couch to watch a video. Drowsy, Ann keeps closing her eyes and falling into a helpless half dream that plays havoc with the plot of the movie. She struggles to stay awake, tries sitting up, but Carl pulls her into a more comfortable position, her head resting on his thigh. At the proximity of her cheek, her mouth, she feels his penis stiffen. "Oh ho," she says, teasing.

"Well?"

"Well what?"

"What do you think?" He raises his pelvis a little, gives her a friendly nudge with his erection, then turns the sound off, stretches. She feels the muscles of his thigh harden under her, and she rubs her head into his groin.

"Great night for a blow job," he says.

"That depends," she says.

"On what?"

"On whether or not you want to redeem one of your gift certificates."

In Carl's underwear drawer are the three little cards Ann gave him for his birthday. Intended as the most lighthearted of presents—especially since Ann is, for all her faults, a generous bedfellow whose favors are unstintingly bestowed and never counted—the little cards have produced an unforeseen revelation about Carl's character. He cannot spend them.

"No freebies?" he asks.

"Not tonight."

"How come?"

"I don't know. Just don't feel like it, I guess."

"But . . ." Carl rubs the back of her neck, kneading the tight muscles. "But you know how I hate to spend them. I want to save them against some future dry spell. A bad mood of yours that might last, oh, six months or so."

Ann laughs. "When did that ever happen?" she says. "My bad moods are fast and furious."

"You never know," Carl says. "Maybe I'll get more of these from you next year," he suggests. "If I knew I was going to get more, I'd part with what I have more willingly."

"Did you get any last year?"

"No."

"Well, can't count on it, then. Might never get any more. Never in your whole life." Ann unzips his fly and slips her finger into his jockey shorts. "On the other hand," she says, "these might have an expiration date, written in very very very fine print." She has his penis in her hand now, close enough to her mouth to pantomime using it as a microphone.

"Please," he says. "Oh please." He struggles up on his elbows; he has slipped half off the couch, his legs on the coffee table and his buttocks suspended over the floor. He looks at her carefully. "But if you don't feel like giving one away, how do I know I'll get a quality job if I redeem one of my tickets?"

"You don't," Ann says. "But I haven't heard complaints in the past."

"Who else did you give these to!"

"You know that's not what I meant!" She withdraws her hand in mock injury.

"No," Carl says, catching her wrist, pulling her back. "I know. And I'd be the first to say that you are a remarkable and multitalented woman."

She traces her finger, wet with saliva, around the head of his penis and he groans. His butt hits the floor, next to where she is now sitting. "A trade," he says, "how about a trade?"

"What kind of trade?"

"Uh. Uhh." Carl clumsily pushes his jockey shorts down over his hips. "You go down on me, I go down on you?" he says.

"Nuh uh."

"I go down on you, you go down on me?"

"Nuh uh."

"Why!" he says.

She holds him in her hand, feels the skin of his testicles draw up and wrinkle under her touch. "I don't know. Not in the mood I guess."

Carl moans. "How about another kind of trade?"

"What?"

"I'll do some other favor for you. Not sexual. Something else."

"You'll give me the sky diving lessons for Christmas?" Ann has taped a brochure to the refrigerator: ten lessons in how to fall out of a plane without dying. Qualified instructor. All equipment provided. A color photograph of five people, holding hands in a circle, faces obscured by goggles and helmets, plummeting through the clouds. Carl has torn it up once and Ann has retrieved the four pieces from the garbage and taped them back together. The only evidence of the tear is a fault line that separates one diver's head from his body so that it hovers slightly to the left of his neck.

"Let's be reasonable," Carl says. "I was thinking more in the line of fixing that leak in your darkroom you've been asking me to look at."

"Umm. I don't know." She strokes the dark hair on his belly, feels the muscles quiver under her hand. "I could call a plumber for that."

"Okay. Okay. Two out of three favors. You pick."

"What are they?"

"Uh, the leak, and that thing on the elevator gate you say keeps snagging your stockings. And one month of dishes, no nagging. I'll do them before you have a chance to ask."

"That's pretty good." Ann tightens her fingers around the root of his penis, and his flesh swells harder.

"What do you mean, pretty good?" Carl squirms. "It's against the law to squeeze your husband's genitals while you barter with him," he says.

"I mean," Ann says, squeezing harder, "that you might not do any of them. That you'll do the dishes twice and then quit, the same as usual."

Ann and Carl's basic understanding is this: she cooks three times a week and cleans the bathroom, he does the dishes. The agreement is successful only in that they are equally remiss in fulfilling their promises.

Carl suddenly pushes the coffee table away from the couch, pins her to the floor. They wrestle for a moment before she gives in and opens her mouth.

Ann lets her tongue linger on the underside of his penis, grazes the head with her teeth: just a greeting, no bites.

"Oh God," Carl says, "oh God." He has his hands in her hair. "You know," he says, "this is . . . the only time I . . . pray." There's saliva running down her chin, her arm. Ann uses her hand as well as her mouth so she doesn't have to feel his penis touch the back of her throat. "Say something," Carl says. "Talk to me." He's twisting his head against the sofa cushions and his face has a strained look as if he's trying to hear some faint music. When he opens his eyes, Ann sees only the whites. She lets her hand take over.

"You know, you're probably the only guy on the planet who expects conversation with a blow job."

He laughs, a short groan of amusement, but she has paused too long, and with one hand on either side of her head he forces her mouth back to his penis. "No hands," he says, and she struggles a little against his insistence. She doesn't like taking him so far in, she can't time the breathing right, the same way she's never learned to swim freestyle: the need for air throws her off. And he doesn't usually ask it of her. That he forces her now makes her wonder if, under the joking, he's angry. She pulls away just as a spasm of what might be mistaken as pain makes his eyes wince closed.

ANN LXXV, 1971*

Two unique gelatin silver prints mounted as a diptych, 40 × 100†
Collection of the artist's estate.

LEFT: Two children, a girl and a boy of approximately twelve years of age, outdoors, in a crude wood structure nailed to the boughs of a tree in full summer leaf. They are naked. The grain of the photograph is evident and suggests the use of a telephoto lens, giving the image a stolen, documentary quality. The girl lies full-length on top of the boy, whose face is turned up toward hers; his neck strains so that the muscles are corded and the veins swell slightly. Her bright blond hair falls across their joined mouths and closed eyes, her hands cover his ears. While the image is not explicit, the children appear to be involved in sexual intercourse.

RIGHT: The girl alone and seated on the floor of what might be her bedroom. In the background is a desk, a chair, an empty bookcase on whose top is an aquarium. She is naked and seated with her arms around her bent knees. The pose is frontal, and as her feet are resting some inches apart, the child's genitals are revealed to the camera. She has no secondary body hair. Her head is tipped back, her eyes closed. In the soft gray light of either dawn or dusk, her face, turned as it is toward the ceiling, or to heaven, suggests an attitude of prayer.

*Unless otherwise noted, editioned prints are courtesy of the artist's estate.
†Dimensions are expressed in inches. Height precedes width.

Texas, 1973

The sessions were long. They set a time when she was to take a
break and eat the sandwich she brought along, but then, at the
appointed hour of four, they often were just entering the most productive
part of the sitting. Often she was lying down and in that position it was
harder for her to know how she felt; she dozed. The first few times it
happened, she never realized how dizzy she had become until she stood up.

She never asked to stop, and her father, monosyllabic while he worked,
didn't think to suggest it. Musing with his camera, making notes about the
exposure on a little pad he kept with a pen in his shirt pocket, he thought
she would care for herself. When she felt herself slipping into an insulin
reaction, she was unable if not unwilling to arrest the process. It was as
if the loss of judgment and perspective were a property of the reaction itself;
and in fact something about the experience implied a transcendence that
was seductive, perhaps to her father also as he witnessed it.

Edgar was never one to acknowledge the frailties of the body. He worked
ceaselessly through colds, the flu, even an attack of infectious hepatitis one
winter, which left him thin and shaken, but still standing, still working.
Sometimes Ann's father was so involved in his thoughts about a picture he
was composing that he himself forgot to eat. Why would he have remembered her hunger?

As soon as the confusion set in—a slight quickening of her heart—there
came the idea that she was late, but late for what? Food didn't present itself
as the answer. The view camera, a Deardorff with its bellows stretched
open, loomed over her like a lunar landing module, her father's legs all she
could see under his black cape. As the reaction progressed, her blood sugar
slipping lower and lower, she began to perspire slightly. Lying down—her
job was to pretend to be dead—it was easy to let the situation deteriorate,
easier, in fact, than arresting the fall: all that commotion, someone running for orange juice, the insult of a finger dipped in honey crammed into
her mouth. And of course, the worse it got and the more passive, pale, and

manipulable Ann grew, the better model she became: the limper, the more absent, the closer, in fact, to death. She looked her part.

Not once, not twice, but too many times—more often than could be judged accidental—the sittings ended in a crisis, but only once in a trip to the emergency room. Her father was angry, something that Ann perceived with a distinct sense of anxiety, on the dim periphery of her consciousness. A large man, he grew small and incidental on the horizon of her perspective. She had slipped too far, past the point where she could answer his irritated "Do you need to eat something? Ann? Ann!" This was a question she always resisted, not simply out of adolescent asceticism, but because what was happening never seemed to have anything to do with something so ordinary, material, and earthly as the consumption of food, the everyday mathematics of the body.

In her mind, what was happening had slipped from the physical to the spiritual; she was ranging on the strange but increasingly familiar territory of her semiconsciousness. The recording figure of her father became almost irrelevant; she escaped her body and learned to walk in this new land, a dull, gray, purgatorial place where sound and light and a sense of the passage of time penetrated only dully. She was at first very aware of her physical self, the spongy thudding of her heart, the expanse and collapse of her respiration, the twisting and gurgling of her intestines. But then all sensations were muffled by a cottony overcast.

Typically, as her father posed her, Ann remained passive, allowed his fingers to arrange her hair, to bend or straighten her limbs and, if she were wearing any, to adjust the material of her clothing. Periodically, he stepped back from her inert form and appraised the composition. Sometimes, it is true, she would fall asleep as he stood above her, thinking with his arms folded. He closed his own eyes sometimes, perhaps to better see the ideal to which he aspired. If he was dissatisfied, as he usually was, he knelt down again on the cement floor, adjusted a lock of hair, a finger's gesture. His hands shook sometimes in concentration, and because he drank a lot of coffee every day and smoked too many cigarettes, more than a pack sometimes. It reminded Ann of the time her broken arm was x-rayed, the technician's careful alignment of the limb against a photographic plate, checking and rechecking the position. Since her father never said, "Ann, uncross your ankles," or, "Ann, I want you to look further to your left," he was unable to gauge her inability to follow simple directions.

———

The emergency room at the hospital consisted of two beds, one doctor on duty, minimal equipment. When her father brought her in, Ann was comatose, far beyond the ability to swallow orange juice or suck on a candy. Mariette held her on the short drive to the hospital. The honey that her father had rubbed into her gums and the inside of her cheek wasn't enough to call her back; and her neck, pale and sticky, had lint stuck to it where the honey had spilled. She wet her pants in the car, as her father told her later, embarrassing her.

Intravenous glucose was administered, and Ann returned to herself on the gurney-like bed behind the curtain. On the rough, sanitized sheets, the words Henfield Hospital Supply marched by her cheek. She realized she felt disappointed to have returned to life. She liked the distance of the experience; she had almost escaped them all as she wandered in the dim, calm landscape of shock.

In the corner of the room, her father looked at her, his jaw tight with anger. She could see the muscle in his cheek. A private man, he was humiliated by all this.

"Where's Mariette?" she whispered.

He took off his glasses, rubbed his dark eyes with thumb and forefinger, and replaced the glasses carefully, as if his nose were sunburned. "God damn it, Ann," he said. "Why did you let this happen? Why don't you carry candy? Why don't you—" He stopped, closed his mouth.

Why don't you, she said in her head.

Why didn't he what? Take care of her? And why did she let it happen? Was she simply trying to force his compassion, to test it? Was it a subtle form of retaliation? In the guise of the obedient model she could get him back by slipping away to this place from which she had to be retrieved. Of its own accord her body conspired with her, led her away from the world: she didn't interfere with it, she let it assert its will over her own.

She turned away from her father's insistent angry questions, looked at the wall, the poster depicting the man bent over the lifeless form of a child. In the first frame, OPENING THE AIRWAY, he had both his hands on the child's head and had positioned it correctly, just so, with the mouth open. The man's lips were painted an unnatural cherry color. The child's, however, were pale, flesh-toned, like the rest of his face. In the second picture, the man looked out of the poster toward Ann, his ear to the child's chest, CHECKING FOR BREATHING. The drawing was not accomplished with the same detail throughout, only essential aspects of the man's and child's physiology were rendered accurately. The child's hands, for example, did not have all four fingers and a thumb but were drawn as clumsy mitts, fingers only suggested.

The fourth frame, MAKE AN AIRTIGHT SEAL, was a close-up of the man's face, his red lips sealed over the child's pale mouth and nose, the child's small chest rising with the man's breath. The drawing made Ann feel sad and confused. She closed her eyes.

In her hand she held a ring of her mother's, one diamond in a thin gold band, the stone so small it was lost in the setting. It was her parents' original engagement ring, the one which, at her mother's death, her father had replaced with a more expensive one—he slipped the new one on her cold finger, Mariette said.

Ann had found the old ring in a box, tucked among her mother's clothes in the attic. It was something she liked to keep with her as she posed, like a charm. Something she couldn't wear, lest he saw it and took it away.

ANN CCX, 1973

Unique gelatin silver print, 60 × 20
Collection of the artist's estate

A girl of approximately fifteen years of age, lying on her side on a bare mattress, wearing underpants, socks, nothing more. Her body is slender and underdeveloped; her blond hair is matted. Folded before her chest, the girl's forearms are scarred. One particularly livid mark suggests a burn; bruises in the form of opposing arcs suggest bites. The subject is apparently awake: at least her eyes are open, but their unfocused stare is that of a trance.

Ann unbuckles the belt she's wearing, deftly freeing the tongue with one hand, and surreptitiously draws the length of it from the loops of her linen trousers. The saleswoman is bent behind the display case, rooting in the stock drawer.

"I'm not sure if I have it in a smaller size," the woman says. Inside the brightly lit case, the tanned goods are displayed like little mummies in an elaborate sarcophagus. "We don't usually carry the more expensive items in multiples," she says.

The alligator belt Ann wants costs nine hundred and five dollars. It lies coiled on the thick glass counter, the ornate sterling buckle shining seductively. Ann touches the silver, runs her finger over the patina of its artfully tarnished filigree. Retrieved from a locked display cabinet, the belt bears no alarm device.

"Mmm. I'm afraid it's just too big," Ann says. "What a shame." She drops her old belt into her camera bag, looks quickly over the counter to see that the saleswoman is still engaged in the contents of the drawers below, and snatches up the alligator one. She works it through the empty loops of her pants, barely getting it buckled and concealed under her jacket by the time other customers press forward and the saleswoman stands.

"No," the saleswoman says. "I'm sorry." She rests her hands on the display case.

"Can I see that?" A woman to Ann's left points through the glass to a green snakeskin belt.

"I need some help," someone else says. The saleswoman looks around in apparent confusion.

"Oh well," Ann says. "I guess I'll just have to take that as a sign, and forget it. My bill is already sky high." She picks up her camera bag and walks off, confident that the sudden, simultaneous demands of other shoppers have abetted her escape. How could the saleswoman know who took the belt while she was busy in the stock drawers? Ann's heart pounds with

illicit pleasure, and she tries to slow her pace. She continues past the
gloves, the scarves cascading down the ribs of a display rack. On to cosmetics and perfume. The belt's heavy buckle insinuates itself against her flesh,
an urgent pressure just under her navel, held tight by her jacket.

At the Chanel counter, she dips her finger into a little glass pot of
moisturizer. The girl behind the counter touches her smooth white neck
self-consciously. She's at least ten years younger than Ann, perhaps even
more. She smiles carefully, not allowing her red, lipsticked mouth to
stretch too wide and possibly mar its precise outline. Clearly, her face is her
greatest asset, and she carries it like a priceless object, something removed
briefly from a glass case for appreciation.

Ann herself is wearing no makeup and, as she fingers the eye pencils and
smells the little bottles of lotion, is aware of the girl's attention to this fact.

"Your bones are exquisite, like a model's really," the girl says. "Would
you like a makeover?" she asks. "You'll look fabulous, really great. I
promise." Ann returns the young woman's stare. The girl's long chestnut
hair is gathered in a barrette and cascades down the back of her white
smock, which is styled to look like a lab coat and thereby allude to efficiency, science: a message of therapy rather than of indulgence. She smiles
eagerly.

"Sure," Ann says. Lately, she's had a number of department store
makeovers. Sometimes feeling too low or impatient to do her own makeup,
she budgets an extra twenty minutes before an appointment. Saks and
Bendel's and Barney's, Bergdorf's and Bloomingdale's, Lord and Taylor
and Macy's. She's made the rounds enough that she hasn't been recognized as a repeat in any one store.

She drops her bags—the one with the heavy videocamera and film, and
the smaller one with her Leica and Rolleiflex and all the junk she can't
seem to go anywhere without—on the floor. If the saleslady from accessories returns with a detective, if they take her to some back room and search
her bags, they'll see her own belt coiled incriminatingly among the film
boxes. But Ann doesn't care: she feels reckless and she's not ready to leave
the store. If necessary, she can always fake an insulin reaction. They'll find
her diabetic ID card in her wallet, read the message it bears: I HAVE
DIABETES. I AM NOT INTOXICATED. IF I AM UNCONSCIOUS OR MY BEHAVIOR IS
PECULIAR I MAY BE HAVING A REACTION ASSOCIATED WITH DIABETES OR ITS
TREATMENT. IF I AM ABLE TO SWALLOW GIVE ME SUGAR IN SOME FORM. The
incident will become, simply, a matter of confusion, of Ann's not realizing
what she is doing.

A small voice questions such suspect reasoning. A voice Ann has heard before, it is growing a little more strident of late. It comes from somewhere over her head and to the left, almost as if Ann has developed an irritating narrator that makes judgmental comments on her behavior. The voice's tone is sarcastic.

Great, it says now. *Just swell. You're really managing your life responsibly, taking good care of yourself. Why not go to the ladies' room, do some more crystal, and go on a real tear? Why stop at Saks? Let's rob a jewelry store, a bank!*

Well, if Ann can't shut the voice off, she can ignore it. She shoves her bags under the stool with her foot and sits down on its firm, white velvet seat. As she draws her legs up to rest her feet on the top rung, she feels the new belt slip a little, the ornate buckle falling lower to her groin. She smiles.

"Great hair," the girl says, offering a steady flow of pleasantries and compliments. "Great cut. Where do you go?"

Ann shrugs as if she can't remember. In fact she cuts it herself—reaching around with the scissors, checking her progress in a double mirror. She gets it colored at Sassoon's. Thick, wavy, and a gold-red for the past ten years, her hair asserts its own form over any style, and she wears it long—past her waist—occasionally twisting it up into a chignon or capturing it in a French braid. Today it's loose and unbrushed, and the Chanel girl gently tucks a few ringlets behind Ann's ears as she readies her face.

"First we'll cleanse your skin," she says, and she pours a pale green liquid on a handful of cotton balls. Clearly, part of the strategy is to demonstrate and instill a spirit of profligacy in customers. Almost half the bottle of expensive astringent is gone. "Now a little foundation," the girl narrates, "nothing oily or heavy, nothing unnatural."

Ann closes her eyes, allows the girl to continue, to make of her face what she will. Each time the girl pauses after announcing her intention: blusher, eye shadow, mascara; she gives Ann a moment to refuse the next ministration, but she does not, she just relaxes under the light touch on her cheeks, her lips, the tiny cold tracing of the eyeliner on her closed lids. It's a strangely intimate experience and one that Ann enjoys, the touch of the young woman's finger on her lips, adjusting the gloss. When she's finished, Ann nods in approval.

"So, what would you like today?" the salesgirl asks. "Perhaps the blusher?" She offers the little compact to Ann.

"Well, I'll think about it," Ann says. The girl's perfect mouth freezes a bit tighter. Most women, after having been so indulgently served, time and skill and cosmetics lavished on them, feel obliged to buy something. A lipstick guaranteed to enhance the complexion, a tiny compact of eye shadow—sparkling powder in a shiny black case. The girl looks puzzled even as Ann picks up her bags and walks off.

When she enters the millinery department, she reminds herself that she doesn't have much time. Luckily, on a Saturday afternoon the aisle between the shining counters is crowded with women trying on hats. They set them carefully on their heads, tilt chins to assess reflections, request hand mirrors to appreciate a big bow in the back or a bunch of silk flowers nodding over one ear. They savor the suspension of a wide Panama over slender shoulders or the pleasing shock of black straw against a long, bare white neck.

Ann herself is lost in enjoyment for a moment before she sees the exact picture hat she wants perched on another woman's head. She looks over the woman's shoulder as she is examining her reflection. "I didn't think so," the woman says and smiles. "I hate to shop, don't you?"

Ann just smiles back, and as soon as the woman puts the hat down on the counter and walks off, Ann snatches it up. There's no alarm device on it, so the woman must have requested it from the case and then lost touch with the overextended salesperson. Ann is in luck.

Lost in the crowd of weekend shoppers, she tucks a lock of hair together with the price tag under the hat's crown and leaves the department. A brisk walk through cosmetics—not too fast and avoiding the Chanel counter—and she's home free. She throws her weight against one of the store's heavy glass doors and, outside, finds herself blinking in the sunlight. She adjusts the brim for shade and hails a cab.

The driver doesn't speak much English and he gets the directions to the wedding confused. Several times Ann has to lean forward to talk to him, putting her mouth to the little hinged compartment for the transfer of money through the barrier of the smudged privacy glass. When he finally seems to be headed in the right direction, she settles back into the hot black vinyl seat and looks at her watch. For someone who worries compulsively about the time, setting all the clocks in her home either five or ten or even fifteen minutes fast, never going without a watch, she is helplessly, hopelessly late.

The experience of shoplifting is changing. When she started last spring, when *it* started, Ann never worried while in a department store. The plotting, the timing, all the little strategies left no chance to consider anything else. But now that she's no longer a novice, she seems increasingly to get trapped in internal arguments or to panic, suddenly, at an unbidden vision of her husband's face, the way his eyes narrow when he is particularly aghast. Maybe, like a childhood illness, the stealing is running its course. It better.

This afternoon she found herself stricken with the notion that she was being followed. But by whom? A store detective? Or had Benny put someone on her because of all the cabs, the fights about where she was, her being late? Had he gotten fed up with her? Had Theo said something? First she thought it was some man handing out perfume samples, then a shoe salesman. Twice she turned around suddenly, but no one was there. Guilty conscience, maybe. Made worse by chronic tardiness.

When she arrives at the church in Riverdale, a squat, granite Episcopal edifice, she's definitely behind schedule, but she doesn't even know by how much because she can't remember how fast she set her watch. Andy— why is Benny always giving her Andy now? There he is, standing on the church's steps as she gets out of the car. Her new belt slips and she hikes it back into place. She'll have to take it off before the service.

"Hi," she says brightly, taking him by the elbow and almost running toward the door to the church. Even his joints feel resistant. They walk quickly up the side aisle toward the bride's mother, whose face relaxes in relief at their approach. At least Ann's hat is perfect; she can see by the woman's expression that she must look good in it.

The church is nearly filled with guests, and Ann dispatches Andy to finish setting up while she goes to the dressing room to talk to the bride. A black actress who plays two roles on daytime television, a sweet ingenue and her evil twin, she is reduced now by stress to a struggle between the two incarnations. Alternately, she chirps and snaps. "Oh thank God," she says when she sees Ann, and then, "You're late, you're *very* late. We're starting in five minutes!"

"Traffic, traffic," Ann says. "I couldn't help it." Why won't she learn to leave earlier? She's reduced a number of brides to tears, which in fact rather become them, but that's beside the point. "You look fine," she says soothingly. "You look *perfect*. And I've done this a million times before. Don't *you* do this too many times?" She smiles, but the girl doesn't react to her teasing. "Nothing will go wrong," she promises. She tucks a sprig of baby's breath back into the bride's headpiece.

Looking out into the church, she sees that Andy has set up. The people sit in the red velvet-cushioned pews, the white flowers look splendid against the red carpet over which the bride and her father will walk. Everything is in place. The bridesmaids stand in a line by the door through which they will walk into the church and up the aisle. Arranged by height, wearing green taffeta dresses with stand-up ruff collars that set off their dark skins to perfection, they look like expensive wrapped chocolates, Ann thinks. They make a dramatic contrast to the groomsmen, all fair-skinned like the groom and wearing black tuxedos.

One of the young men is staring at Ann. He sees that she's seen him and steps forward suddenly. "I . . ." he says. "You're . . ." He stops. "What is your name?" he asks finally.

"Ann Rogers," she answers, sure of what will follow.

"There's a photograph of you in my parents' house," he says. "It's— That *is* you, isn't it?"

Ann smiles, a professional manipulation of her features, a pleasant expression she has perfected in the mirror. "Probably," she says.

"I mean, you're the daughter, right? Edgar Rogers? The one whose photographs are going to be shown at the Modern? My parents are . . . well, they've always been interested in photography," he explains.

"Yes."

He nods. As usual, her confirmation ends the exchange, and he steps back awkwardly, taking his place beside the second bridesmaid.

It happens sometimes, the collision of Ann's separate worlds. Not often enough that she doesn't have to marshal herself to respond politely even as she imagines some unhappy document of her past hanging on a stranger's wall. Posed as if dead. Naked, perhaps. The thing is, while some people change, Ann still looks very much like the teenager she was; and black and white photographs make a different hair color less significant.

The groomsman unbuttons his jacket, adjusts his cummerbund, rebuttons. He looks unhappy, and his cheeks are red. Perhaps, like Ann, he is thinking of the young woman who set herself on fire. Ann has called New York Hospital several times since the incident, but they will not release any information about the girl. Ann wants to know if she survived; but the newspapers have said nothing more, and she cannot bring herself to ask Doris to do the detective work.

The bride appears with her father, and Ann nods at them. "Two minutes," she says. The prelude music is just ending, and she hurries up the side aisle to take her place.

Andy is waiting by the altar, standing in a semblance of attention by one of the two camcorders the service will require. The cameras, heavier and more complicated to use than home equipment, are set up on tripods, and there are standing lights as well, which he's managed to set at a discreet distance from the altar; still, the minister squints in irritation. Some churches do not allow lights or cameras near the altar or even in the aisles, and Visage promises to accomplish a wedding video with minimal intrusion. But many church interiors are too dark to film without auxiliary light, and Visage also guarantees a broadcast-quality film of any event; the company does not employ low-light cameras, whose fidelity is compromised. Even carefully placed, the necessary equipment blocks the congregation's view; but some couples are more concerned with having a good tape than with the aesthetics of the event itself or the comfort of the guests.

Ann trains her camera on the altar, looks through the viewfinder. A battery cable lies too close to the priedieu where the couple will kneel, and Ann gestures to Andy, making a sweeping motion with her hand. As the wedding march begins and the congregation stands and turns to the rear of the church, giving him a moment unobserved, he steps forward and shoves it aside with his foot.

The ceremony is a short one, interdenominational and very understated, considering that it's for TV people. No organ, no flutes, no sopranos, just a tasteful Bach recording that Ann will borrow for the score of the little film she'll create. She gets a good shot, a close-up of the groom's hand as he tucks the same stray sprig of flowers that Ann adjusted before back into the bride's headpiece.

———

Four hours later, back in the editing room at Visage, Ann is pleased by the afternoon's work. She's scanned both the tapes, the one she made and auxiliary footage taken by Andy: the guests seated for the ceremony, the cake, the pyramid of presents, the flowers—all useful for inserts into the final product. Key moments from the reception—the first dance between the bride and her father, the best man's embarrassed retrieving of the garter from the bride's silk-stockinged thigh—have been taped twice, from different angles.

Ann likes to edit, reviewing an event she's just experienced, seeing it through the always mysterious and sometimes sly eye of the camera. She runs three color monitors at once—two for the original tapes, one for the final. Visage has enough equipment to accommodate simultaneous editing of more than one finished tape: seven monitors, a character generator, audio mixer, a big gadget called a toaster that offers hundreds of different editing cuts, wipes, and fades. Benny is the brains of Visage, the electronics genius who actually understands how the whole system works. Ann knows only which buttons to push for the effects she wants. On occasion she's gotten trapped in technological snares and has even accidentally erased footage. Of course, with video all the editing is done electronically, no messy splicing, no evidence of cutting on the proverbial darkroom floor; but for Ann the job requires a calm solitude, and she often chooses to do it on the weekend, when she can have the editing room to herself.

Today's ceremony went well, and making a nice wedding into a perfect one is relatively easy. Her job is more challenging when things go wrong, for Visage is not in the business of creating warts-and-all portraits, and Ann has had to become adept at creating tapes that entirely misrepresent a less fortunate celebration. Brides who weep throughout their vows are dubbed over with inserts of their smiling, restored faces, mascara smudges wiped away, fresh blush on pale cheeks. She leaves enough tears to suggest the dew of emotion and erases the rest. If the bride looks perfect except for her fingertips—nails bitten to the quick and cuticles bleeding—Ann uses an auxiliary, staged recording of the maid of honor's hands slipping the ring on the groom's thick finger or clasping the frosting-smeared cake knife. Separate audiotaped material—music from the ceremony or a recording from Visage's classical music library—is spliced into a soundtrack that obliterates any discordance or indication of woe. Weddings are made harmonious right to the final burst of applause; for Ann has discovered that people who want their vows professionally recorded tend to invite audiences rather than mere congregations.

All this subterfuge requires a good deal of time and patience in the editing room, a willingness to play the recorded event over and over, harvesting each good or usable instant, sometimes resequencing shots, dubbing over a clumsy moment. This time, seconds in which the groom's hand groped for the ring are replaced by a close-up of the bride's father hugging her tearful mother. She ends the tape with a shot of the bride's arm waving out from the tinted window of the limousine.

As she turns off all the equipment, she realizes that she's been working for the last hour or so with one hand covering her left eye. It's the second time she's caught herself doing this. Last time, she couldn't explain the behavior other than that it was more comfortable working that way. The hand creeps up when she's preoccupied and stays. She looks around the editing room. Her vision seems fine, but there's a sense that her eyes are at cross purposes.

She feels a sudden squeeze of anxiety, like a hand at her throat, and she covers her left eye, looks around. The right's report is perfectly normal. But when she repeats the test with her hand over the other eye, she notices a subtle peculiarity: lines that should be straight—the edge of the table, the seam where the walls meet—are wavy.

Ann moves her left eye slowly over the room. Everything is in focus, but the slightly disrupted vision, the *warp*, makes her feel dizzy and nauseated. Or perhaps it's just anxiety that's making her sick.

If it isn't better—and even if it is—she'll have to call Ettinger's office first thing Monday morning.

Y*ou could never stand to be home alone and sometimes you would pick me up out of my bed and take me to sleep in your room. Not in the bed, no, that wouldn't have been proper—and you never did anything that wasn't proper, so you laid me down on the floor next to the bed. I'd wake up later with my hands in your slippers, the old braided rug around me. I was cold, but grateful that you wanted me, if only to lie on the floor near you.*

Your room was so dark with those blinds, no wonder you didn't want to be in there alone. Your eyes tightly closed under the further guarantee of a sleep mask: absolute black night. You guarded your sleep so jealously; ear plugs made your escape complete.

The night you died, Papi, the moment you died, I was fucking a boy. Not a nice boy, not a handsome boy, not even a boy I knew very well, but still I was not alone. And I wasn't being good.

So many hours lying there, posing. I would drift sometimes, and that made it bearable. I would think any crazy thing, try to imagine what the best thing would be. Fucking an angel, I thought. That was as close as I could come to the idea of God. A very beautiful boy. I would feel the air on my face from the beating of his wings. When angels come they beat their wings, it makes a noise like a flock of birds lifting off the water.

Your favorite piece of music was Malaguena. *You made me take lessons twice each week from that old man who cut my fingernails so short it hurt to pick up a spoon. "When will you be able to play* Malaguena?" *you'd ask. "Can you play* Malaguena *yet?"*

I learned it. At your request I played it perfectly, repeatedly, until I couldn't hear the notes for the screaming inside my head. One day, about a month ago, it was broadcast on the radio in a cab, and though I could not make the connection, did not know what I was hearing, my fingers started throbbing just like the first hours after the lesson and Mr. Leonard's little German scissors. An hour later I was recording with a zoom from a church balcony. The wedding gown's train was very long, it fell down the six stairs from the altar and behind it bright sunlight on the floor made the white satin seem to go on forever. It was a beautiful shot and I ruined it, pushed the wrong button when I remembered suddenly why the music in the cab made my fingers hurt. Seconds later, the sun was behind a cloud, the magic light was gone, and you had exacted a little cost from a young bride you never knew.

What did you want? What would have made it all work? It wasn't enough to play the piece carefully, or to lie so still.

It's the people who hide themselves so thoroughly from you, they are the ones that possess you. They make themselves mysterious, ever receding, eluding perception, and you chase them forever. And who am I thinking of, Papi? You? Or me?

You took the lock off the door to the bathroom Mariette and I shared, broke the knob. There was one on the outside of my bedroom door though, so I could be locked in. I hated that room and all its closets where you stored your chemicals. You said you didn't have enough space in the darkroom. That wasn't true, you wanted a reason to come in anytime, checking to see: what was I doing? My pathetic little secrets. What were you waiting for? Of what did you think me capable? I was just a girl, like a million others.

Sometimes I hid on the floor in the big closet where my clothes were, the door open just an inch or two. You'd come in the room, and as you passed you'd close the closet door, shut me in that safe place where you couldn't see me.

You were smart but never took the time to consider. Really, it was perfect to be a photographer: so fast, the blink of a shutter, you don't think about what you're saying. Well, there's composition, I suppose, you took enough time with that, but did you think about anything else? Photography was your compulsion, a construct that blocked your view even if you said it was the camera that let you see.

Now you're dead and you never had an idea who I was. I was so far underground you never caught me, I went under deeper and deeper. There was a feeling of triumph sitting next to you on the couch and knowing that I was safe, that you had no idea really. I came home every day from school, I submitted to your vigilant lens, and we never talked about what my life was, what I cared about.

The three of us around the dinner table. "May I please be excused?" I would say, standing before you had a chance to put down your fork, look up from your plate. "Ann!" Mariette said if I hadn't eaten enough. And I would sit again, or my body did as Ann slipped away. Sometimes I felt Mariette's hand on my knee under the table, a furtive hello, but I was too far distant to acknowledge it.

Texas, 1973

"Please, let's not talk," Ann said. She reached out, put her hand over Mark's mouth. She could feel the moisture of his breath under her fingers, his ribs as he squirmed against her, tee-shirt riding up over his stomach. Deep in the gulch between two grassy hills separating the west Texas towns of Jessup and McKittrick, they had only a few minutes left before she had to be home. Their rusted ten-speeds lay in the broom weed, and the wind teased a strip of unwound tape hanging from one of the handlebars of Ann's bicycle, making it snap.

Ann held him tight, so tight, then let him go. Having escaped, for a moment, the demands of school and father, Ann wanted only to lie in the weeds with Mark. Leaning on her elbow, she traced the vein at his temple, a blue ghost of life under the skin, followed it just to the point where it disappeared under his brown hair.

She rolled with him in the dry grass. "Okay, time to pay up," she said, sitting on his stomach, sealing her lips over his and stealing his sweet, heavy exhalation, letting it fill her lungs. She didn't love him, at fourteen years old, not exactly, but she wanted his breath inside her.

Every minute that she could slip away, she spent with Mark. Waited for him on the McDunnoughs's porch as he finished his chores. The whine of thousands of cicadas was loud and furious, like a buzz saw, and the big cottonwood's boughs were full of them, its trunk encrusted with their abandoned exoskeletons, tiny armored suits split neatly down an invisible seam to free the growing insect.

Sometimes, in his little brother's tree house, they took off all their clothes. And whenever her father or Mariette let her go, Ann ran down the alley that cut behind all the houses on Sutter Street and banged breathlessly on the frame of the screen until Mark's mother answered.

"Just come in, come *in*," his mother would yell. She didn't even look up from the novel she was reading at the breakfast table, holding the book open among the dishes. Ann passed Mark's twin sisters' room, the floor strewn with toys, the little girls on the floor, their identical heads together. They whispered and laughed, manipulating the limbs of tiny plastic dolls, speaking a secret puzzle language that no one else could decode.

Half-unpacked cartons narrowed the hall to Mark's room into a dark passage through which even Ann had to pass sideways. He would be lying on his side reading or listening to the radio amidst the clutter of books and clothes, everything heaped on the floor where he slept. His bed, the mattress bare, was covered in coins, tarnished spoons, patent medicine bottles, two with labels intact. Mark had discovered the original town dump, and with a shovel he dug deeper and deeper that summer, searching through the last century's garbage.

"Let's go," he'd say when he saw her, pulling his shorts up to cover the elastic band of his underwear, but they immediately slipped down again, exposing the crests of his slender hips, slipped down just to the root of his penis. When they were alone in the weeds, she'd trace her finger slowly, limning the line of his pelvis, feeling the bones under his skin. The essence of him was so close to the surface, too close—that architecture upon which hung his life, breath, being. It made her feel like she couldn't breathe deeply enough, like she was suffocating, and she'd jump on him and pummel his back.

In his bedroom he worried his dirty, sockless feet into sneakers, never bothering to undo the knotted laces. "Let's go," he said again, and Ann followed him past the girls' room, their matching dollhouses disgorging tiny furnishings onto the yellow shag carpet, and out into the stupefying heat.

They walked to the dump where Ann sat in the shade as Mark dug and sifted through the junk. Then they lay in the empty lot behind his house until dinnertime. "So why're your folks always having dinner at six?" he asked.

"Because my father wants it that way."

"Why?"

"Because he goes into the darkroom after dinner, at seven."

"I've never seen your dad," Mark said, musing aloud, not really challenging her.

"I don't see yours much," she answered.

Evidence of Mr. McDunnough's existence, however, was everywhere in Mark's house: a box of ammunition—.38 wadcutters—in the den's desk drawer, foil-wrapped prophylactics under the socks in the tall walnut bureau, cigarettes that Mark filched for Ann from the carton in the cupboard over the refrigerator and which she kept in a Band-Aid box along with those she stole from her father.

Mark came over to Ann's house only after her father was working, safe in his darkroom. They watched TV in the den, and she unzipped the fly of his brown corduroy shorts.

"Hey," he said, "your aunt's in the kitchen." But he let her put her hand inside his jockey shorts, touch the skin at the tip of his penis; and he kissed her as he did in the tree house, the oily smell of his infrequently washed hair staying so palpably in her memory that Ann would forever find the smell of dirty hair arousing.

When Mariette went out for a walk, they took their shirts off and lay chest to chest on the floor of her room, the heat of their skins magnified by touch. She put her mouth on his neck, listened to his heart.

At nine Mark said he had to go. Ann remained lying on her side on the carpet of her darkened room, her hands tucked between her knees. She dozed. Sometime later, eleven, midnight, her father walked down the hall, his steps paused outside her room. Mariette had gone to bed already, calling goodnight, closing her door.

Her father's silhouette was just visible, the light from the street came through her window and caught the frame of his glasses, the buckle of his belt. "Ann?" he said, and she sat up from the floor.

For a long while neither of them spoke. She began to reach for her shirt, and he said, "It's bedtime, isn't it? Why don't you just put on your pajamas?"

When she was dressed for bed, she switched on the light. "You missed a button," he said, and when she looked down to check, he left her.

The next day, Sunday, Ann met Mark under the tree house. He had his gun—a .22 with a scarred, real wood stock and bluing on the barrel—and a box of the small bullets. He reached for her hand as they walked through the brown grass. Wet with dew, it left their pant legs sodden and heavy with moisture, slapping against their shins. They walked past the border of Jessup to the fields behind the feedlot where a couple of oil rigs slowly pumped the earth, their insectlike heads dipping, rising, dipping in the weak, early sun. They kissed for a while, forgetting the gun.

"So, he just stood there?" he asked when she told him about her father. "Uh huh."

He shrugged, looked away. "Come on," he said, finally, "I'll show you how to shoot straight."

They loaded the gun and crouched in the grass until their thighs ached before Mark finally saw his prey: a large, ugly lizard. Sluggish in the morning cold, it was moving too slowly to avoid its fate, and when he shot it, it flipped up into the air and fell on its back in the dirt. They inspected the dead animal which had been gutted, white belly gashed with red, dry tail whipping in the weeds.

"Now you," Mark said, and Ann practiced for a few rounds until she could repeatedly hit a Coke can from twenty, even thirty, yards. The gun was light. After a few rounds, she hardly felt the kick. "You're *good*," he said admiringly. "Okay. Now we wait for something better."

Ann was staring at the jackrabbit for some moments before she saw him; his coat was the same color as the dry grass, his wet eye winking. With the gun's barrel propped on her knee as she sat waiting against the wall of a well cap, she didn't even have to aim. The rabbit hopped into the sight, and was dead before the thought registered that she had shot him.

Ann and Mark walked slowly to the place where the body lay in the grass. Its ears were long and tattered—someone else had taken aim at him before—and it was astonishing that he could have lived or run at all, his long legs were so scarred with shot. The tendon rising from one powerful back foot was bare of fur and pink with old wounds, nothing more than the will to flight had propelled him forward. In death his eyes remained open and bright.

Later, years later, Ann was surprised to see a photograph her father had taken of her standing in the quiet Sunday fields, her hair blowing forward into her eyes, a few strands sticking to a smear of blood on her forehead. A telephoto lens had produced a picture too grainy to report the subtlety of emotion, and the black and white film rendered the blood black, like soot. Shocked to see it.

Shocked also to see other photographs of what she had thought was her private, secret life. To know, finally, that nothing she did was private. Nothing had escaped her father.

How did he do it? How could he have followed her, and what had he thought of her as she lay patiently under his hands as he posed her? What had he thought of her pretense of docility as she submitted each week to his bleaching her hair which had turned brown at the approach of puberty?

When she got home that Sunday afternoon, leaving Mark at the tree house, she washed her face, changed her clothes. At four, she knocked on the door to his studio. Her father was at the darkroom sink, mixing the bleach. He sat her at the darkroom sink and began working from behind, where she couldn't see him.

"You'd think he'd cut his tongue on your braces," her father said. He dipped the applicator in the purple-paste and painted it along her scalp where the part in her hair exposed the secret dark roots.

She ran her own sore tongue over the wires, said nothing.

So that not even a hint of brown hair would show, they bleached her roots every weekend. Before he finished making the twenty or more parts from forehead to nape, the first application began to burn.

Ann kicked the legs of the darkroom stool. Her eyes watered; "I hate this!" she cried in exasperation.

"Do you want to stop being my model?" her father asked. He paused in his painful ministration, the applicator in his hand.

"No," Ann answered.

"Okay, then. Sit still."

He rinsed her hair. The sink was hard against her neck and smelled so strongly of fixer that it almost obliterated the burn of hydrogen peroxide in her nostrils. The towel, folded in eighths to pad her neck, slipped as it always did.

After her hair was dry and before Mariette called her to come in and wash for dinner, Ann escaped and climbed the trunk of the pecan tree in Mark's backyard. He wasn't home, she knew he wouldn't be. Her scalp, pink with irritation, burned. It would itch for a day in the spots where the bleach had remained the longest, and she tried not to touch it. Lying on her side on the gray boards, she put her hands over her eyes, bit her lips to keep from crying. The tree rocked slightly in the wind.

Ann could not see where her father kept his camera, and the pounding of her heart, the wind in the leaves, the voices of distant children, all conspired to obscure the one clue to his presence, the click of the shutter's instant theft.

IN THE SUPERIOR COURT OF THE STATE OF TEXAS
IN AND FOR THE COUNTY OF ECTOR
114TH JUDICIAL DISTRICT
IN SESSION AS A JUVENILE COURT
BEFORE EDWARD L. APPLEBAUM, REFEREE
DEPARTMENT 12

— — —

IN THE MATTER OF   )
ANN ROGERS, a Minor) *TEMPORARY MANAGING CUSTODY*
)

Reporter's Transcript of Proceedings

ECTOR COUNTY PROBATION CENTER
1200 Main
Odessa, Texas

July 16, 1973

APPEARANCES:

FOR THE DEPARTMENT OF HUMAN SERVICES:	MR. JOHN MILLS, Assistant County Attorney
FOR THE MINOR:	MR. ALBERT LORDAN
ALSO APPEARING:	MRS. EUGENIA DAVIS, Child Welfare Worker
	MR. EDGAR EVANS ROGERS Pro Se Respondent

ABIGAIL WOLF
Certified Shorthand Reporter
#2727

STATEMENT OF FACTS
VOLUME II OF 3 VOLUMES

On the 16th day of July, 1973, a hearing was held in the matter of the above entitled and numbered cause before said Honorable Court, Judge Edward L. Applebaum, in the 114th Judicial District Court, Ector County Courthouse, and the following proceedings transpired:

PROCEEDINGS

THE COURT: Is the Petitioner ready?

MR. MILLS: Yes, Your Honor.

THE COURT: Is the Respondent ready? Is the Respondent here?

MR. ROGERS: Yes, Your Honor. I have no lawyer.

THE COURT: That's all right. Are you ready?

MR. ROGERS: Yes.

THE COURT: Is the Intervener ready?

MR. LORDAN: The Intervener is ready, Your Honor.

THE COURT: At this time the Petitioner may proceed.

MR. MILLS: Your Honor, we're calling the Matter of Ann Rogers. In that matter, we'd call Mrs. Davis first.

THE COURT: I've read the Report of the Agency. You are recommending the father's custody be reinstated?

MR. MILLS: That is correct, Your Honor.

THE COURT: So, in terms of need for continued detention, this is to be regarded as an accident of negligence, not just on the part of the parent, but also on the part of the Minor who, at—what is it?—fourteen years of age?—has been managing adequately on her own for some time.

MR. LORDAN: However, there is Dr. Aldrich's statement, Your Honor, dated July 10. We absolutely feel that the Minor should be placed under temporary foster care.

MR. ROGERS: Can I say something, Your Honor, I'd like to be given the opportunity to describe the incident with a clearer mind than I had at the time of the, uh, accident. I'd like—

THE COURT: You'll get your turn, Mr. Rogers, sit down, please. Mr. Lordan, you are recommending the Agency detain the Minor?

MR. LORDAN: I am. Dr. Aldrich's initiating report and the report of the attending physician at Jessup Emergency Services both indicate that the

Child suffered severe insulin shock, which is life endangering. Pending further medical investigation, I object to the Child's being released to anyone who has had custodial care of the Child in the past.

THE COURT: All right, Mr. Lordan. Thank you. Let's just proceed with the hearing. Mr. Mills, call your first witness, please.

MR. MILLS: The state would call Mrs. Eugenia Davis.

THE COURT: Step forward, Mrs. Davis, and be sworn.

EUGENIA DAVIS
called as a Witness by Mr. Mills,
being first duly sworn, testified
as follows:

THE CLERK: State your full name.
THE WITNESS: Eugenia Davis.
THE CLERK: Please be seated.

Direct Examination by Mr. Mills

Q. Mrs. Davis, where are you employed?

A. I work for the Texas Department of Human Services in Child Protection Services.

Q. Will you tell the Court, please, what your educational background and training is?

A. I have a bachelor's degree from Rice University. I did postgraduate work at Baylor University and I have been working for the Department for eleven years. I've had all the training and then some for a CPS worker.

Q. And as part of your job responsibilities is it standard that you go into people's homes and conduct investigations for the removal of children?

A. Yes, that's true.

Q. And did you conduct such an investigation in the matter of Edgar Rogers?

A. I did.

Q. From your investigation of Mr. Rogers's home, would you tell the Court what your recommendation was in reference to Ann Rogers.

A. I recommended that Ann Rogers be returned to the custody of her father, Mr. Edgar Rogers.

Q. When you were in the home, how did the Child appear?

A. Ann seemed happy, healthy—appeared to be. She was described by her aunt, Mariette Crane, as high-spirited.

Q. And what was the condition of the home in which they were living?

A. It was clean and comfortable. There weren't any—nothing was spared materially for comfort.

Q. Now, in that this is a hearing to determine medical negligence, I need to ask if you have concluded—through your observations and discussions with health care professionals and what-all—that the juvenile diabetes of Ann Rogers is being adequately managed by the family?

A. In sum I do.

Q. In sum?

A. Well, obviously there has been a sort of unfortunate incident, but I think after observing that it was accidental, not negligent, and that future care will correct any problem. It can be looked at as a warning which everyone heeded—to say, well, to say that adequate attentoin wasn't being paid before, but is now.

Q. In short, do you see any problem with Mr. Rogers and his daughter if she continued to live in that home?

A. No, I do not.

Q. Mrs. Davis, if this Child is to be placed, do you think it preferable that she be placed with her father or in foster care?

A. We are very resistant, you know, to separating families without good, I mean really good, cause. I feel that the parent should have the Child.

MR. MILLS: Thank you. That's all we have of this witness.

MR. LORDAN: Am I going to be next in line, Your Honor?

THE COURT: (Nods head up and down.)

Cross-Examination by Mr. Lordan

Q. Do you know where Ann Rogers is living right now?

A. I know where she was several days ago.

Q. And where was that?

A. She was in foster care with the Carmichael family.

Q. And why is that?

A. Because the—because CPS removed Ann Rogers from the custody of her natural parent following a report to the Agency from her pediatrician. It was, well, it was a protective measure pending investigation.

Q. And what was that investigation?

A. Well, it happened that—there was—the pediatrician of Ann Rogers made a report to the Agency that he felt it was warranted that we investigate the Rogerses because of the frequency with which Ann had had these reactions, incidents in which the insulin of a diabetic isn't monitored well enough. The last such incident led to Ann's being treated at Emergency Services.

Q. And are these reactions life endangering?

A. It's my understanding that they can be if they aren't arrested.

Q. So this custody hearing is one that is trying to assess the possibility of medical neglect?

A. Yes, that's my understanding, sir.

Q. And will you define medical neglect for the Court?

A. Well, Priority One referrals, such as this, warrant immediate removal because the situation is deemed life threatening by a CPS specialist. But it's—

Q. Thank you, Mrs. Davis.

A. Your Honor, I just want to add one more thing.

THE COURT: (Nods.)

A. A long-term removal of a minor on the grounds of medical neglect is warranted only when the parent is uncooperative, and I did not in my study conclude this to be the case with Mr. Rogers. The pediatrician is required by law to report any serious suspicion that he might have, and that's how a whole thing like this happens, that's what happened here. But—

THE COURT: Thank you, Mrs. Davis. The Court is familiar with the process. Let's just allow Mr. Lordan to proceed. There are others in line today, and we don't want to send everyone else home without a hearing.

Q. (Mr. Lordan) Thank you, Your Honor. Now, Mrs. Davis, am I right that the transcript of your investigation contains a summary of your interview with the reporting physician?

A. You are.

Q. Will you please read that summary starting here where my finger is, so that we can hear a little about juvenile diabetes. Because it's more complicated than we—I mean we might think we understand it, but a little time spent on explanation won't hurt.

THE COURT: If you'll please, Mr. Lordan, only take as much of our time as necessary.

Q. (Mr. Lordan) Yes, Your Honor.

A. Here?

Q. Yes, go ahead please.

A. Okay. Diabetes mellitus is a metabolic disorder that inhibits the body's manufacture of insulin which is necessary for the conversion of food to energy. To survive, a diabetic like Ann relies on injections of pork insulin. But it's a hit-and-miss process, sometimes the injection is less, sometimes more, than she actually needs at a given time. The resulting imbalance can be critically significant. If Ann gets too little insulin in comparison to the sugars she ingests, then the blood sugar will be too high—high enough and she'll go into a coma. If she gets too much insulin, then she will go into what's called insulin shock. Is that right? Shall I stop here?

Q. Go on, Mrs. Davis. Skip down to the definition of insulin shock.

A. Insulin shock is a rapid fall in blood glucose levels which results in sweating and palpitations, tremors in some people, headaches, nausea, pallor. Sometimes it looks like intoxication, with slurred speech and inappropriate, excitable behavior. Reactions to insulin vary a good deal from individual to individual. But if insulin shock isn't treated with sugar, candy, or some form of simple carbohydrate, then it results in a loss of consciousness, even brain damage.

Q. Thank you, Mrs. Davis, you can stop there. I think we can agree then that Ann, being of—how did you describe it?—high spirits, rebellious perhaps, needs an extra measure of guidance to prevent what could be a life-threatening occurrence. Would you say that's accurate?

MR. MILLS: I object, Your Honor. The attorney is testifying.

THE COURT: Sustained.

Q. (By Mr. Lordan) I'll rephrase. Given that we all can agree that Ann's condition is one that requires monitoring beyond her own capacities—

MR. MILLS: Your Honor.

THE COURT: Overruled.

Q. (By Mr. Lordan) Thank you. Is it your opinion that adequate care is taken of the Child?

A. Yes.

Q. And on what do you base that judgment, Mrs. Davis?

A. Well, there is more than one adult in the home. The aunt has been a surrogate parent to Ann for all her life. She is the one, in fact, who accompanies Ann to medical checkups.

Q. And you are confident that the Child is cared for adequately within this arrangement? Evidently Dr. Aldrich was not so confident, in that he made the initiating report to the Agency.

A. I am confident, yes. Dr. Aldrich had what he felt was a reasonable concern and as such it was his duty to call on the Agency. And the Agency has responded, investigated, and it's my, our, conclusion that Ann Rogers is adequately cared for.

MR. LORDAN: Thank you. Pass the witness.

THE COURT: Do you have any questions, Mr. Rogers?

MR. ROGERS: No, no questions, Your Honor.

THE COURT: Very well. Who is the state's next witness?

MR. MILLS: Mr. Rogers. Edgar Rogers.

THE COURT: You may proceed.

EDGAR EVANS ROGERS
called as a Witness by the Petitioner,
first duly sworn, testified as follows:

THE CLERK: State your full name.

THE WITNESS: Edgar Evans Rogers.

THE CLERK: Thank you. Please be seated.

Direct Examination by Mr. Mills

MR. MILLS: Can you describe the incident involving Ann that led to your taking her to the emergency room last Friday evening?

A. Yes. For some years now Ann has been my model—I am a photographer—and we have set times during the week when she helps me, poses, and I make pictures of her. Friday afternoons is one of those times.

Q. How many hours a week does your daughter model for you?

A. It depends. Eight or ten.

Q. Go ahead.

A. On Friday I was taking a picture that required Ann to lie still for an hour or so, maybe an hour and a half. Not an uncomfortable position, and I imagine the work might be boring for her, but Ann has always said she didn't mind, and I've even known her to fall asleep. I try to remember that she needs to eat, but when I work I am thinking about the pictures and when I think of Ann it is as a model. We have talked about this. I have reminded her of this and asked that she be an adult about her needs, that she ask to stop when she needs to and that she take breaks and eat. On Friday when we were through for the day, she was clearly in a reaction. She was very pale when she stood, and she did faint then. When I tried to revive her I could only bring her around halfway. So I took her to the hospital.

Q. Has anything like this ever happened before, has Ann ever had a reaction so severe that she has needed medical treatment?

A. No.

Q. In the context of your work as a photographer using your daughter as a model has Ann had a reaction that you have successfully treated at home?

A. She has complained before of feeling unwell after the sittings. On those few occasions she has eaten something and then taken a nap before dinner.

Q. So you are aware of the daily possibility of an insulin reaction and are prepared to stop and care for your daughter.

A. Yes, I am. I rely on Ann to tell me what she needs, but I respond to those needs.

Q. Thank you.

THE COURT: Do you have any questions, Mr. Lordan?

MR. LORDAN: Yes, Your Honor.

THE COURT: Proceed, then.

Cross-Examination by Mr. Lordan

MR. LORDAN:

Q. Mr. Rogers, how often does your daughter Ann ask to take a break during your photo sessions?

A. Not very often. Rarely.

Q. Do you remember the last time Ann asked for some sort of recess to eat something, walk around?

A. Not offhand, no.

Q. Do you believe your daughter is competent to care for herself?

A. She is fourteen.

Q. That's not what I asked. I asked if it was your opinion that Ann is competent to care for herself.

A. Yes, I do.

Q. But you know that diabetes is a potentially life-threatening ailment?

A. Yes.

Q. And you understand that whether or not your daughter says she is hungry or indeed even feels hungry she should, as directed by her physician, eat regularly to prevent insulin shock?

MR. MILLS: Objection, Your Honor. The attorney is testifying again.

THE COURT: Overruled.

Q. (By Mr. Lordan) Thank you. Mr. Rogers, do you understand that Ann must interrupt whatever work she is doing to eat, whether or not she says she is hungry?

A. Yes.

Q. Then can you explain why it is that you did not make sure she ate on the afternoon that preceded her hospitalization?

A. Yes. I understand now, as a result of Ann's collapse, what I did not understand before.

Q. Tell me, Mr. Rogers, would you notice while photographing Ann if she were to become pale?

A. I might. But we often use makeup.

Q. Was Ann wearing makeup on the night she went into shock and you took her to the hospital?

A. I'm not sure. She may have been. Yes.

Q. Was she or wasn't she wearing makeup?

A. Yes, she was.

Q. Are you sure?

A. Yes.

Q. But you say that afterwards you noticed that she was pale.

A. That was when we were finished and she stood up. She was so pale that it was obvious that she was ill even with the makeup.

Q. Can you tell me why it was that you did not notice earlier that your daughter was going into insulin shock?

A. As I said, she was posed as if asleep. And sometimes she does go to sleep. Not unconscious, asleep. A normal sleep. We'd been working toward a photograph that required that Ann lie very still and I had stopped to put more film in the camera, and as she usually does, Ann held the pose. It was entirely usual that she behave that way. I took the last exposures for that day and went to help her up and then I found that she was ill.

Q. Thank you, Mr. Rogers. No further questions, Your Honor.

THE COURT: Okay. Redirect? No, uh, wait here a minute.

(There was a brief interruption.)

THE COURT: Let me see counsel a minute here.

(An off-the-record discussion was held at the bench.)

THE COURT: Ladies and gentlemen, this case is going to be discontinued until eleven o'clock on July the twenty-third and it will resume at that time in the district courtroom at the facility on Main and Bowie, that's 574 Main, about ten blocks north of this building. And so if you will mark that, it will be necessary for you to be available at that time. We will not have time today to finish the case in order that both sides be able to present all the testimony that they all have.

Counsel, if you would, have the witnesses identify themselves for purposes of the record so that we know who all is here and who I've just instructed.

WITNESS: Dawn Davis.

WITNESS: Darrell Young. Two r's and two l's.

WITNESS: Jeannie Alton.

(Whereupon the proceeding was concluded.)

State of Texas   )
County of Ector   )

    I, Abigail Wolf, court reporter in and for the State of Texas, do hereby certify that the above and foregoing contains a true and correct transcription of the proceedings in Cause No. 17,779, styled In the Matter of Ann Rogers, a minor Child, which took place on July 16, 1973; all of which occurred in open court before Honorable Edward L. Applebaum and was reported by me.

    WITNESS my hand this the __17__ day of _July_, 1973.

Abigail Wolf
_____
Abigail Wolf, CSR, RPR
Court Reporter
Certification No.: 2727
Expiration Date: 12-31-75
P.O. Box 1085
Odessa, Texas 79603
915/789-4344

Ann sits with unusual patience in her eye doctor's waiting room, its four abstract paintings obviously chosen for the pleasure of people whose vision is so poor that they can appreciate little more than pure color. Fearing blindness over any other possible ravage of diabetes— the amputation of a toe, a foot, the failure of a kidney—she arrived for her appointment with time to spare. Foolish, because Ettinger always runs late. After waiting half an hour, she calls Benny at the office to let him know that he'll have to get someone to cover for her if she doesn't get out in time to make her booking. When she returns to the waiting room, she picks over the coffee table's selection of large-print magazines—*Reader's Digest, Horizons,* and the *Daily Word,* a monthly devotional reader with a snippet of scripture and an uplifting message for each day. She reads the current issue, marveling at its good cheer and willful optimism in the face of any disaster. "I am confident in the love of Christ. I let go and let God's harmony and peace be expressed in my being." A simple homily follows; a story of a dancer who lost her legs in an accident and found greater happiness teaching from her wheelchair than she did on the stage. After it a box in which are the words LET GO, LET GOD.

A weekly large-print edition of *The New York Times* offers top news stories, editorials, book reviews, all in bold, large letters that have the effect of making Ann feel as if she is just learning to read, sent back to first grade where she stumbles over tricky combinations of consonants and tries to form letters between the lines of the widest-ruled paper. Even *The Times*'s crossword puzzle is writ large, difficult clues rendered imbecilic in large print. Ann completes it, wrecking the puzzle for other patients, and out of boredom and the nervous imperative to avoid thinking about the diagnosis she awaits, goes on to an oversized omnibus of !MORE CROSSWORDS!. She is stuck on "_____, let down your hair," a name she knows she knows but can't remember, when her own is called.

Inside the examination room, the framed pictures are different: clinical representations of the eye, its microscopic, bloody plumbing, and one photograph of the organ's iris. Illuminated, the eye's perfect corona blazes like a solar eclipse, a beautiful fire that bears testimony to the delicate, artistic surveillance of the surgeon. On Dr. Ettinger's immaculate mahogany desk is a gargantuan eyeball whose lid comes off like a toy's, revealing intricate works inside.

Dr. Ettinger has cared for Ann's eyes for six years. He is a kind man who seems more discomfited than Ann by any grim prediction he feels he must make. He winces as he warns her of what could happen to her eyes if she does not reform the myriad bad habits of which he suspects she is guilty— correctly, although he is ordinarily without absolute proof. Now Ann worries that he'll find out she's done drugs, that some chemical change will be written on her retinas and revealed by the light of his ophthalmo- scope.

It is Dr. Ettinger's specialty to care for the eyes of diabetics, to preserve their vision for as long as possible against the ravages of retinopathy, neovascularization, secondary hemorrhagic glaucoma, macular edema, and other complicated words that add up to the same thing: blindness. Ettinger has described what Ann will see if enough of her retina is de- stroyed: simply light, not vision but light, like swimming through a cloud. Not blackness—the way she had always imagined blindness—but a pearly, luminous nothing, ghostly, with no landmarks by which to guide oneself: a shadowless fog of light. Light without shadow, light without dark: pur- gatorial, not black or white but gray.

"So," he says now, "let's talk about this problem you're having."

"It's weird," Ann says. "Something that's never happened before. My vision is as sharp as ever, but when I look through my left eye, straight lines look, well, wavy."

"What do you mean? Could you describe it more fully?" Ettinger leans forward as if she has reported something genuinely interesting.

"I don't know. Like when I'm writing a check or something, I know the blanks are drawn with straight lines, but they look crooked to me. Clear and sharp, but crooked."

"Umm hmm," Ettinger nods, squinting at her. His own eyes peer over a curious pair of spectacles, two crescents of glass that magnify the pouches of skin beneath his bloodshot eyes and make him look wearier than he might without the glasses. He retrieves two ruled index cards from the drawer and stands from behind his desk, walks around to where Ann is sitting. Covering her left eye with one card, he holds the other before her right. "Straight or wavy?" he asks, repeating the test she's performed countless times on herself.

She squints at the little blue lines. "Straight," she says, and he tests the left eye, confirming it as the culprit.

"We'll take an FA today," he says.

"FA?"

"Fluorescein angiogram, a picture of the inside of your eye."

Ten minutes after this determination, Ettinger injects one of the prominent veins in Ann's arm with an orange dye that travels to her eyes and illuminates their minute vessels with a blue light at which the doctor grunts and mumbles. She feels a wave of nausea as the dye enters her bloodstream, not a psychological response—Ann isn't bothered by needles, God knows—but as Ettinger explains, corporeal, a tremor of revulsion somehow communicated from her veins to her stomach. The doctor has thoughtfully placed an emesis basin in her lap; which she hopes she won't have to use.

The angiogram machine produces a picture of what it sees: on its screen the vessels of her left eye are lit up like some freakish tree hit by lightning, the burning bush. Whenever God reveals himself, man is blinded; Carl once said that to Ann. The only person she knows who's actually read the Bible, all of it, Carl has a tendency to say ponderous things when she least expects it. He's not so much a religious man as a contemplative one, and this quality in him attracts her. Even if he hasn't kept her honest, she thinks that at least with him she's less of a liar than she might be otherwise.

The machine shudders and ejects a flimsy photocopy of Ann's eye. Ettinger looks at it and purses his lips. Holding his ophthalmoscope over the offending eye, he lets his cool fingers rest lightly on the bridge of Ann's nose, steadying the tool and making her shiver. The antiseptic he uses smells pleasantly of almonds.

The angiogram's report of a possible aneurysm in one of the veins in her left eye dictates that Ann endure a numbing series of peerings and probings: a pilgrimage of two floors, five rooms, and eleven diagnostic apparatuses of the Kitteridge Kennedy Eye Hospital. After calling Benny again to say that there was no way she'd make her booking this evening, she reports to room 201F for the first test.

For hours, it seems, Ann kneels under snares of hardware that trap her head and look into her eyes; she sits bathed in unearthly light and assumes obeisance to various machines. In the dark, Ettinger apologizes for the rigorousness of the tests, even as he searches the depths of a dilated eye, using his thumb to compress the resilient orb of her eyeball and force its usually hidden concavities to present themselves.

After this, Ann is dismissed to the private hospital's cafeteria with the direction to have something to eat and return at five P.M. She sits alone in the surprisingly tasteful room whose only other occupants are nurses, all of whom wear pastel cardigans over their uniforms in defense against the aggressive air conditioning.

The food isn't bad, but Ann can't eat. She picks halfheartedly at her sandwich of mozzarella and basil and sun-dried tomatoes on eleven-grain bread. Are there eleven grains?—she can only think of four, she'll remember to ask Carl. She should have taken him up on his offer to come with her to the hospital; at least he might have made her laugh at some of this. She takes a bite of the cheese, eats one tomato and the orange slice garnish. She realizes she's scared.

At 4:55, checking her watch compulsively against the slightly slower clock on the wall, she leaves her tray on the tiered cart by the door. At five exactly, she is sitting before Ettinger in his office.

"Macroaneurysm," he says, without preface. He delivers bad news quickly, as if to spare them both the pain of a falsely hearty prologue.

"What does that mean?" Ann says.

In response, Dr. Ettinger takes the lid off his big show-and-tell eyeball and runs his index finger along the perimeter of the plastic retina. He lays the tip of his finger somewhere in the middle of the concave red area behind the big eyeball's lens. "It's a bubble in a vein right about here," he says. To clarify, he pulls the FA photocopy from Ann's thick chart and with his pen indicates a nodule on the white-etched tree of vessels. "We'll go in with the laser and cauterize it," he says. He reaches across his desk and pats her hand in a gesture that is so paternal that it nearly makes Ann cry. She looks away. "It's almost foolproof," he says. "The risks are minimal— they exist, mind you—but it's far more dangerous to leave it. It's leaking already."

Ettinger explains that her vision may be compromised by the procedure, that the advance of laser surgery—that knife of light that can heal what no scalpel can—is yet crude when compared to its target, the eye, which is more wondrous in its infinitesimal complexity than a crowd of proverbial angels waltzing on a pin. Lasers can repair damage, but they often leave interruptions in the restored vision—blank areas. Ann met a woman a few years ago who had recently had another in a series of laser surgeries. She moved her head constantly while talking to Ann, explaining that she was mentally getting a composite view of what she saw. "It's a pain," she said.

"But I'm getting used to it." Ann is scared enough of laser surgery that she'd willingly settle for wavy instead of straight lines, but the risk of doing nothing—blindness—is too great to wait more than a week for the surgery. Ettinger argues for the next morning, but Ann wants time to detoxify, let her blood pressure settle down. When the nurse took it this morning it was 160 over 90, higher than it's ever been before. It could be nerves, but it's probably crystal.

Ettinger unlaces his long fingers and separates his hands, white hands that always look so clean. He tilts back in his reclining chair, pivots a little, hinges squeaking. He faces the wall to Ann's left, but his eyes look sideways at her.

"Ann," he says, "I'm concerned about some of the changes I see in your eyes this time." He turns back and looks significantly at her. "Your circulation is compromised in ways I wouldn't anticipate in an otherwise healthy diabetic woman your age."

Ann shifts nervously in her chair across from his polished desk. Could a couple of months of dissipation have taken a toll already? He's wrinkling his forehead meaningfully, as he does when discussing the inevitable wages of her disease, those same which will someday require his performance of complex microsurgeries, correcting scar tissue caused by tiny vessels growing in the wake of hemorrhages, the ignorant body's attempt to heal itself. Eventually, Ettinger once told her, he could suck out her vitreous and replace it with salt water, but it would be a shame to have to take such measures sooner than need be.

As Ann recrosses her legs and pushes up the sleeves of her shirt, Dr. Ettinger sits quietly in his suede-upholstered chair, waiting for her to speak. "How do you mean, *compromised?*" she says finally, attempting nonchalance.

"Well, this is the scenario we discussed when Dr. Sanders first referred you, but it's something we weren't expecting yet." He shuffles through her chart, peruses the written report of diagnostic tests, a couple of printouts and notes made in his own illegible hand. "Your blood pressure's a little higher than last time. How's your sugar been?" he asks.

"Okay," Ann says. "Stable enough. You know." She licks her lips, worries a shred of chapped skin with her tooth. "So," she says, changing the topic, "what are the risks? Ten per cent? Five? One?" she says hopefully.

"Somewhere in there," Ettinger answers.

"I am a photographer," she says, her voice peevish in the attempt to forestall tears. "It's not like I can afford to lose the sight in one of my eyes."

"I know," Ettinger says patiently. "That's why I'm especially concerned. I want you to know what's going on."

No indicator of the ill health of her eyes, Ann's vision is an enviable 20/10, and she needs that vision. She needs it to read the insanely tiny readout in the camcorder's viewfinder. She needs it to see the God damn scale on her syringes. She needs it because she knows she's too disorganized to wear contacts and too vain to consider glasses. If she is not blinded by the surgery, her left eye could still lose its focus, an outcome at whose likeliness Ettinger is unwilling to guess. Usually so specific, predicting hypothetical outcomes to the percentage point, the eye surgeon retreats into vagaries when faced with an actual case. This irritates her, and she feels unjustly angry at his considerate translations of medical jargon into lay imagery that she can understand. A wet sponge. He describes the intricacy of Ann's eye in such terms. Doctors. They all make her feel as if illness were some measure of character. As if she suffered from poor judgment and unreasonable expectations. What was it the orthopedist had said when she almost lost her toe? "You've lived with diabetes for nearly twenty years, Ann. The disease takes its toll."

Ann stands. *Rapunzel,* she thinks suddenly to herself; of course it was Rapunzel who let down her hair, a rope for the prince to climb the tower and rescue her. "So, a week from tomorrow, then?" she says.

"Nine A.M.," Ettinger answers. His voice has returned to its hearty self, and he seems as relieved as she is to have changed topics. "Be there a half hour earlier, please, and we'll get the paperwork out of the way."

"Eight-thirty? If I'm up in time to get here, you won't need anesthesia, I'll be in a coma."

"Oh, we can't use anesthesia anyway," he smiles. "We need you to be alert for this."

"Like with brain surgery," Ann says, and Ettinger smiles.

"A little."

―――――――

When Ann comes in the entrance to their loft, she scrapes her shin on the hinge of the elevator gate that Carl never fixed. "God fucking damn it," she says, dropping her bags.

"Ah," Carl says from the couch, "there she is, my better half."

"Why didn't you fix this God damn thing?" she says.

Carl cranes his neck to look at Ann where she is standing by the elevator gate, pointing at the offending hinge. "I'm sorry," he says, "Jesus." He returns to what he's reading, a true-crime book with a picture of a freshly dug grave on the cover. His long legs are resting on the coffee table, his feet propped on a pile of photography books, expensive monographs that are not replaceable. Ann pulls the books out from under his feet, and he sits up. "You're right," he says, "I went back on my word. I don't think you should have sex with me again. Ever."

She looks at his feet. Carl is the only man in Manhattan who wears wool socks in July. "How can you possibly be wearing those?" she says. "And why don't you have the air conditioning on? It's about eighty degrees in here." She looks at his blue eyes behind the wire-rimmed glasses and starts to cry.

"What's wrong, Ann?" he asks, sitting up.

She drops heavily onto the other end of the couch, kicks off her shoes, and draws her feet under her. "I have to have my eye cauterized," she says.

"Cauterized? I thought that was for noses." Carl marks his place in his book, puts it on the coffee table.

"*Photocoagulated,* then. Whatever. There's some aneurysm thing that's leaking."

"Oh, Ann," Carl says with sudden alarm. "Which eye?"

"What does it matter which eye, I need both of them." She picks up a throw pillow and holds it. "The left," she says.

"Ann." Carl puts his arms out. "Come here, Ann," he says. "Closer." When she doesn't move, he sighs, drops his arms. "Isn't this a procedure Ettinger does all the time? It's laser surgery, right?"

"There are still risks. And, anyway, it's not so much the thing itself as what it means. I'm only thirty-three and already more stuff is going wrong."

Carl frowns. "Well, did Ettinger seem concerned?" he says.

"He didn't exactly act like it was par for the course."

Carl stares at her, then reaches forward and pulls off her sunglasses.

"Stop it. My eyes are still dilated," she says, and she puts the glasses back on.

For a while Carl sits next to her on the couch with his arms folded; neither of them speak. Finally, she lets her head rest on the sofa back. Through the dark lenses of her glasses the clouds look luminous as they float overhead, framed briefly by the skylight.

Carl says, "Say something," but Ann remains silent. Words surface as she looks at the light overhead, things she might say, should say. *"Carl, I've been slipping a little lately. You know, the same problem as before. Speed. I'm afraid I just can't get the hang of it—life.*

But she says nothing. Carl, she practices silently, I'm afraid I've . . . I'm afraid.

"Look at me," Carl says, and Ann lifts her head and looks at him. She realizes he's being patient only with effort. His voice has that supernaturally calm tone.

"Let's just talk, Ann. Really, it's easy," he says. "I say, Ann, what's up?, and you say, Carl, I'm worried about my eyes. I say, Why? You say, Well, they seem to have deteriorated faster than my doctor thought was expectable. I say, Why do you think that is, Ann? You say, Why Carl, what do you mean? I say—"

"Please!" Ann says. "Please."

"Something's going on." He looks at her. "I know you don't want to talk about how you're stressed out about the retrospective. Or about how you're not taking care of yourself. Or about anything else. But this can't go on indefinitely." He stands, paces around the coffee table, comes back to the couch. "Something else is going on here," he says. "Something besides—besides your having become, at the very least, a compulsive shopper."

Ann says nothing and Carl reaches over and takes off her glasses again. "You're doing drugs," he says.

"Fuck you," she says. "I'm just trying to tell you that I'm scared about something."

"And I'm telling you I think you're taking speed."

Ann says nothing, but her injured posture is as good as the lie she doesn't speak. *Compulsive shopper.* Does he mean he's worried that she's buying too many clothes, or that he suspects she's *not* buying them?

Carl stands up and walks around the loft, goes to the window, sits down on the sill; she can see him only in silhouette, his arms crossed and his head bowed. When he speaks, his voice is soft.

"Look," he says. "I'm not going to appeal to any normal sense of self-preservation because that's something you don't seem to have. But since your eyesight is the one aspect of your existence that has some value to you, I'll say it again: *If you're doing drugs, you're nuts.* If that's why one of the little veins in your eye has popped, then you'd damn well better take it as a great big warning." He walks over to where Ann sits in the corner of the couch, the pillow still clutched to her chest.

He's silent for a moment and then he sits down suddenly on the coffee table in front of her. "How can you think so little of yourself when I love you so?" he says. "You have so much talent, Ann. You say you respect my taste in other things—in design, in art, in . . . in dishes," he says, pointing to the Venetian glass bowl on the table, an anniversary present. "Why not believe me about people?"

"Don't be melodramatic," Ann says. "And why do you assume I'm doing drugs? I'm the one who should be upset. I'm the one who has to have an operation, the one being unjustly accused." It's absurd, but having decided to reform upon news of the aneurysm, she already feels a prick of self-righteous indignation.

He looks at her studiedly. "I don't know," he says. "There's just something." He pauses. "You're acting like you did when your aunt died. There's that same sort of accelerated passage through the bathroom in the morning. I lie in bed and listen and it's like you're playing Beat the Clock or something, doors slamming, things dropping. You used to spend an hour in the bathtub, now it seems like the shower turns off as soon as it's on. And you're so irritable. I wake up to the sound of you swearing. This is the first time I've seen you sit still in a week." The phone rings and Carl stops speaking, arms crossed, clearly intending not to answer it.

Ann stands and picks up the receiver just before the fourth ring, which triggers the answering machine's response. "Hello," she says.

"Am I speaking with Ann Rogers?" says a voice. Unfamiliar, male, slightly British accent.

"Who may I tell her is calling?" Ann says.

There's a pause, a little cough. "Bill Millman," the voice says "I'm calling from *New York* magazine. I'm doing a story—"

"She's not home," Ann interrupts and puts down the receiver.

"Who was it?" Carl says.

"Some journalist. I don't know how people get this number."

Neither of them speak for a moment, and then Carl goes on as if he were never interrupted. "I have never asked you to take care of me," he says. "It's always been clear that you weren't that kind of person. But you have to take care at least a little of the woman I married. Don't you love me enough to protect the only thing I care about?"

"I love you, Carl, you know it. And I'm clean. Why oversimplify everything and reduce it to the same old questions? I don't have diabetes because I don't care enough for you. Or for me, for that matter. You make everything sound too simple."

"I'm not talking about diabetes, and what I am talking about *is* simple." Carl stops talking, but his mouth remains open as if he intends to say more. As if he is breathless, panting.

She wants to go to him, close her eyes, and put her arms around his neck, her head against his chest, but she can't. What is it about her that makes it impossible to reach out? It's just like hiding in her closet, ignoring Mariette's hand on her knee. When things go wrong, she only knows how to be alone.

"Look," she says, "I'm going to go lie down. Why don't we do this some other time." She regrets her words even as she speaks them, but still she leaves Carl sitting on the coffee table, goes into the bedroom, and shuts the door.

———

Ann flies to Mexico the next afternoon. She's made up with Carl the easy way, in bed; she's told him she needs a vacation before her eye surgery. As she informed her grumpy partners, she can't work anyway, and she's vowed to herself that by the time the aneurysm is repaired, not only will she have stopped taking speed, but she will be better about her insulin shots, will try to eat healthy food; and she will stop stealing.

Behavior modification seems impossible without a change of scene, so she heads south, where, as the travel agent promises, or warns, it's too hot even to move, let alone get into trouble. She drags a suitcase packed with novels that make few emotional or intellectual demands, a bottle of tanning lotion, two bikinis, tee-shirts, one sundress, and some underwear. She leaves her crystal at home.

In Cancun, she doesn't stray once from the narrow strip of beach directly in front of her hotel, doesn't take the hotel bus to look at the famous ruins, doesn't shop, doesn't shoplift, doesn't eat anywhere but from the seemingly clean plates wheeled onto her own private terrace on a room-service cart. Every morning she takes her shot of insulin—measures out the forty units after pricking her finger and monitoring her blood sugar. She orders breakfast, which she hates, and she eats it. Then she puts on her bathing suit, goes down to the beach, and lies in the heavy, humid sun, closing her eyes against the bright blue of the sky.

Ann is tempted to look directly at the sun, to commit the transgression of looking at the one thing she's always been told not to look at. "It will burn your eyes," Mariette used to say. She was about to pay someone a lot of money to do just that.

Don't look at the sun. Don't get into a stranger's car. Don't put money in your mouth. Don't run with a pencil. Don't swim right after you eat. Simple exhortations to keep children safe. She's tried to subscribe to the easy formulas, generally has granted taboos their authority. But evidently she failed. Slipped, somehow, from safety.

Don't look at the sun. In her compact's mirror, applying sun block to her nose, she can see the dying star, high and white like a blister on the blue skin of the heavens. When she finally closes her eyes, the reflection of the sun is hot enough to remain before them for some minutes: a black disk, all burned up.

———

The eye hospital's release form is rendered in large print, something Ann cannot help but interpret as an ill omen at the hour of eight-thirty in the morning, when even the slant of the sun's rays is nauseating. Past the paperwork and sitting in the laser wing, eyes dilated by the nurse and swimming with tears, Ann jumps at the sound of Ettinger's laugh.

"I have to hand it to you, Ann," he says, his smooth, almond-scented hand under her chin as he looks at her eye, but from a normal distance and without some diagnostic tool between their faces.

"What?" Ann feels piqued by his good humor so early in the morning. She moves her head in irritation as he peels her lower lid down with his thumb to reveal the conjunctiva.

"I've heard of vanity, but you are the only woman yet who has shown up for eye surgery wearing mascara."

"Pride," Ann replies tartly. "Not vanity. Besides, Doctor, what if it was just a gesture of morale? Isn't it insensitive to short-circuit what is perhaps my pathetic little attempt at bolstering self-confidence?"

"You're too smart for that. And you don't even wear eye makeup for regular exams. This is the first time I've ever seen you in it. You're just contrary, as Dr. Sanders warned me."

"Perhaps it was important," Ann continues, "even essential to wear it today. Perhaps—"

"You were right, you never should have to get up this early, it has a negative effect on your personality. Wash your face." Ettinger hands her a poisonous-looking green bottle of PhisoHex. "There'll be enough in your eye without the added insult of makeup," he says. The pretty nurse titters.

But Ettinger is right. Ten minutes later, her head harnessed into the grim architecture of the laser mount, a Velcro-secured bridle preventing any movement, Ann's eye is filled with a clear, stinging gel that allows place-ment of a thick contact lens over her cornea. The gel spills over her lower lid and runs down her cheek and over her lips, tickling, but the small annoyance of that sensation is lost in others. Ettinger's good humor evapo-rates under the exigencies of the procedure, and if Ann so much as twitch-es reflexively at the sound of therapeutic artillery, he barks her name. At one point he stops and removes his mask.

"Ann," he says, "I don't want to frighten you, but if you move at the wrong moment, I could blind you. My target is infinitesimally small." Ann sits still.

The laser is activated by an acceleratorlike pedal under the surgeon's foot and goes off every few seconds, a rapid succession of loud clicks almost obliterated by the background noise of running water that cools the hot equipment. It sounds like her father's darkroom sink.

The light Ann sees is bright, blinding, the kind she associates with the literature of near-death experiences. Her chin goes numb against the metal plate to which it's lashed; her neck aches. The fifteen-minute procedure takes, she is sure, a year off her life. When Ettinger removes the stabilizing lens, her eye closes automatically in shock, gel squeezing out like tears.

"Fuck," Ann says.

"Excuse me?"

"Sorry." She can't see the refined doctor's expression, but she can imagine it.

Ettinger puts a tissue in her hand and she wipes the gel and tears and mucus from her face. Her nose has been running in sympathy for the duration of the process, but before when she moved a hand to wipe it the nurse grabbed her wrist. "Caught you," she said. "We use Velcro hand-cuffs for children," and she let go.

Try as she might, Ann cannot convince the lids of her left eye to part. Having allowed such an invasion, they seem determined against future slipups. She opens the eye manually, but sees nothing. A half hour later, as she lies on a bed in a dim recovery room, the eye begins to burn. A slight amount of vision has returned, and Ettinger has pronounced that the procedure is probably a success, but she's in a kind of pain for which she was not prepared. When she can't stand it anymore, she makes her way to the nurse's station, groping along the corridor as if she were blind, or crippled, or both.

"My eye really hurts," she says.

With her right eye she sees the nurse nod.

"I mean *really*."

"The anesthesia's wearing off, that's all. The cornea gets scratched a little in the process. Just lie down, and I'll be in with some antibiotic ointment."

"I thought there was no anesthesia with this process."

"Well, none *per se*, but the gel has an analgesic in it, otherwise we'd never get that big lens in your eye. It's not even adjusted to the curvature of any particular eyeball."

Ann nods. "Can I use the phone?" she asks. "I mean, could you dial a number for me?" Carl is due to pick her up at one, and she tells him that she's ready to leave early. When he arrives, with a cab waiting downstairs, she's wearing her dark glasses to cover the patch on her left eye and is propped rather than sitting on the waiting room couch. She has a tube of ophthalmic ointment in her hand which she gives him to carry, along with her bag and coat. It's all she can do to get herself to the elevator.

Once the doors close, she leans against him. "The only thing in the world I want to do is to go to bed for about a month. Please, can I just do that?" she asks.

"Jesus," Carl says. He touches her cheek, puts his lips to her hair. "You're so pale, I've never seen you so pale."

"Tell me everything is going to be okay," she says.

"Everything will be okay," he says, and stops at "okay," his inflection indicating that the words are the first half of a qualified statement: everything will be okay *if*. If what? Ann thinks, *If you don't do drugs. If you take care of yourself.*

———

Ann sleeps from two on Wednesday afternoon to eleven the next morning. When she gets up, her left eye is still half closed—not swollen, but on some level of pure reflex unwilling to open more than a crack. She pulls on Carl's bathrobe and makes her way to the kitchen. Carl has prepared and left on the dining table a shot of insulin, a muffin, and a banana. When even a third cup of coffee does nothing to offset her mood of black despair, she begins pacing the loft's living area, circling her camera bag.

Why didn't you throw it out? If you'd meant it, you'd have thrown it all out. I did, I did mean it. If I can only just wait, it will be better. The eye will be better. Life will be better. *What about you? Will you be better?* Shut up, I don't need this.

Jesus, I must be crazy, she thinks. Almost as much as she worries about taking speed, she resents these interminable internal struggles. The energy wasted on arguments with herself, attempts to justify her behavior, to rationalize whatever failure to resist, or to forestall for just a day, an hour, a minute, the next transgression. She sits on her hands on the green couch and looks at the bright badge of light coming down from the skylight. *Look, you can't do it today because of the surgery. If you do it today, you've really lost it. You have to take control.* No, I'm fine, I'm fine. I'm just discouraged. What do other people do when they get discouraged? Watch TV? Read? Eat? I can't see and I'm not hungry.

She curls on her side on the couch, holds a throw pillow to her face. I can't, I won't. Not today. Just please not today. If I do it today, the little vein might bleed, and then what? Ann doesn't know this to be true, but she says it to herself, hoping the dramatic sound will give her some discipline.

She sits up again. Like a naughty schoolgirl, she sits on her hands for one hour and a half. Finally, she stands and gets the little bag of crystal from her camera and takes it to the bathroom. After holding it over the toilet for what seems like forever, she goes into the bedroom and opens her closet, drops the little bag into the zippered lining of her trench coat. She rehangs it in the farthest corner of her closet. There's enough in there now that the coat is heavy and lumpy. Just as soon as she has the energy, she'll have to come up with a better place.

F or a time after your death I went through a period of telling staggering lies. The stories I fabricated were elaborate. On the plane back to college, I sat next to a woman whom I told, in a slightly British accent, that I was a student from Kenya. That my father had been one of the last great white hunters on the continent of Africa. I spoke of a house full of Kikuyu servants, said that I deplored my father's hunting of course, but that life on the Serengeti was very beautiful. At night the noise of monkeys was delightful. The lions were fierce but did not trouble us.

I went on, I don't think she asked me any questions. I was scrupulous about maintaining the accent. It was important to me that she believe what I said.

I told the cab driver who took me from the airport to Evanston that my father was a famous archaeologist and that he was in Pompeii at the moment. That he drilled holes into ancient lava until he came to a cavity which he filled with plaster of Paris. When he dug the hardened plaster from the mold, he would have a statue of a person long dead, a man or a woman who had expired in the eruption of Vesuvius in 79 A.D. I said that our house was full of these statues. That lying on our coffee table was one of a man and a woman embracing. When the lava came, they were caught forever in one another's arms. The driver let me out by the door to my dorm. He said, "Okay then," and handed me my change which I gave back to him.

I felt responsible for your despair, your death. The sane reaction would have been anger, but I didn't feel anger. Just guilt. Oh, I know how guilt is a response that seeks to smother rage, I've tried to find my anger.

I still feel responsible. Even though I know you cannot hold another's happiness in your hands, on your shoulders. At the time it was so unbearable that I insisted it was an accident. I explained to Dr. Alda that you didn't mean for the insulin to kill you. I told her that I knew this because you used Polaroids only to set up a shot, to check composition, and never for a final print. That you were going to make some self-portraits, document yourself since you'd fired me. That if it were going to be the last picture, you'd have gone out in style, used the

Deardorff with the timer. That you were too vain to leave nothing better than a few crummy Polaroids scattered on the studio floor.

It wasn't just other people that I told elaborate lies.

You know, I wanted to be touched not because you had to, posing me, but because you wanted to, because you couldn't help yourself. I put up with the modeling because I wanted to feel your hands on me, I hoped you might betray some affection. It was so boring and painful sometimes.

I wish we had all been happier somehow. Even Christmas, it was hard when you couldn't guess what my wishes were. Always looking for a sign, I took that as proof you didn't love me.

At the office, I found on my desk calendar a note, in my writing. Two words: Christmas Island, *the only notation for July 9, a day on which I had no appointments. Sometimes when I'm on the phone I draw or write things without realizing it.*

There's a place in the Indian Ocean called Christmas Island. You told me that one Christmas and said you'd send me there, and that then I'd always get just what I deserved. That was the year that you pulled the stockings down from the mantel. "But—" Mariette said. "She's too old now," you answered.

We put the tree up, Mariette and I, and in protest never took it down. At Easter it was still standing, the trunk and branches at least. Needles all over the carpet. You never gave any indication that you noticed, you had that quality of obliviousness, when you weren't pursuing something you wanted, that is.

I spent my life hiding from you. I hid from everyone and made sure they didn't know who I was, but then I blamed them for it, too.

I put out decoys—little props to give you the idea that I lived in our house. That the real Ann inhabited the body you saw. Clothes on the floor. Fish tank. Radio playing. I brought the honor roll certificates home from school and left them where I earned them, on that desk I hated. I wanted the rolltop with the little secret drawers and pigeonholes, sitting in the attic, unused. Why couldn't I have it? Because I wanted it? It was Mother's of course.

The only present you gave me that I liked was that watch for my sixteenth birthday. For years I've turned it over, looked at the engraving, not remembering that it was I who chose the words on the back of the case: For Ann, Love Papi. Wrote it on a little piece of paper and pushed it, silently, across the jeweler's glass counter. He squinted at it under his light, then stapled it to the order.

For years I told myself that you knew my heart's desire and chose the gift for me. I wonder when it was that I forgot the truth. Did I forget it in pieces, or all at once? Did I forget things even before you died?

I can see you now, waiting in the car outside the jewelers, one hand on the wheel as if to pull away from the curb. "Don't take all day," you said. You signed the blank check, tore it from the book which you replaced in your pocket, and handed it to me through the window. I stood for a moment on the corner, looking at the check. Then I went into the store.

You were always angry when I couldn't read your mind, those few occasions that I didn't anticipate your wants and fulfill them. I was selfish, I guess—I was a self, even when I struggled against it.

And perhaps what is surprising is that I saved Ann at all, that my adaptation, costly as it was, worked. For by going underground, I survived you, I think.

Somehow I always knew that if I let you have your way completely, use me up as you seemed to think it your due, there'd be nothing left for me, you'd eat me up. You were like a wild animal: very quiet, but I felt it in the room with me, your hunger.

You were ravenous, you ate and ate without getting fat, but you never seemed to taste anything Mariette cooked, it could have been dog food out of a can. And when you'd eat a banana or pudding, something soft, I would hear your teeth come together, a little click, you bit so hard.

Mexico, 1886

Michael Rogers emigrated to Mexico with his family, part of a splinter group of sixty Amish who fled the United States in 1864, disgusted with the ubiquitous evidence of their young country's moral decline. They left the warring union and established an isolated agricultural community in the Sierra Madre, a small outpost near Esperanza on the Yaqui River in northern Mexico. Michael was fifteen. His adopted country was tolerant of the separatists, but the land itself was rocky and hostile, unlike the rich black earth of Pennsylvania, where orderly thriving orchards were thick with fruit each September. The Amish brought seeds and seedlings, but the apples they grew in Mexico shriveled on the branch, and the insects in the mountains were unchecked by the choking smudge pots they burned in the hilly orchards all day, all night. The harvested fruit was small, mealy, and pocked with black holes.

The middle child of his mother's five sons, Michael was a malcontent. His delicate build and grudging performance of chores made him the most expendable member of the hard-working commune, and as he had no talent for mutiny—no desire to have his name expunged from the family Bible—one afternoon, a week after his seventeenth birthday, he lay down his hoe. Carrying nothing, he walked the rutted dirt road from the tiny Amish community named *Manzana*, for apple, and followed the swarming, muddy river to Esperanza. In that it was not what he fled, the neighboring town was far enough away, and he went no farther than those twenty miles.

Unlike his fair brothers, Michael had dark enough hair that, sunburned, he could blend in with the townspeople. He took a series of odd jobs, learned to speak Spanish, and changed his name to the native *Manuel*— not a translation to the equivalent, *Miguel*, but the name his current *patrón*, the plump, mischievous Rosario, called him. By his eighteenth birthday, he had apprenticed himself to señor Delgado, a mysteriously wealthy recluse who lived in a grand and peculiar house on the outskirts of town, in a chalet built by two Swiss brothers who went on to Cuernavaca and other rich fools. Delgado's cavernous parlor was filled with the playthings of an idle, lonely paranoiac.

Michael, now Manuel, was hired as a gentleman-scientist's assistant. The gentleman, having exhausted the diversions of botany, spiritualism, and herpetology, had taken up the pleasures of the new scientific art of *Fotografía*. He had a studio and a darkroom outfitted with equipment shipped from Europe, crates of chemicals sealed in amber glass bottles and packed in straw—potassium iodide, potassium cyanide, silver nitrates and halides, pyrogallic acid—a locker filled with variously sized beakers and a leather-bound volume of Estabrooke's standard text, *The Ferrotype and How to Make It*. It was for this manual that Manuel was hired—a silly pun that his new employer favored, *Manuel and the manual*—to translate it and guide this gentleman who would become his benefactor in his newfound vocation. Simply put, it was Manuel's job to explain to José Jesus Delgado how to operate all the expensive equipment he now owned.

Manuel managed to teach only himself how to operate the view camera and its sulfuric, exploding flash, the complexity of preparing the little metal plates, before José Jesus abruptly died, after a dinner of crayfish, leaving the boy alone in the decrepit house crammed with decades' worth of diversions: laboratories and workshops, a greenhouse filled with carnivorous plants, a dusty library of books in German, French, English, Spanish, even Latin and Greek.

Manuel hung a black wreath on the gate, with a notice of señor Delgado's passing and a request that the señor's relatives make themselves known. But no one contacted Manuel, even after advertisements were placed in Mexico City's newspaper, notices nailed up in surrounding towns. The one legal scholar in town, señor Bernardo, declared that the property—the house and grounds and banana grove—belonged to Esperanza. The contents of the chalet Manuel could keep.

Away from his Amish roots, Manuel discovered in himself a lively entrepreneurial talent. He sold the dismantled locomotive to an aspiring revolutionary, the distillery and microscopes and the three hundred and forty-two snakes preserved in alcohol to various local *curanderos*. At his all-day snake auction, he made as much as twenty-seven pesos for more remarkable specimens, and the unheard of sum of one hundred pesos in gold for the fetus in a bottle—that went to Rosario's grandmother, Esperanza's town witch. With the money he made, Manuel established himself in a small studio which he set up between the bakery and the casket maker's. He ordered a marquee from the Ellery Brothers Sign Company in Baltimore, Maryland, a Spanish translation of the American Daguerreotypists' popular slogan, "Secure the shadow ere the substance fade," a saying already writ on the Mexican heart.

Soon Manuel had a thriving business. He charged very little for his portraits, for he was not greedy, and his peculiar inheritance had provided a lifetime supply of developing chemicals and enough guncotton, alcohol, and ether to make ten lifetimes' worth of the collodion he used to coat the metal plates he had sent from Mexico City—his sole expense. It seemed everyone in the small town of Esperanza owned a stiff and formal likeness of his or herself posed on a little wrought-iron bench in front of the painted backdrop of a mysterious landscape, one not unlike the melancholy lakes and trees behind *La Gioconda.*

It was during the meningitis plague of 1886, when he was thirty-seven, still a relatively young man, that Manuel had his most lucrative year. Confronted with so many dead, Esperanza discovered—as did most Mexican towns enjoying the new luxury of photographic portraiture—that the highest calling of the ferrotype was in memorializing the departed with a last likeness. The miniatures were placed in the family shrine against a backdrop of candles, flowers, jewelry, trinkets, sweets, and petitions written to the dead on scraps of paper. Especially on the first and second days of the eleventh month—All Souls' and All Saints' days—were these pictures celebrated, another prop to add to the festive mania of the Day of the Dead, to accompany the sugar skulls and paper flowers.

Most popular, most indispensable, even for the poorest people, were pictures of the *ángelitos,* the dead children dressed in little black suits and white lace frocks, babies in their christening gowns. It was not odd that people wanted such keepsakes. The bodies children leave are beautiful, and having been on earth so short a time, they leave nothing else. The children who perished in the meningitis epidemic died so quickly that their flesh was left intact, plump and blooming even as their spirits fled, the blush of fever enlivening their cheeks. They seemed asleep in their finery, the girls with earrings and their mothers' necklaces wrapped twice, three times, around their throats, sometimes a cross held in their arms or their fingers garlanded with rosary beads. Children who had never sat so still in life posed prettily, with hair brushed that would never before tolerate a brush. They lay with their eyes shut in their mothers' laps, heavy fringes of lashes highlighted by an extra flash that exploded overhead—an innovation of Manuel's. They lay on little beds with ornamental pillows supporting their solemn heads. They lay idle, or if brought to the studio before rigor mortis set their bones, they played, posed with one or more of the expensive European toys that Manuel kept in his gallery as props.

Seven months into the plague, a new doctor moved to town. This Dr.

Laarsen, a Swiss, decried the practice of carrying the dead through the streets to the photographer's gallery, saying that it spread the fever. Undoubtedly, he was right, but many of the townspeople wouldn't believe him. Adamantly unwilling to forego the final portrait, their only consolation, they continued in their custom. The situation grew acrimonious: the bereaved were attacked by those who would reform them, even as they carried their dead children to the studio, and parents took to bringing the little corpses to Manuel's shop in secret.

One summer night a señor Zapporo was carrying a large hatbox down the main avenue of Esperanza where all the businesses were located. The man tripped and dropped his burden; out of the box fell the body of his infant son. Unluckily, this transpired outside the *pulquería* on a Saturday night, when Manuel, hoping for the occasional live portrait, closed shop late. Out of the bar flowed an angry crowd. Señor Zapporo's child was taken and cremated for the destruction of germ agents, Manuel's gallery plundered.

Such was the beginning of the end of the photographic business of Manuel Rogers. Riots began, and corpses were snatched and burned despite the protests of the priest that the little children must be spared their bodies for the afterlife. The gallery's shop window was broken and replaced four times; and after three months Manuel emigrated north, back to his fatherland.

Afflicted with chronic dysentery from the Yaqui River's water, Ann's great grandfather was too weak to travel further than across the United States border. He settled on the other side of the Rio Grande, married a young widow from El Paso; and despite his broken health, left her with one son when he died in 1909. Sixty-three pounds, four ounces, he was less than half the weight of the mahogany casket that his old friend Ignatio, proprietor of the funerary shop next door to his in Esperanza, made for him, and which he had used as a chest to transport his few possessions—his camera and the likenesses he had managed to save—back to the United States. His son, Ann's grandfather, became a lumber salesman and settled in Jessup, Texas, where Edgar Evans Rogers was born.

———

In the box that Ann found after her father's death were one hundred and sixty-seven portraits, mostly of children, all taken by Manuel in 1886. Aside from a few letters to his dealer, this was the only personal legacy left by her father, the only hint of his past, his heritage.

Ann sat on the floor of his office, the room that held all of his own negatives filed in metal boxes with the year of the exposure written on a gummed label affixed neatly to the top of each. She sat and went through the cardboard box of pictures. The children appeared as angels, and it was some minutes before Ann realized that they were dead. One little boy was dressed in paper wings; spread behind his white robe, they seemed almost to lift him from the lap where he lay.

After she had looked all she could, Ann put the ferrotypes back in the box and packed it away in her suitcase. Years later she would close her eyes and see the dead children of Esperanza—even though she couldn't have named the images, which, like little ghosts, simply flitted through her consciousness. She shared the pictures with no one, mentioned their existence to no one, until Eric Elsin, curator of the retrospective of her father's work, seized upon them.

Edgar Rogers had never met his grandfather, but Ann could imagine what her father felt at the discovery of the photographs. While packing up the contents of his parents' attic, he would have come upon the pictures, hidden away, an embarrassment, really, pictures of dead children, so ghoulish.

But her father would have found them beautiful—any artist would have, anyone who cared for good photography. Like the work of Julia Margaret Cameron or Lewis Carroll, each was lovely, and the passage of so many years excused affectation. The pictures Edgar took of his wife, Virginia, her milky legs, attempted the same mystery and grace, the beauty of the *ángelitos*, of flesh arrested in innocence. All that might have been, all that had never disappointed. No one had ever had to explain how it was that Antonio grew up embittered and beat his wife; that Sarita was, it must be admitted, not merely slow but a half-wit; that Maria had slept with her sister's husband; that José, disappointed in love, had drowned his sorrows and then himself. All confessed with a heavy sigh.

It was as if, somehow, he knew what was coming. Sad about Virginia, no? You heard, didn't you? Ah, she died, such a shame, and her husband wasn't the same afterward. You remember how young she was, always laughing, those red, red lips! Lips parted in a smile, forever.

Ann's father, kneeling among the debris in the attic—dusty mason jars and chipped Christmas ornaments, old sheets and sprung mousetraps— the ferrotypes spread on the floor before him. He would have stared at the portrait of the one young man in his middle twenties seated on the wrought-iron bench. In his lap he cradles an infant. The child might be asleep; but the devotional icons—the chalice, the loaf, the crucifix—indicate that the baby is dead. The lace border of the child's white gown is outlined starkly against the young man's trousers. His black suit is formal, complete with celluloid collar and watch chain; his dark hair is parted neatly in the center; but his dress is belied by his gauntness and crude leather sandals. Observant of such details, Edgar would have seen that he was a poor man.

His full lips part as if he would tell us something, and his eyes are opened so wide that the white sclera shine under the dark irises. Behind father and child is a canvas backdrop painted with a moody landscape of dark hills and cypress trees, mounting storm clouds, and their position on the ornate bench is thus made precarious: the two poised on the border of that inscrutable land which is the mystery of death.

Or what about the double frame of the two tiny twins? On the left, they lie in the cradle they shared in life; on the right, they are in their next bed together, a jewel box casket imported from the north. They hold matching rosebuds, and the white lace of their identical christening gowns—so long that they must have swept the floor when they lay in their mother's arms, when the priest's holy water anointed them—overflows the sides of the cradle, the foot of the coffin. Due to an overly long exposure, the gowns are luminous, so bright with light that they glow beyond their outlines.

Ann could imagine her father holding the picture to his lips. Perhaps that day, that solitary hour, was the start of everything that followed.

A s soon as I was home from college—Thanksgiving, winter break, summer, whenever—I'd kiss Mariette in the kitchen and go immediately to my room where I'd drop my bag. The first time back, the first Thanksgiving, Mariette followed me down the hall. "Ann," she said, "say something. Talk." "What do you mean?" I answered. "Your accent," she said. "It's gone, completely gone. Only two months away, and you don't sound like you're from Texas anymore." She shook her head. I shrugged.

You were in the darkroom or your shuttered bedroom, your little office, you weren't waiting to greet me, but I didn't expect it. What I did was I climbed up to the attic before you knew I was home and I went through the boxes again. The contents were always undisturbed, no evidence that anyone had touched a thing since last I'd looked.

Before I was home for even an hour I would have opened the suitcases of Mother's clothes packed neatly away, stockings rolled and tucked into corners, underwear folded to hide crotches stained dark like any other woman's, shoes placed with their soles together and reminding me of hands in prayer. Dresses and blouses folded just so. As if she were going on a trip.

All of it together up there—the suitcases, the old rolltop desk with letters from her sisters in the drawers, the double bed with the soft mattress. I told myself as a child that my mother lived in the attic. That one day I would catch her there, sitting at her desk or napping on the dusty pink spread.

Mariette used to tell me about how you and Mother took trips together in the car, and while posing for pictures I would imagine putting my head in Mother's lap. We'd be in a car, driving slowly, a pleasant trip. You behind the wheel. Lying on the seat, all I could see out the window would be the endless swoop, swoop, swoop of telephone wires connecting poles. I'd think of all the invisible voices burning through the air, and my head was no longer on the cold studio floor but in my mother's lap, and her hand was on my forehead. Such a warm, smooth, pretty hand, the fingers lightly playing with my hair. She would have loved my hair, simply because it was mine, not because it was pretty. It wasn't pretty, it was brown and unremarkable. But she loved it—me—and when I could make myself feel that hand on my forehead, stroking my hair, the wrist with a dab of some perfume, fading but still sweet, I felt the thing that I never felt otherwise: that everything was going to be absolutely all right.

Of course, nothing was right.

That whole thing with the insulin shock—we conspired together, didn't we? The court hearing never examined what really happened. You thinking that my guard would go down, that it was as good as spying on me, and me knowing that I was never better hidden than when I let my body take over.

Or maybe it was worse, maybe you wanted something terrible to happen. Maybe I did.

———————

Before you knew I was back from school, I'd shuffle quickly through the boxes of papers in the attic. A Christmas card someone had sent to the two of you twenty years before. A bill for a new water heater. Checks kept in tight rubber bands that broke away lightly before I could remove them. Mother's written in her nearly indecipherable hand. $7.00 to Samantha's—that must have been a beauty parlor. $2.50 to K. D. Shoe Repair. Yours printed in block letters, pen pressing so deep into the paper that, were I to turn one over, I could read the words from the indentations they made. Such tight control. Even your signature was printed. $97.28 to Stadler's Emporium for: Crib. 10/17/59. It was a lot to spend. You didn't have much then.

Maybe I'd already started forgetting things, because during those homecomings it was as if I were searching for something, something I'd lost, I didn't know what. I looked at it all. Looked at all the pairs of shoes you'd worn over the seventeen years you'd lived in that house: eleven pairs, all lined up. Black wingtips that you wore from morning to night, a peculiar choice for someone who never had to work in an office. Only one pair at a time in your closet, set heel to heel when not on your feet.

You were the fastidious one, not Mariette, so I knew it must have been you who packed Mother's suitcases after she died. So many clothes. The dead leave so much behind. It was hard to imagine you emptying her dresser drawers, slipping her dresses off the hangers, putting them all away. But only you would have folded the underwear to hide the stains, placed the shoes just so.

Your own you wore just until a hole developed in the right, never the left one's sole; then you retired them. Pairs and pairs of shoes neatly lining the attic's west wall.

You paced your darkroom—a quiet, thoughtful walking. My ear to the door, pausing before calling you to dinner, I could hear the sound of your feet on the cool cement, could hear how your gait was slightly off, the reason for the uneven *wear of your shoes. Sometimes I listened for some other sound. Once, it seemed to me, I heard you weeping. I crouched so still, holding my breath, trying to hear, until the sound of my own pulse roared in my ears. "Papi?" I called finally. You didn't answer, but that was not unusual.*

Up in the attic, I would pick up one of your shoes, look at the hole, just about the size of a dime, and the way the heel was worn down on the outside edge.

Shoes, clothes—they tell a lot about who wore them. In the cabs, sometimes, I wonder what people think about the clothes I leave behind. In my haste, are buttonholes torn? Do the depths of a pocket reveal an open seam, never mended, through which I might have lost something I valued—an earring, a phone number written on a matchbook? Does anyone hold up a skirt that bears the very shape of my flesh, do they look at it carefully, do they smell it? Does anyone go through life the way I do? Stopping to pick up a scrap of paper on the street, to read a note dropped by a stranger as if it might have a message for me. Does anyone else look so hard, everywhere, for clues?

Inside the salon on Sixth Avenue, Korean manicurists sit at identical pink laminate tables lining the walls of the small business, making two neat rows of six tables. The manicurists all look the same, of no particular age between twenty and thirty, their skin smooth and pale, their black hair cut into short Western styles. They all wear the same uniform, cotton top and drawstring pants—like surgeon's scrubs, only pink: a message of industry and hygiene. The whole enterprise has the order and efficiency of a bank.

Ann considers manicures a waste of money, but after ten days of virtue she is desperate for activities to replace her vices. Thank God she'll be back at work tomorrow. Of course, the first person she'll see is Theo, but how much temptation can he represent when she's put the crystal back behind the mirror of her camera? She can't bring herself to throw it out, and there's no other hiding place that she trusts; if Carl were to find the drug, she'd be in trouble. *What the fuck are you doing to yourself?* she can hear him ask.

Yesterday she went to the market, leaving him at home, the crystal in the lining of her trench coat; she got so nervous waiting in the checkout line that she came home without any groceries, saying she'd forgotten her wallet. "Aren't you going back?" Carl said as she sat down on the couch. "There's no food in the house." She shook her head. Too tired, she'd told him. They ordered dinner in, and she went shopping this morning. She put the groceries away, paced the loft for a while, and then went out to get her nails done.

The manicurist takes Ann's larger, rougher hand in her own two soft ones, and after soaking Ann's fingertips in a dish of warm, soapy water, begins to massage her hands with lotion. Ann glances around the room, looking for her reflection. Opposing mirrors suggest endless repeating aisles of manicure tables, the actual and the reflected almost undistinguishable, and the illusory space created by so many multiplying reflections—the lie that this little world of order goes on indefinitely—makes Ann suddenly claustrophobic. She finds her own stricken face among all the others, her hands caught over the white towel with the hands of the manicurist folded around them.

"You pick color and pay now," the manicurist says, as she blots the cream from Ann's fingers.

When Ann doesn't respond immediately, she says, "You pay now. Later nail are wet, no good, no good for new nail to touch money, yes."

"Yes," Ann says finally. "How much?"

"Fifteen dollar."

Ann hands the woman a twenty-dollar bill. The money feels dirty to her freshly creamed hand, proof that this is not a communion between women, but a little business transaction. The bill, limp and faded, almost tears as Ann removes it from her wallet; as if to imply the frailty of the exchange, she thinks, and is immediately disgusted with herself for looking everywhere for significance, for everywhere finding evidence that the fabric of life is threadbare and that she is about to fall through. And there's another reason I like speed, she thinks, I never think such stupid things when I'm on it.

The manicurist hands Ann five crisp one-dollar bills, and she returns them. "For you," she says, and the little woman nods thank you and hides them in her clean pink pocket. She again takes Ann's hands in her own, which are so soft, and uncurling Ann's fingers, she begins to shape her nails with a pink emery board.

————

Two hours after the manicure, Ann has already picked the polish off all the fingernails on her left hand. She's in a phone booth in Grand Central, calling Doris. "Can I come up?" she says.

"Sure," Doris says. "Anything wrong?" Ann can hear her smoking on the other end of the line, deep inhalations that introduce inappropriate pauses in the conversation.

"Nothing really," Ann says. "I'm a little stressed out, I guess. I go back to work tomorrow. I thought I'd maybe use this afternoon to sort through the rest of the stuff in the archives."

"I'll pick you up," Doris says. "Which train?"

Ann looks over at the big board listing departures from the city. "I'll catch the three-forty," she says.

Doris meets Ann at the station in Greenwich in her old, battered Mercedes, rust spots bleeding through the white rocker panels. Her car winters outside because the garage of her house has been converted to a controlled humidity environment for the disposition of photographs and negatives, everything protected and insured against fires, floods, theft, and all manner of catastrophe. Ann owns about sixty percent of the body of her father's work, and she keeps it all archived in Connecticut, along with other documents pertaining to his career. Doris represents Ann's interests to people such as the curator of the upcoming retrospective, journalists, and anyone else who wants to transact business with the estate of Edgar Evans Rogers.

Ann met Doris her first week of graduate school. She had just arrived in New Haven after two days of driving east without a break. It was late afternoon, she'd stopped at a bookstore for a copy of the *Yale Daily News*, and was back behind the wheel, driving while looking through apartment listings—the two columns of ads folded open on her steering wheel—when she rear-ended a white Mercedes stopped at an intersection. A woman got out of the car and walked over as Ann stared through her dirty windshield, shoved the newspaper down between her legs. The woman was wearing a tennis dress; she had short gray hair and was built like a man with muscular legs, trim hips. Her large breasts had the quality of an after-thought: they looked too big, as if they had been added on to lend credibil-ity to the idea that she was female.

Ann got out of her car. "Well, I guess we know who's fault this is," the woman said. Her bottom lip was white with zinc oxide.

"I'm sorry," Ann said, and she began to cry.

"It isn't that bad." The woman took her sunglasses off, smiled.

But, overtired and having started to cry, Ann couldn't stop. As she became more incoherent, inexplicably telling the woman that classes began the next day, that her car's radiator had a small crack and had to be refilled every fifty miles, that she'd never been in the East before, Doris ended up sitting her down on a curb while she moved their cars to the parking lot of a small shopping center on Temple Street.

"Is there something wrong?" Doris asked from across the Formica table in a coffee shop. "Something more than denting my fender, I mean?" She ordered a piece of pie, and when it came she pushed it toward Ann, handed her the fork.

Ann looked at her. "I haven't, I'm not . . ." She looked down at the pie. "My father died," she said. "Not recently. It's been more than two years, actually. But I seem to be . . . well, I've been a little disorganized since then."

Doris said nothing, nodded. She beckoned to a waitress, ordered herself a tuna sandwich. By the time it came, Ann had finished the pie, and Doris put half of her sandwich on Ann's plate, watched her eat it. "Did you stop along the way?" she asked. "For food, I mean."

Ann looked up. "Sort of. I mean I had to stop for the car. I guess I just wasn't hungry until I got here." Ann put the remains of the sandwich down, shrugged self-consciously.

By the time they left the coffee shop it was dark, and she followed Doris back to her house in Greenwich. She spent a week there; when she finally moved her stuff into a little apartment just three blocks from Yale's art center, she had an attorney.

Doris had been the first person to suggest that there might be a way to better manage at least some of Ann's peculiar heritage. All the mail, for example: cards and letters and modeling offers, questions, threats, proposals. Although she was only twenty-one, Ann's credit rating was shot; she had allowed herself to become delinquent on bills simply because she couldn't stand to sort through her mail.

Within a month, Ann transferred the administration of her father's estate to Doris. Four boxes of files arrived from the Texas lawyer, along with a letter whose tone was openly relieved. "I am retiring my practice in the spring," read the last line, "so I'm pleased that you have found an able custodian for your late father's affairs."

Doris looked fifty when Ann met her ten years ago—too many cigarettes, too many hours in the sun, and hair that had turned gray before she graduated from law school. Lately, now that she really is fifty, she looks unexpectedly younger; she plays tennis every morning, and is often still in her shorts and court shoes when Ann sees her in the afternoon. She jokes that she's the only lawyer she knows who owns only one business suit.

For the past year much of Doris's time has been spent on red tape occasioned by the retrospective. Art handlers. Insurance. Photographs damaged in shipping. One lost, or stolen. And publicity, of course, along with the complications that attend it. Since the show was announced, Doris's house has been splotched with red paint, repainted white, and splotched again, presumably by the same group of radical feminists who called in a bomb threat to the museum two weeks ago. The group, identifying themselves as "Crusaders for a United Terrorist Sisterhood," or, more informally, CUNTS, must have gotten Doris's name, along with information that photographs were archived at her house, from a gallery that once represented Edgar Rogers. To be safe, the police evacuated Doris to a local motel and insisted that she remain there for twenty-four hours following the threat. They were unable to find out whether the young woman who had set herself on fire in the museum's sculpture garden was one of these "crusaders," but interpreted that event as evidence that rabid feminists might well do anything they threatened.

Doris responds to such inconvenience with good humor, or perhaps she's just trying to offset Ann's fears. "Horrible, aren't they?" she says of the ugly Rottweilers that now pace around her house and the photograph archives. She laughs. "Not exactly what you had in mind when you suggested a pet?" She and Ann walk carefully, making no sudden moves, from Doris's car to the kitchen.

The dogs—on duty one at a time for six-hour shifts—work within an electronic fence, an invisible barrier that triggers a transmitter collar to shock the animal if it ventures beyond twenty feet of the house and storage facility. Familiarized with Doris's and Ann's scents, the dogs are guaranteed not to hurt them, but their malevolent gold eyes and conspiratorial, ursine grins inspire little confidence in the trainer's promise. "The force of their jaws is calculated at 1800 pounds per square inch," he'd said.

"You just don't like anything you aren't allowed to take care of yourself," Ann says when they're safe inside.

Of course, it's been obvious from their first meeting that Doris is a compulsive caregiver. Unmarried, childless, she uses whatever extra time she has to represent illegal immigrants, at least one of which is usually living in her house, the work and the destitute strays both supported by Ann's money.

Before she goes out to the archives, Ann sits with Doris at her big trestle table, pushing away pieces of a muffin Doris keeps nudging toward her. "Stop it," she says. "You're worse than Carl."

"Just trying to be helpful," Doris says. "So, how's your eye?"

Ann doesn't answer immediately, sips her tea, looks around the well-appointed kitchen that she knows is seldom used. Doris comes down to the city and buys up Dean & Deluca every Tuesday; she never dirties those shining copper pans hanging over the stove. Every once in a while one of the immigrants she helps is sufficiently skilled and courageous to approach the big restaurant stove and produce meals, as a way of thanking her. But the current one, Lupe, rarely leaves her room.

After reading an article about South American girls shanghaied into prostitution, earning two hundred dollars a day for their pimps, ten for themselves, Doris spent an afternoon in one of the seedy neighborhoods of Queens that warehouses bargain sex. She left her card in the local bar, grocery store, beauty parlor, random mailboxes—anywhere someone might find one. Under the words ATTORNEY AT LAW she had printed the message "I can help you get a green card and a job." Lupe is the sixth prostitute to have called this summer. She says she is eighteen, but she looks twelve.

"The eye is okay," Ann says finally. "But I'm scared it might happen again." She holds her tea, feeling the warmth through the cup. Briefly her eyes meet Doris's unblinking gaze, and she puts down the tea.

"You've been pretty scarce," Doris says. "Lately, when I want to know how Ann is, I end up calling Carl."

"Well, the eye thing," Ann says. "And I've been working hard. You know how summer is for weddings." She stops. "I've been running around trying to be too busy to worry about anything," she says after a moment.

"I'm here, you know," Doris says, "if you want to talk."

Ann nods. "I guess maybe it's time to think about things that I had the luxury of ignoring for a while." Ann puts her hand out to Doris's. "You know, you've made it possible, for the past ten years, for me not to have to face up to being Edgar Rogers's daughter."

Doris looks away; gratitude embarrasses her. Ann stands up and stretches. "Well," she says, "I'll just get out there." She looks at the dog through the window; its black sides heave as it pants in the heat. "I wish there were a tunnel," she says.

As she closes the back door behind her, Ann sees that Lupe is coming tentatively into the kitchen. The girl does not enter the room directly but creeps along its perimeter, keeping a hand on the edge of the counter, the back of a chair; it's as if she's blind, feeling her way in. Ann is surprised by a sudden stab of jealousy as she sees Doris stand and put her arm around the girl.

In the storage facility, Ann retrieves the Bell & Howell projector from the closet. It's old enough that when she plugs it in, it smells as if the electrical insulation is smoldering, and she hopes it doesn't pick this day to finally give out. She points the projector at the white wall and gets out a crate of tiny film cans.

Of course, there are no family *snapshots*, a term her father used to deride the work of others; but there are these movies: tiny sixteen-millimeter reels bearing only twenty-five feet of film, two and a half minutes of history.

Burning her fingers on the old projector, the bulb making the brittle film so hot that it often breaks and has to be spliced, Ann squints at the first reel. Last month she embarked on a project to catalog these old movies of her father's. She can't remember ever seeing them as a child, but when fragments of the past started intruding on her workday, her sleep, even while reading a novel or worse, during sex with Carl, she decided to go through the old movies. Maybe they could tell her something.

Last time she came up to Greenwich to look at them, she got through about twenty reels before she was too tired to continue. The films are mute, untitled, full of mysteries, and while she's made a list detailing the content and presumed dates of the ones she watched before, each description, followed by a question mark, is useless. *1958? One of Mother's sisters? Mexico? Man in hat = father?* As soon as Ann has one reel in the projector, she's hooked, stuck in the quagmire of the past. Running them forward, running them backward, hoping to find . . . what? Something: she'll know it when she sees it.

In color—lovely, lush, vulgar color, saturated and fat with color—the films are the antidote to her father's starkly elegant black and white stills, and she likes them for that reason alone. Likes them, too, for their sentimental quality that video doesn't impart. The tapes Ann makes are smooth, polished, and almost antiseptic in comparison. Perhaps because it is Ann's job to correct for spontaneity, and truth.

She threads a cracked leader under the gate latch behind the lens. She looked at this film last time, it's the only one she can identify positively as to date and event: her parents' honeymoon, beginning with her mother at the wheel of a convertible. Driving slowly, slowly, languorously, Virginia is wearing a hat that could never stay on in any wind and she keeps one hand firmly on the crown. Ann's father must have held the camera while he walked backward in front of the car, walking on the shoulder of the road in the hot Texas sun. The scene changes: he is at the wheel and her mother rides on the hood of the car, decorously at first, as if sidesaddle; then, with a little acceleration, she falls back on the hood, knees spread, laughing, "Stop! Stop!" Ann can see her lips form the now silent words. Who held the camera when they were together? And whose car were they driving? She will never know.

They approach a gate made of two old wagon wheels set in a frame and painted white, the entrance to the ranch run by the Giant, a man her father told her about years later. She doesn't know his real name, only that his hands were so big that a child could sit on the palm of each. Ann was disappointed at her first sight of the man, smiling affably in his freakishness for the camera: not a real giant at all—no more than nine feet tall, standing at the door to his regular-sized inn. Still, he dwarfed her father, and he opens his arms as if welcoming two children.

Her parents are then suddenly in a garden, where wind makes the leaves tremble, shadows move seductively over flesh. Bare arms, and sunshine so bright, bright with happiness—it's as if the sun that shined for those movies never shines anymore. And Ann has never seen flowers in colors so extravagant, big, big zinnias, their heads heavy, dropping with color.

Red zinnias, a red blouse. Her mother is plump and flirtatious, every gesture suggests that she knows it is becoming, this abundance. Under a willow tree is that kind of intense shade possible only on the brightest days, the area under the foliage absolutely black so that when the couple strolls under the tree they are momentarily gone, vanished, disappeared.

Doris comes in the studio after the first couple of reels, leans against the counter running along the back wall, arms crossed. "So," she says, "what are you looking for?"

"Nothing. I don't know. Just looking."

Her mother's eyes, squinting prettily. They play a game, tag. Chasing through the garden, bees buzzing, caught for a moment before the lens. Who is holding the camera? In the vegetable garden, lips on a tomato's bright skin, the fruit breaking under white teeth. Red, red mouth, red blouse, red fingernails, red shoes getting dirty in the garden. Her mother's head tipped back, her white throat moving as she drinks water from a glass. The bright sun, too, is trapped in the glass, she is drinking sunshine, drinking life. Her lips move, she begins to speak even as she takes the glass from her lips. The film is silent, but Ann can imagine her San Antonio accent from the way her lips move. She tips the glass into the flower bed, and the last bright drops disappear into the dirt.

When they chase into the dark leaves, shadows dapple their faces, her mother's white arms. Her father in his perennial white shirt, black pants, but he seems like a different man wearing the familiar clothes: happy, laughing, *cutting up*, chasing her mother through the vegetables, taking off his glasses to kiss her among the tomatoes. He kisses her cheek and his mouth is open for the kiss, so that it looks as if he bites her.

Ann hears Doris leave the room quietly, the studio door's latch clicks softly. She doesn't raise her head, even, so absorbed is she. Ann runs the film backward, looking for what might have eluded her when it went forward, the way you notice the familiar only when you yourself are turned around: ill, feverish, something. She turns the knob to slow down the film so that the figures move in reluctant deliberation, a hand coming up to the lips, taking too long to brush a hair away. Forward then backward again: watching lips part even as they had joined just frames before, the surrender of an embrace replaced by the bright-eyed expectancy that preceded it. Her parents stroll backward and out of the garden as Ann makes her parents grow younger by the second, her mother a few cell divisions less pregnant; both of them, all three of them, just that much further from death and unhappiness, the clock of the body running backward toward childhood.

The close-ups make her throat ache with longing, the desire to touch these people she never knew. Her father is young, his shoulders thick, muscular, the only wrinkles those of amusement around his eyes. The slight gap between her mother's front teeth is sexy, alive, a promise of her generosity. She wears a bracelet that Ann now has packed away with all the other objects too freighted with memory to handle or display—a silver bracelet with western charms, too many of them, horseshoes and broncos, cowbells, a tiny coiled lariat. The bracelet of someone who is young and carefree, it jangles loudly on the wrist. Behind her mother, the heads of flowers shudder in the breeze, cabbage roses as big as dinner plates, roses long dead, their petals falling, blowing across the grass. The bright sun floods everything, it is all drowned in sunlight.

Her father swings his coat over his shoulder; reverse, and he takes it off again; forward, on. What can be learned about someone by the way he throws his coat over his shoulder? Anything? Nothing? The way he settles his glasses on the bridge of his nose as if it were tender, sunburned.

Ann grows dizzy with looking, her hand over her left eye—not necessary but a bad habit by now. She realizes she has been frowning in concentration for an hour, even more.

These aren't like the pictures her father took of her, the stolen ones.

Even in home movies, there exists a self-consciousness: a hand brought before the mouth: Not now when I've just taken a bite of this tomato! Waving the camera away: Don't remember me with my cheeks bulging, juice running down my chin! Her parents laugh with extravagant glee, happy, yes, but aware of the camera's eye, their emotion magnified by the idea of preservation. They double over with mirth, as if in pain.

Only happy days are recorded, that is all one could say of the movies. Happy sunny afternoons, her parents walking forever in a happy land. Pulling a piece of twine for a cat to chase. When Ann reverses, the animal dances acrobatically, impossibly backward. The father Ann knew was a man who did nothing but work; the father in these movies does nothing but play. Her mother still nearly a girl, turning a cartwheel, underwear flashing white.

Stepping off a prop plane onto a small dusty runway, hair blowing in her eyes, shading her eyes with her hand: Where are you, Edgar? Seeing him with the camera: Oh there! Running to him. Backward: let her disappear up those metal stairs, close the shining door, let the plane take her back into the sky.

If that girl, looking so guileless, loved her father, then . . . then what? Then he couldn't have been unlovable? But Ann knows that, she loved him herself. Ann is aware, as she packs up the films in their tiny cans, that

Doris has returned and is sitting in the back of the room, head cocked to one side. What is Ann looking for? Is that what she wonders? The one movie that isn't there, wasn't filmed. The one that answers all the questions. That's not possible of course, so why not, then, the pivotal scene of her mother, never fully described to Ann but which she has imagined too often.

She died in the kitchen, kneeling in front of the cabinet under the sink as if she were about to retrieve something: a sponge, the Ajax. In a white dress, her aunt told her, and she thinks of her kneeling, her head falling forward as if in prayer. What's it like to bleed to death? The life ebbing out of you like air from a balloon? Blood—so much blood! They say the placenta tore away when she went into labor, tore away from the womb. Blood in a symmetrical pool around her knees, her white dress soaked in her blood, her life, so that it looks as if she wears a red skirt. She kneels on a magic red carpet that carries her away.

Where do we all go, and why? Ann asks the questions of a child. Why do some of us die and leave others behind? How can it be that only she is left, alone? The sole keeper of her history, she cannot remember even half of it. No more Mariette to call and ask, Do you remember if we had a cat, a dog? Did we used to go away in the summer, did I go to camp? Was that an elm tree in the back by the fence or a maple? Such questions are significant only because no one can answer them.

Mariette died in her old Toyota, on her way . . . where? Heading east on a highway in Missouri. Mariette Crane, forty-nine, an unmarried schoolteacher. A box came for Ann from whoever packed up her aunt's belongings—there was no letter, no return address. In it were Ann's baby shoes, clumsy drawings from first grade, a little undershirt: junk precious only to a mother.

Ann is about to crack a joke, something to make light of her self-indulgent forays into the past, and she turns, grinning at Doris, when something like a black spiderweb slides down in front of her vision. She feels the smile freeze on her face.

"What is it?" Doris says, slipping down from the counter where she was sitting. Ann closes her eyes, opens them. She can't tell if she sees Doris behind the web or if she sees Doris with the right eye and the black net with the left. She blinks and rubs her eyes, as if the obstruction were a real cobweb, something she could brush away.

"I don't know. I don't know," she says. She covers her eyes with her hands. "Please . . . please call Carl."

———————

The second laser surgery is performed that night and keeps Ann in the eye hospital for two days. The spiderweb, despite looking black, turns out to be blood, or at least the effects of bleeding: the repaired aneurysm has ruptured and leaked.

In the hospital she wears a patch over her left eye. Carl is standing by the window. With her good eye she can see the sun on the East River sparkling around his head.

"What do you mean you don't know?" Carl says.

"I mean I don't know."

"You don't remember?"

"That's what I'm saying, yes."

"But when we talked about the photographs a long time ago, you said it was all staged, faked. Airbrushed, painted negatives, double exposures. You pointed out examples, you explained how it was done." He takes her forearm, traced with old scars: white, indistinct, too faint to be felt. Nothing anyone would notice upon meeting her. "God damn it, Ann, you said these were from a bike accident, you said you fell on some glass in the road." His fingers tighten painfully around her wrist.

Ann pulls away, turns on her side and closes the good eye. "Jesus, Carl," she says. "We'd only just met. And I think I thought that *was* what was true. I think it must have seemed like the best answer to the question everyone always asked, and then I began to believe it, too."

"But if that's not what happened, what did?" Carl sits on the side of the bed. "I mean, he didn't hurt you and then record what he'd done, did he?"

"I *don't know.* I'm not saying they *weren't* faked, I'm just saying that I've realized I don't remember it at all, nothing." She rubs her head. The slight but constant pressure of the elastic holding the eye patch is giving her a headache.

Carl exhales loudly, as if he's been holding his breath. "But maybe you will," he says. "I mean, if some things come back, maybe others will, too." He puts his hand on her knee through the blanket.

'**ve** been lying to Carl. I do remember. I just can't talk about it, say the words aloud. Not yet.

I was scared at the dealer's, Papi. When I saw those pictures, saw myself naked, when you showed me what I'd done to myself, I could smell the fear on me, rank, like a dog before a beating. When, when did you take them all? So many. I thought I had hidden what you learned.

How long had you been dead? A week?

Sitting there, considering my inheritance, I found myself referring to the girl in the pictures as "she." "Her." Not out loud of course, that wouldn't have seemed normal. And besides, I didn't say anything out loud.

You do have that desire to keep a person you love with you forever, even the ones that poison you, maybe even especially them—you want to drink that poison. I tried to hate you, Papi. It would have made everything easier if I had. But somehow, I couldn't.

All those years it was you who threatened to eat me up, now I find I have swallowed you, kept you inside me. I went on, I made a life, I thought I wasn't thinking of you. But now I cannot help myself, you've come back.

I wish I had been braver, had asked you more questions. All that I'll never know about your past, all that I can't remember about the part of it we shared. Were you really more mysterious than any other person? Was I? Did you take pictures of what you found mysterious as a way to try to know it?

Of course I didn't pose for the pictures, not the ones about which everyone asks. And they weren't faked.

I can feel it again, the way I did so many years ago.

Bending a Coke can back and forth, back and forth until it tore and made a knife. Cutting myself. Doing it carefully, very carefully, so that just a line of red opened behind my blade's slow progress.

Or a little burn, perhaps, the edge of the iron as I was pressing a skirt for school.

It wasn't masochism so much as a sort of drug. The small, specific sensation, the red color, was calming to me. That strange way pain can make you taste metal in your mouth. Not from licking the blood, that's not what I mean: just a taste that comes into your consciousness along with a smell like ammonia, something you might be thinking rather than sensing. It didn't hurt, not really, it felt.

I didn't know why I did it, not then. But now I do. I longed for a wound that showed. I used to fantasize that you beat me—you who never touched me except to turn my head this way or that—I imagined that you beat me until I was black and blue. Because I wanted wounds, stigmata. I never spoke out against you— that was a matter of honor—but I wanted my pain manifest. And I wanted to feel it.

For almost a year after you died I stumbled, I stubbed my toes, I closed fingers in drawers, knocked my head. As if to break through the terrible numbness, I was always calling myself back into my body, reminding myself that yes I was still here. I never knew what month it was. I knew the day of the week, and even the date perhaps, but it was just a number. I didn't know where in the year I had fallen, and I would have to extrapolate, saying, for example, Oh, a greeting card: it must be Christmas, winter, the end of the year.

Now, sometimes, walking down the street, looking in the mirror, I catch my breath in the realization that you're really dead, you're gone. It's been long enough, certainly, but you took up so much of me—is it possible that you could have died and left me behind, intact?

The first wedding I recorded took place in a private home, a twenty-six room apartment in the East Eighties. Checking on the bride in her silk-upholstered dressing room, I put my hand up to adjust her headpiece. No mother, sister, or friend was there to help her; the one bridesmaid was applying mascara. As I raised my hand, the bride winced and ducked her head: the sign of someone who had been hit too often, by a parent perhaps, or maybe by the man she was marrying that day. Maybe both.

We looked at one another and just as I was going to speak—what would I have said?—she put her hands up and lowered the veil over her face.

A hundred, no, a thousand happy weddings, but when I close my eyes, it is those two lace-gloved hands lowering the veil between us that I see. I was scared. Scared for her, but also, I realize now, for me. As if for an instant I knew that all this was coming, that like her, I had lowered a veil. And would have to take it off.

So, is this going to happen again?" Ann asks Dr. Ettinger.

"It could happen again," he says, "but not for a long while, I hope."

She looks at him, chewing her lip. Without the patch, she is constantly fighting the urge to cover her left eye with her hand. It's been a week since the surgery, and while her vision has returned, it isn't as it was: there's a blank spot a little to the left and up. It's the kind of thing that when she tries to catch it, moving her eye quickly, it disappears. She sees what was missing before, and some other detail falls away.

"What about the hole?" she says.

"The hole?"

"Yes, the whatever-it-is, the missing part."

"Well, we've talked about this, Ann. The disrupted field of vision is something you'll get used to—your brain simply fills in what your eye misses and soon you won't know that you aren't seeing everything." His words have a rote quality, probably because it's an answer he's given twice already, once in the hospital before the patch came off and again just an hour ago in the examining room.

He crosses his arms. "Let's talk about your health in general," he says. "Have you seen Dr. Sanders lately? You look thinner to me, and your blood pressure is consistently higher than it was last year."

Ann shakes her head. "I have checkups twice yearly, the next is in October. I'll mention it."

"Maybe you should go early this time. Have him look at your kidney function." He takes his little crescent glasses off, rubs the bridge of his nose, replaces them. "Eyes and kidneys tend to deteriorate simultaneously," he says.

She nods. She knows this: in either organ it's the same minute blood vessels that are damaged by diabetes. "I thought the blood pressure thing was maybe just nerves," she says.

"Nerves?"

"Well, you know, stress or something." Ann looks at Ettinger's desk. A diagnostic report rests on top of her open file. She figures out the words "rare dot and blot hemorrhage" typed next to the date of the last surgery. She's considering asking what the words mean exactly—Is what she has something rare? Could it have to do with the speed?—when Ettinger speaks.

"What stresses?" he says, closing the file. "Anything unusual?" He leans back in his chair and looks at her rather pointedly, she thinks.

"I don't know. There's this show of my father's photographs coming up. And it's been, well, there have been—" Ann pauses. "Here," she says finally, rooting in her camera bag for the article about the woman who set herself on fire. She hands it, crumpled by now, to the doctor and watches as he reads it.

Ettinger frowns, folds the article, hands it back to her. "I'm sorry," he says. "All this must have been very unpleasant. When does the show open?"

"In two weeks. They moved it up to avoid more trouble."

"Why don't you plan a little vacation? Go away with Carl, get away from the city for the week around the event?"

"I really can't do that."

"Why not?" Ettinger leans forward, elbows on his desk as if settling in for a long conversation.

"Well, aside from not being able to miss any more work, since all my partners seem ready to kill me, I'm involved in the show. You know, I've cooperated with the curator, loaned photographs, helped make some decisions. I'm going to go to the opening."

"Do you think that's a good idea?"

"I did. I mean I still do. It's just that I'm a little tense. I mean—I didn't really expect the friction. Maybe that was sort of naive or wishful thinking on my part because my father's work has always been, well, caused problems. But I'm managing," she says.

Ettinger looks at the ceiling, nods, then looks back at her. "I can refer you to someone. I think you should talk with someone about all this." He writes a name on a pad advertising a new ophthalmic product and hands it to her.

"I don't really think so," says Ann. "But thanks."

"Well, keep the reference. If you change your mind, you can set up an appointment. At the very least, Ann, I want you to think about ways in which you can protect yourself from what it appears will be a difficult experience."

Ann nods as she stands to leave.

Descending in the elevator, she still has the crumpled article in her hand. Since she clipped it, she has carried it with her everywhere. She shoves it in her bag—she's stopped rereading it by now, but she knows it by heart. And everywhere she goes, she imagines she is followed by the young woman, who slips after her through the air-conditioned aisles of a store, sits with her at the breakfast table, peers over her shoulder as she draws insulin into a syringe. Her hair in flames. Her blind, burned eyes. A tee-shirt that reads, Ann Rogers. At times it gets so bad that Ann wonders if the girl has died and she is being genuinely haunted. And what if there are more of them? A whole army of crazy young women wearing shirts with her name on them. Terrorist Sisterhood.

Maybe this show was a bad idea. Maybe she should have realized that she was just asking for trouble.

It was Doris who had helped to set up the retrospective, Doris to whom the curator came when he wanted photographs. An art historian and professor at Southern Methodist University, Eric Elsin knew Edgar Rogers's former dealer. As Doris later pieced together, late one night the two men were drinking Jack Daniel's and complaining about the provinciality of Dallas—that all the exciting art was in New York—when the dealer let it slip that there were a number of provocative Rogers photographs controlled by the estate of the late photographer. Photographs that would cause a stir if released to the public.

Two days later Elsin sent a proposal for a retrospective of Rogers's work to the Museum of Modern Art. In it he claimed he had access to photographs no one else had seen, photographs that would guarantee press and crowds. The museum took the bait: if Elsin could produce what he claimed, they'd organize a show. Elsin got Doris's name and address from the dealer's secretary. He sent a polite letter asking if the estate would consider loaning works for a major show. When he received no answer, he sent another.

A retrospective was something that was bound to happen eventually, with or without Ann's approval. At the time of her father's suicide, there had been a number of smaller shows, but never an attempt at anything comprehensive. And, as Doris told her, after musing privately for some months over Elsin's letters, this man might offer Ann a means to say something: to reveal some things, to hide others. At least that was how it had seemed almost two years ago.

"Why shouldn't you guide or make public opinion, sort of manipulate it the way it's manipulated you?" Doris said. They were standing at the counter in Dean & Deluca the November before last. For all the seemingly pivotal things she's forgotten, Ann still remembers that day; the snow falling, falling so slowly, spinning in draughts between the buildings.

She stuck her finger in the foam on her hot chocolate, then finally said, "You think?"

"Why not?" Doris struggled with the remains of her brownie. She'd eaten half, intending to throw the rest away. "Christ," she said, and she stuffed the remaining half in her mouth, washed it down with cappuccino. "No self-discipline." She smiled. "Well, what do you think?"

"Okay," Ann said.

And so Doris wrote back to Professor Elsin. The estate would be willing for Elsin to review its archives, including the works which no one else had seen. In return for certain concessions, these photographs might be included in the retrospective. Approval of all written material accompanying the show, occasioned by the show, and appearing in the catalog would be the trade. Elsin went back to the museum, got the deal approved. The contract was executed within a month.

But instead of feeling the confidence of control, as the prospect of the show became increasingly real, Ann felt afraid. She didn't tell Doris this— how could she? The show was booked into seven major museums through 1996. And she didn't talk to Carl about it because she knew she couldn't articulate the fear; it was almost something physical. She lost weight, but all of her clothes felt too tight: turtlenecks or anything touching her throat made her feel dizzy, breathless. The day she was to meet with Elsin up in Connecticut she woke at dawn, sick with anxiety.

"Ann?" Carl said outside the bathroom door.

"It's okay, it's okay," she gasped. "It's nothing. It's something I ate."

He put her on the 2:50 train with a pocketful of dry crackers. She'd be late—she'd missed the previous train because they'd bailed out of one cab en route to Grand Central when Ann thought she was going to throw up again.

From her seat, behind her sunglasses, Ann saw Carl looking after her as the train pulled away from the platform. She feels like he's been looking at her oddly ever since.

Ann and Professor Elsin went through all the photographs. She kept her sunglasses on during the first half of the meeting, standing to one side as he lingered over documentation of her adolescent sexual curiosity, her loneliness and what solace she had found. At the time of her father's death, as directed by his will, all the photographs except these—the ones which were explicitly sexual—had been released for sale. These others, bequeathed to Ann, had been lying in their dark drawers for years, looked at only often enough to ensure that they remained safe, that their value was not compromised by damage to the delicate emulsion.

After an hour she excused herself, leaving Elsin in the studio, white cotton gloves pulled over his thin, hairy wrists; she slipped out the door and into Doris's pantry, which was adjacent to the storage vault. Stocked with a few imported goods, a restaurant-supply size jar of artichoke hearts in olive oil, some fancy vinegars with various sprigs of greenery pickled inside, a wine rack bearing dusty bottles of Chianti, it was a small space devoted to cultivated pleasures. She put her hand out and touched the glass jar of artichoke hearts: cool, smooth. She took off her sunglasses, laid them on the shelf. When she could, she returned to the studio.

"So" she said, startling Elsin, closing the door.

"Yes? Yes?" The professor jumped up from the print he was examining with a magnifying lens, his eyebrows just inches above the image of Ann's face, her bare chest.

"Nothing. Just wondered if you'd finished." Ann dropped into a chair.

"Uh, yes. I have." The professor stood from the table where, she saw, he had made four piles of prints, each replaced in its envelope.

She put on gloves and they went through his choices one by one. Aside from pictures of Ann, he had set aside eight of the ferrotypes taken by her grandfather and some early photographs of Ann's mother, her shoulders and ankles and a monumental print of one breast that revealed an unfeminine scattering of hairs around the dark aureola. Ann paused at that one, the way it filled the frame of the print, swelling against boundaries. She parted with it finally, along with a few loose sheets from her father's ledger, tiny calculations in his fine printing, the amount paid for a box of Ilford paper, the pennies traded for stamps: no transaction too small to include. In the absence of a daybook or any more direct communication of his interests and passions, the ledger would have to suffice.

"Okay," she said, allowing him all of it. Elsin nodded, they shook hands awkwardly. He looked surprised that she had agreed to all his choices, but of course he didn't understand just how adamantly Ann cared about what was said about the pictures, didn't know how many hours of argument would attend each paragraph of the introduction to the catalog. Or that three writers would be fired in the process of trying to get an essay on which everyone could agree: one for using the introduction as a forum for feminist invective; another for referring to Ann as "America's dead sweetheart"; and the last for not referring to her at all.

The essay upon which everyone settled, by a photography critic whose words appeared in many of the texts on Ann's own bookshelf, ended in saying almost nothing. All the sentences looked to be crammed with complex ideation and big words; but, as with the mixture of certain highly potent chemicals, the end product was neutralized to the point of being inert. At least he had a big name, and Ann tried to console herself that not many people read introductions to art books anyway. Thinking about it now, she's sorry she ever asked for approval over the essay or anything else. What words could ever have exposed her more than the photographs themselves? Besides, she can't control the nut factor—demonstrations by extremists and young women who set their hair on fire—any more than she can prevent the constant flow of offensive mail that comes to her care of Doris or, lately, the occasional one that makes it to her own address.

This very morning the doorman handed her an envelope as she left her building. "Some guy, he dropped it off," he said. She opened the letter in the cab on the way to Ettinger's office.

> *Let me in*
> *And I will fuck you*
> *On the cold marble blanket of your tomb,*
> *You dead angel,*
> *I will fuck the teeth out of your head . . .*

No hole in her vision large enough to obscure that. She folded the page without reading the rest of the poem. A block later she reopened it, checked that her name didn't appear anywhere on the page, and when the cab pulled up in front of the eye hospital she left it lying open on the seat.

———

By the time she escapes Ettinger's office and his questions, it's almost two. She'll have a hard time making her Tuesday time slot at Bellevue Hospital. It's pouring with rain, and without an umbrella, she's soaked by the time she sees a free taxi. She tries to make it across the street but loses the ride to someone else.

It's either the subway or a company car, and she's out of practice with the subway. She's taken it only once this summer, and she got off a stop early and walked the last ten blocks. Something about the gelid air conditioning in contrast to the heat of other people's flesh coming through their clothes as they sat on either side of her, pressed tight.

She fishes in her camera bag for a quarter. In the past she's felt no qualms about making indiscriminate collect calls to the office, but it's another thing that irritates Benny, and she's on a new, ingratiating course.

"Benny Benny Benny," she greets him from a dripping public phone booth, "I need a car."

"Excuse me, princess? A what?"

"A car, you know, four wheels, driver." She twines the cord nervously around her fingers.

"A *car?*"

"Yes, Benny, car, c-a-r, car. Can you send one? I'm at—"

"Who'm I taking to?"

"Look, it's pouring and I don't have time for any more bullshit." She's missed work, she's screwed up everybody's calendar, she knows it, but eye surgery is hardly a flimsy excuse for someone whose job is to hold a camera. As she talks she struggles with the broken mechanism of the Rolleiflex, phone receiver held under her jaw. It's jammed. "Fuck," she says.

"What?"

"Not you. There's something wrong with my goddamned camera," she says. "Look, I'm due at an appointment. Will you please just send the car? I'm having a bad day and you're making it worse, if that makes you feel any better."

"Much better," he says and he hangs up on her.

Ann stands for a moment before the phone, Rolleiflex in hand, receiver still tucked between chin and shoulder. Benny is out to get her, he must be. As soon as she returned to work, before she'd even had a chance to put her camera bag down, he demanded a record of her business expenses for the past month, all the receipts, everything.

The Rolleiflex's mirror finally yields to pressure from her thumb—just a matter of paying attention—but once the tiny bag of crystal is before her eyes, she stops herself. She's opened the camera reflexively: no rationalizations, just a knee-jerk response to stress that entirely bypassed her conscience. Not only that, but she was apparently about to do drugs on an uptown street corner after almost three weeks of abstinence. "Christ," Ann says to herself, and starts to cry.

She has never missed one of her Tuesday dates at Bellevue and she has never shown up at the hospital on drugs. She puts her forehead against the dirty pay phone. She can't get a hold of herself. It's impossible. Despite the last weeks, she's just getting worse. If she could lose it like this, on the street, she'll never be able to go on fooling Carl. And then what? Will he leave her?

After a minute, a voice behind her makes her realize that she's weeping in public. She puts the camera away in the one dry corner of the phone booth, wipes her face on her sleeve, and turns her attention to finding the closest subway stop.

Ann gets to the hospital late, runs panting up the stone steps that lead to the big double doors. It is the dispossessed who end up behind these doors—babies born to mothers with AIDS, mothers on drugs, mothers who can't cope with being mothers because they're too selfish, too immature, too something. Or not enough of something else. Patient. Loving. Brave. Despite her fantasies of adopting a child, Ann is afraid that she herself might be one of those unfit for the dailiness of parenthood, a woman saved by her biology from becoming a bad mother. She thinks of the work as an anonymous attempt to help the women she knows must hate themselves for abandoning their children.

Even if they are fed and changed and medicated when sick, children who are not held enough fail to thrive. If they aren't held at all, they die. And most of the babies in Bellevue are disadvantaged from birth by a host of physical ills that will be complicated by retardation, or at the least emotional and behavioral problems.

Ann goes through the locker room where she drops her wet bag and coat in one of the cubbyholes reserved for volunteers. After washing and putting on a smock and mask—protection for the babies, not her—she enters the nursery. "Hi," she says to the duty nurse. "Sorry I'm late."

The nurse, tired toward the end of her shift, shrugs. "It's raining," she says. "Everyone in New York is late when it rains." She indicates which baby Ann is to pick up by pointing with her clipboard to the furthest crib in the glassed-in room. Ann walks over and reaches down for the rigid little bundle. Some of the babies are quiet, but this one is crying raggedly, as if for some time.

Who's to say whether a stranger's arms offer any real comfort? Does it matter that these children who haven't much of a chance from the very start are held? Is too little better than none at all? These are questions Ann never asks; she believes in this. The baby's head rests on her arm, and Ann looks into her dark blue eyes, sparse lashes shining with tears. She does not believe in original sin, she knows that in their brief lives these children have yet to do anything wrong.

Once on her shoulder, the baby squirms until her face is wedged up under Ann's jaw. Ann feels the down of the baby's warm head under her chin, the wet cheek on her neck. She feels the little body begin to relax, slowly. The baby is still crying, but her sobs have lost their conviction, and Ann can feel her succumb to the fatigue of grief. She'll be quiet soon.

Sometimes the babies Ann holds cry for the whole three hours. She used to think this was evidence of her doing no good at all, but she's decided that that isn't necessarily the case. Even if their interaction—Ann's and the baby's—is never articulated, it is yet one in which one person witnesses the pain of another. And it must be better to cry in someone's arms than alone.

SAMANTHA SPIERS
Specializing in Private Surveillance
803 West End Ave, #12E
New York, New York 10024

Mr. Carl Graves
Box 1598, General Post Office
James A. Farley Building
New York, NY 10116

August 16, 1992

Dear Mr. Graves:

Enclosed please find the surveillance report for 8/13–8/15, 1992, as well as a copy of the invoice forwarded to Doris Ashton, Esq. As per our phone conversation of 8/15, Benita Amons, who made Saturday August 15th's report, judged the subject to be extremely nervous and was concerned that Ms. Rogers seemed to have some suspicion of being followed. As you suggested at our initial conference, I withdrew supervision immediately (as of Saturday at 10:34 P.M.), so as not to possibly further alarm the subject. If you prefer that surveillance resume, please inform me of this at your soonest convenience.

None of our detectives found reason to conclude that Ms. Rogers is using any controlled substance other than insulin.

Per your request, establishments other than Bergdorf Goodman and Co. were compensated for all items removed by the subject. A separate invoice (copy attached) detailing these incidental expenses was forwarded to Doris Ashton, Esq., along with the receipts for said purchases. A pair of silk evening pajama pants, recovered from a waste can by Benita Amons, was forwarded under separate cover to Doris Ashton esq. (See 12:35 PM notation for Saturday, August 15.)

Sincerely,
Samantha Spiers

Thursday, August 13
2:20 P.M. Subject entered Saks Fifth Avenue department store, and proceeded via elevator to the 4th floor Ladies' Lounge. Remained in facilities
for six minutes and left two magazines, five Q-Tips, and a Rexall Pharmacy
receipt inscribed with the following non-working numbers: 572-1616;
336-2770; 442-7892 in the sanitary receptacle.
2:28 P.M. Subject descended via escalator to third floor where she loitered
for some minutes in the Georgio Armani boutique, then asked the saleslady
in attendance to check the stockroom for a size not on display. In the
absence of personnel, subject removed a sleeveless blue linen dress from the
rack and secreted the garment in her camera bag. She exited the department and continued down the escalator to the first floor, leaving the
premises through the East 50th Street exit.
3:12 P.M. Cab [TLC# 9H55] to Broadway & 95 Street. Subject emerged
from vehicle wearing the stolen blue dress under her original jacket.
Browsed at "Bernie's" magazine and candy store at corner of 95th and
Broadway, where she removed *Startling Detective, Elle,* and *Interview* without paying.
4:10 P.M. Subject entered Argo Coffee Shop at 244 Broadway, ordered
coffee and pie, neither of which she consumed. Read magazines which she
left in the booth.
5:15 P.M. Cab [TLC# 4J13] to Riverside Church, met Andy Gustafsen,
Visage employee, at 490 Riverside Drive entrance.
6:20 P.M. Cab [TLC# 6A93] to 47 West 28th Street, entered lobby.

Friday, August 14
2:00 P.M. Cab [TLC# 4W69] to 86th and Columbus.
2:37 P.M. Cab [TLC# 6Y93] to Bergdorf Goodman and Co., 5th and 57th.
3:05 P.M. Subject proceeded via elevator to 7th floor where she removed
and secreted on her person a wrapped box of eight La Reine Belgian
chocolates from the Gifts department. Went directly to the Ladies' Lounge
where she left candy wrappers and three uneaten chocolates in facilities'
sanitary receptacle.
3:13 P.M. Subject made three calls from the fifth-floor public telephone,
two of short duration, one longer, argumentative call, 3:27–3:39.
3:40–4:53 P.M. Subject took an extended, agitated walk through the
boutiques on the fourth and fifth floors of the department store and returned to the seventh floor where she had tea sandwiches, which she
charged on her Bergdorf Goodman credit card, in the Café Vienna. Left the
store without removing any merchandise.

5:12 P.M. Cab [TLC# 5T67] to 49 East 11th Street, ESO World, a business which rents the use of sensory deprivation tanks.

7:45 P.M. Subject walked to 47 West 28th Street.

Saturday, August 15

11:15 A.M. Subject left lobby of 47 West 28th, walked north on 6th Avenue to 33rd Street.

11:30 A.M. Subject met Elaine Briggs, Visage employee, at Cosmic coffee shop, corner of 6th and 33rd. Ordered coffee and discussed camera angles for wedding scheduled at 1:00 P.M., St. Patrick's Cathedral Chapel.

11:45 A.M. Cab [TLC# 7Q99] to St. Patrick's, 5th and 51st, with assistant Briggs.

11:50 A.M. Subject asked Briggs to remain at St. Patrick's to receive delivery of auxiliary video equipment. Walked six blocks north to Bergdorf Goodman department store, entered through the south door into Cosmetics department. Proceeded via elevator to third-floor Escada shop where she removed a suit of silk evening pajamas from the rack, cutting the cable when the saleswoman was involved in a conversation with a coworker. Subject secreted garment in her camera bag and proceeded to Sonia Rykiel boutique where she examined and removed a lavender silk sheath dress from a locked rack after cutting the cable. Descended via escalator to the first floor and exited through the north door.

12:35 P.M. Subject walked six blocks south to St. Patrick's Cathedral Chapel. Met with family of bride on front stairs and excused herself to change in church dressing room. Taped wedding wearing the stolen lavender sheath with the jacket from the silk pajamas. Left pajama pants in dressing room waste can.

2:15 P.M. Cab [TLC# 7Y55] to Plaza Tea Room for afternoon reception. Subject quit reception via personnel locker room.

3:45 P.M. Gypsy car service [unidentified vehicle] to 86th and Broadway.

5:50 P.M. Gypsy car service [unidentified vehicle] to Our Lady of the Redemption Catholic church at 112 East 92nd Street. Met Assistant Briggs at church's south door.

9:12 P.M. Cab [TLC# 9Y73] to 28th and 5th, Rexall Pharmacy. Subject picked up prescription for Humulin NR, box of 100 ct., B-D diabetic syringes, 50 cc size, paid with PCS/Blue Cross card. Removed three packages Reese's peanut butter cups, Cutex nail polish remover, and cassette tape—*Twenty Unforgettable Hits* by Nat King Cole—without paying, secreting items in camera bag and jacket pockets.

9:34 P.M. Subject walked one block west to 47 West 28th Street and entered lobby.

SAMANTHA SPIERS
Specializing in Private Surveillance
803 West End Avenue, #12E
New York, New York 10024

Doris Ashton, Esq.
129 Framington Avenue
Greenwich, CT 09715

Surveillance Charges
August 25–August 29, 1992

Thursday, August 13: 10:00 A.M.–7:40 P.M.	9 hrs, 40 min
Friday, August 14: 10:00 A.M.–7:45 P.M.	9 hrs, 45 min
Saturday, August 15: 10:00 A.M.–9:30 P.M.	11 hrs, 30 min
	30 hrs, 55 min

30 hours and 55 minutes @ $85.00/hour............	$2,635.50
Deposit..	− $1,500.00
Total due	$1,135.50

cc: Mr. Carl Graves

SAMANTHA SPIERS
Specializing in Private Surveillance
803 West End Avenue, #12E
New York, New York 10024

Doris Ashton, Esq.
129 Framington Avenue
Greenwich, CT 09715

Incidental expenses:

August 13, 1992:

"Saks Fifth Avenue,"		
1 Armani dress	@	$695.00
sales tax		$55.60
"Bernie's" magazines,		
1 *Elle*	@	$3.50
1 *Interview*	@	$2.95
1 *Startling Detective*	@	$1.95

August 15, 1992:

"Rexall" pharmacy,		
1 Cutex Nail Polish Remover	@	$1.89
1 Cassette: Nat King Cole	@	$6.99
3 Reese's Candies @ $.65		$1.95
sales tax		$0.87

TOTAL $770.70

cc: Mr. Carl Graves

Texas, 1975

When Aperture published an expensive monograph entitled *Ann: Fifty Photographs*, Birch Books in Odessa sold all of the copies it ordered within a week of their arrival. Of course, Edgar Rogers was by then a local as well as a national celebrity, and the fuss over his daughter's health, the small flurry of publicity surrounding the court hearing, had secured his place in the memory if not the affections of the neighboring towns of McKittrick and Jessup, towns that had no bookstores of their own. People who never bought books came in to at least look through the glossy, heavy-stock pages.

One resident of Jessup bought two copies. He kept one for looking at, removing the dust jacket and storing it in his bedside table drawer, and the other he left sealed in its plastic wrap. It wasn't that he was a connoisseur of the photographic art or process: he looked at the pictures of Ann while masturbating.

He was thirty-one. His name was James Sullivan, and he taught science at the high school Ann attended, the one shared by three small Texas towns and located on a service road that ran between them. He lived in Jessup, and when Ann was taken into the custody of Child Protection Services two years before, he heard the gossip at the school, eavesdropped when the guidance counselor told the principal what a shame it all was, something wrong there, even if nothing was proven.

James Sullivan watched Ann at school and saw that she was quiet, a loner. One day he talked to her in the hallway outside the chemistry lab. "Those are something, those pictures, aren't they?" His voice was strained with excitement, a little breathless. "How do you do that?"

"Do what?" Ann answered.

"You know, make them up or whatever. I mean, *you*'re not dead, are you?" Ann looked at him, his gray hair which seemed at odds with an unlined face, the way his forehead was high and smooth, even when he raised his eyebrows in question. She shrugged.

"I just do what my father asks me to," she said. "He makes them up. I just lie there." Ann was used to interrogation. So many people asked so many things—some, like the social worker, because it was her job to ask questions, most just out of curiosity. Ann had learned that the best way to silence them was to answer right away and matter-of-factly.

"Yeah? It always works that way, then?" His eyes were squinting at her in concentration, as if he were trying to picture it.

"Mostly." She looked at his pale blue eyes. "I have to go now," she said. "I'm late for practice." She had plenty of time to suit up for track, ran extra laps while the others dawdled in the locker room, but she wanted to get away from this Mr. Sullivan whom she'd have next year for twelfth-grade chemistry. He was odd, overly friendly, and had offered her an apple the week before.

"Can you eat it now?" he had asked.

She looked at it in his hand. "What do you mean?" she said.

"Well, I know from school records about the diabetes and all. *Diabetes mellitus.* It means a flow of sweetness, the last part. Did you know that? Pretty. A pretty word." His hand still held the apple.

"I can eat what I want," she answered. "It's no big deal, diabetes."

"You take insulin shots?"

"Yes," she answered. Everyone knew, she knew that. The whole thing about the emergency room, the hearing. A small town had nothing better to think about, her father said. Ann took the apple to end the conversation. She thanked him and then threw it in the Dumpster behind the girls' locker room.

"There's this guy at school," she said to Mariette that night, but when Ann saw that her aunt misunderstood, her bright "Yes?" meaning that she expected Ann to uncharacteristically reveal a crush, she didn't continue.

"Nothing," she said. "Something about a teacher. Never mind."

"Ann?" Mariette followed her down the hall to her room, sat expectantly on her bed as Ann flicked on the radio.

"Really," Ann said. "Nothing. Not what you think."

———

James Sullivan smelled her wariness and backed off, looked the other way when she passed through the hallways. Months passed, and Ann forgot about him. Then on Valentine's Day when she passed him in the parking lot, he stopped her, offering a little box of chocolates wrapped with a red bow. There was a card under the ribbon.

Ann stood before him, arms at her sides. She was taunting him, she knew that. She found herself enjoying the mean pleasure of his discomfort, his awkwardness, and his inability to leave her alone. She stood, expressionless as his eyes moved over her nervously. He held the box out, and she took it finally. "Thanks," she said, and she walked away.

The card was blank inside, unsigned. She opened the little box in the girls' lavatory, looked at the dark chocolates. Cherry Cordials, it said on a slip of paper tucked under the lid. She squeezed one over the sink, and its shell broke open, revealing an almost white cherry, bloodless and shriveled, drowned looking. A clear pink liquid fell from the broken chocolate onto the white porcelain. It looked medicinal, and she threw the candies away.

———

James Sullivan walked from his apartment to where the Rogers lived so he wouldn't have to worry about concealing his car. He sat all night sometimes in the alley behind their house where the trash cans were. A cement gully filled with dirty water ran down the middle of the little service alley, and bits of trash eddied along. He watched them as he sat there: gum wrappers, leaves, a Styrofoam cup. He noted when the Rogerses' kitchen light went off, when Edgar Rogers came out of the garage, sat on the steps and smoked a cigarette. He knew the garage had been converted into a studio and darkroom for the photographer. Sometimes Rogers had a photograph in his hands, a print he considered in the light from the street lamp for some minutes before tearing it into four pieces and dropping them into the trash can.

The girl wore shorts, her feet were often bare. Sometimes she carried a plastic bag of garbage out from the kitchen and dropped it into one of the metal trash cans. The street lamp made empty hollows of her wide-set eyes, revealed how straight her nose was. The gym shirt she wore was cut for a boy, and deep armholes exposed her sides as she lifted the trash bag. On the weekends, she read, lying on a towel in the backyard. Her legs were clumsily long.

James Sullivan stole the Rogerses' trash; he collected Ann's used syringes, the empty vials of insulin. He read a book about diabetes and practiced injecting an orange with distilled water.

———

On June twenty-third, two weeks after Ann graduated from the eleventh grade, Ann's father was in his darkroom, unwinding the morning's work from film canisters. In the absolute dark, the red safelights off and the doors sealed against light by a black rubber gasket, he gently coiled the exposed film onto the metal spools that fit inside the little round developing tank. Sometimes he let Ann do it, guiding her hands in the dark when she couldn't get the film properly attached to the spool. That morning her hand slipped, possibly scratching one of the negatives. She felt his hands tightening on her wrists in anger and she gave up, handing the spool back to him in the dark. When it was in the tank, her father agitating it slowly, Ann went outside into the light.

The June sun was warm on the grass, not yet too hot. It had been a wet spring and the plains were intensely green. The day smelled good and the sky was a high blue canopy stretched tight. Mariette was out shopping. Ann wandered, idle, through the yard.

She was sitting on the porch, bored, when James Sullivan pulled up. He rolled down the window of his car, reached across the passenger seat to crank the handle. He beckoned to Ann.

"I found some stuff of yours," he said.

"What stuff?" Ann said.

"Books. They were in the lost and found."

"I didn't lose any books."

"Sure you did. They have your name in them, *Ann Rogers*. I'll run you over to the school and you can bring them back."

Ann stood up from where she was leaning down to talk through the window. She was sure she hadn't lost anything. "That's okay," she said. "I'll get them later. They can't be too important if I haven't even noticed that they're missing."

"Come on," he said. "Why wait? Besides, it's a nice day for a drive. You don't want to spend your whole life sitting on the porch. I'll drop you at the McKittrick pool afterwards. I saw that a lot of kids were there, swimming, having fun."

Ann looked at the darkroom. Her father would be in there for hours. What harm could there be in it? The science teacher was a little peculiar, but he had always been kind. She pictured her father standing in the dark, one hand on his stainless steel sink, the developing tank in the other, shaking back and forth, back and forth, as even as a metronome. She could go if she wanted—if he noticed she was gone, well, it would serve him right, maybe make him worry. Ann went back to her room for a pair of sneakers and her bathing suit.

The high school was about twenty minutes outside of Jessup. James Sullivan wasn't the best driver, that was for sure. When he pulled into the school parking lot, the car's back wheels fishtailed on loose gravel, and Ann was thrown against the passenger door.

"Hey!" she said. He was driving too fast, and he had a stricken look on his face, like he'd lost his way. He made a wide circle over all the parking places painted with faded white lines, and suddenly they were back on the service road that connected Jessup to McKittrick. "What are you doing?" she said.

"Open the glove compartment."

Inside: no gloves, no map, no ice scraper or candy wrappers, no change. Clean like the rest of the car. One thing only: a box with the familiar Lilly pharmaceutical label. Twenty little vials of pork insulin.

Ann looked at James Sullivan. They passed quickly through McKittrick's tiny business district, the one gas station's sign receding in the mirror on the passenger door, the small figure of the attendant growing smaller. "Where are we going?" she asked. "I think we better go back." He had a funny grimace—as if the car weren't behaving the way he expected, as if the brakes had failed and the two of them were hurtling forward under the machine's power rather than his.

"I want to turn around," she said.

But he kept driving. When the car approached a break in the long fence of some ranch, he slowed finally and turned the car over the cattle guard and through the open wire gate. The wheels slid a little on the dirt access road; he stopped about a hundred yards off the main highway, seeming clamer once the engine was turned off. After a moment, he pulled a syringe from his pocket and took one of the vials of insulin from the box in the glove compartment.

"Time for your shot," he said.

"No," she said. "I mean, I only have two a day, when I get up and before dinner. It's too early."

"But it wouldn't be, if you ate right afterward. Something sweet." His breath was halting, and he spoke in short bursts. "I brought you something to eat. Candy. I bet you don't get much." He smiled. "It's okay, if you take the shot. You can eat it if you take the shot."

Ann looked at him. Was this going to be it, then, just some insulin and some candy, and then she could go home? He was weird, obviously. Maybe it would be smartest just to take the insulin, to play along with him, eat the candy. Maybe that was all he wanted, maybe then he'd drive her home.

Ann picked up one of the little glass bottles. The color of the stopper through which you drew the insulin into the needle was different than usual, but it was the same brand as she used, the same make of syringe, too. Just like at home. Was that scary? She wasn't sure. How many different brands were there? The pharmacy in Jessup only stocked one kind of syringe, which Mariette always ordered in quantities of one hundred.

James Sullivan held the syringe and the vial in his right hand; his left rested on the steering wheel. He looked at Ann blandly.

Maybe this was all because of the whole thing with the hearing, the business with the social workers. Maybe she'd brought it on herself; everyone in town knew about Ann's insulin reactions, James Sullivan along with everyone else. Maybe he thought he was doing her a favor, holding out the two variables of her body's unbalanced equation. Maybe he imagined he could take better care of Ann than her father. Ann took the syringe.

"I'll fill it," she said, and she took a different vial from the one he held out. She checked the label to make sure it was U40 and drew nine units into the syringe.

"That's not enough," James Sullivan said.

"Yes it is. It's too early to take more. I don't usually have any for another three hours."

"But you're going to eat candy. You need more." He reached behind Ann's seat and pulled out a box of chocolates, a one-pound Valentine heart. She thought of the others he had given her, the thin pink syrup running down the white bowl of the sink.

"Look," Ann said, "what do you want?" She was frightened now, a thin, thready feeling like a fuse burning along her spine. When it climbed as far as her neck, her head, she would scream. "I want you to take me home," she said.

"It's okay to eat them if you take your medicine first. Just a couple more units."

Ann looked at him and at the candy, at the wide empty field all around them. Cattle were clumped together in a small valley under the shade of a few scraggly mesquite; their tails twitched at flies. Every so often a car passed, going fast. Ann pushed the needle back through the vial's neoprene plug and drew another two units into the syringe. She stuck it with practiced nonchalance into her thigh and depressed the plastic plunger and handed the syringe back to James Sullivan.

"There," she said. Uncharacteristically, it burned a little at the site of the injection.

He inspected the empty syringe. "Okay," he said. "Now we can wait up to a half hour for the candy, right?"

"Right." Ann sighed and leaned her head back on the warm vinyl seat. "You did your homework," she said.

He looked at her face carefully, as if waiting for some palpable narcotic effect. She stared forward out of the windshield. The thick grass moved under a breeze and a cloud traveled in front of the sun. Ann shivered at the brief shift from light to shadow and back to light.

He didn't try to make conversation but seemed calmer now that she had taken the shot. It was bad timing, actually, because the morning's insulin would be peaking soon. She had a funny cold feeling, and her thighs, even while stuck to the warm vinyl seat, were getting goose bumps.

"Is it time?" she asked. She knew no more than a few minutes had passed.

"I guess it is," he said, and he smiled at her and handed her the box. It was very light, and before she opened it, she knew it was empty.

"I need to eat something," she said.

James Sullivan shook his head.

"Please?" Ann asked, and her voice sounded strange to her, high-pitched, as if squeezed from a toy. He didn't say anything, he just looked at her. He wasn't smiling, he was just watching, as if he expected something dramatic to happen.

In the two years since the hearing, she hadn't had one bad reaction. They'd all been so conscientious about avoiding any trouble, Mariette packing her a snack for school, the guidance counselor meeting her in the hall after her sixth-period class to remind her to eat it. Her father even asked routinely now during the sittings if she felt all right.

Ann struggled against the insulin. She remembered the words of her doctor, probably exaggerated to scare her, but still, what had he said? Severe hypoglycemia could cause brain damage in less than ten minutes. How much insulin added up to severe hypoglycemia? All the reactions she'd had before were from her morning shot, from just having skipped lunch or her snack. Now she'd taken twice the usual dosage.

She tried to breathe slowly and evenly. She had to think, she had to make him be reasonable, convince him to take her back to her house. Mariette would be home from the store by now. "Look," she said, "you don't want anything bad to happen to me. That would just mess up your life."

He turned to her. "We're here because I have something to show you," he said, and he reached between his legs, under his seat; he felt along the floor for a second, pulled out a manila envelope, opened it.

A photograph, torn in four pieces and repaired with tape. He handed it to her.

It was recent, from a series her father had taken in the spring. In it, Ann was naked except for a black scarf tied around her eyes. She was lying in a mowed field, farmland east of Jessup. Next to her body was a top hat, the kind used by magicians, and a white rabbit in a cage.

"How did you get this?" she asked.

"I got it," he said. "I don't think your father should take pictures like that. I don't think it's right. Do you?"

She didn't answer.

"What's it supposed to mean, anyway?" he said. "I don't understand it."

Ann shook her head. "It doesn't mean anything," she said. "It doesn't mean anything. It's just a picture." She started to cry. "Please," she said.

"I'll take care of you," he answered.

Ann and James Sullivan sat in the car for what seemed like a very long time. She had no watch, and the clock in the dashboard was broken. All afternoon it read 1:15, and the sun, which had seemed mild when she left home, came harshly through the window, making her eyes and head ache.

The last thing she remembered was leaning her neck back against the sticky seat and looking at the head liner, at the pattern of perforations in the white vinyl.

James Sullivan took her to the emergency room in McKittrick at 2:50. "She doesn't weigh that much," he said to the doctor on duty, refusing the help of an attendant to get her on the gurney. "Insulin reaction," he told the nurse. "She's a diabetic."

He gave false information as to her identity, claiming she was his brother's child who was staying with him. But the nurse recognized Ann Rogers, remembered seeing her picture in the local paper, both in connection with the emergency and the release of the book of her father's photographs. Recognized Ann, but not James Sullivan. She called the police and he was arrested.

Semiconscious when Sullivan brought her in, Ann was revived to the point of hysteria by the glucose drip. Crying and choking, she screamed for her father; she thrashed her arms and repeatedly pulled the IV tube out of her left wrist until she was sedated. She was crying so convulsively that she had trouble breathing.

She put her arms around the nurse, her head butting up against her bosom. "He touched me," she said. "He dragged me out of the car."

The nurse took Ann by the shoulders and looked at her. "He what?" she said.

Ann put her face into the nurse's chest, held tight to her. "He, he pushed me, and I hit my head. He pulled my clothes off. He did things to me." She continued to speak, but her words were incomprehensible, she was crying too hard.

Ann was examined thoroughly by two doctors. Each used a swab to take a sample of cells from the wall of her vagina. They undressed and examined every inch of her skin. They looked for a bump on her head. On questioning, they found her oriented with respect to time and place and identity.

They found no evidence that she had been raped or otherwise physically abused. Her clothes were clean; they were not torn. The next day, at home, Ann remembered nothing except the little black holes perforating the vinyl ceiling of James Sullivan's car. A week later, interviewed by the same social worker who had talked to her about her father just two years before, she said that James Sullivan was quite kind to her, that he was peculiar but gentle.

———

Tests revealed that all the vials in the Lilly box were filled with distilled water. Sullivan had restored those he had found in the Rogerses' trash, fitted them with lids from veterinary medications he stole from a previous job at the zoo in Odessa; Ann developed nothing more serious than a local infection at the site of the injection. Whatever insulin shock she experienced resulted from her skipping lunch after her regular shot.

When Sullivan's apartment was searched, officers found one hundred and sixty-three photographs taken by Edgar Rogers and identified by the artist as failed prints he had torn up and discarded. Some were taped together with such care that only close scrutiny revealed the damage; the best ones, those that an amateur would have been proud to make, were framed.

12 June 1976

Harry Elliott
Elliott-Adams
1257 Briarridge
Dallas, TX 79301

Dear Harry,

I've given our conversation a good deal of thought. I remain convinced that it is time to stop. Ann's awareness of herself as a woman, now that she has *obviously* become a woman—I mean her sexual maturity—makes the end inevitable. Whatever success the photographs have enjoyed thus far rests in my daughter's being one of those rare creatures who seemed to embody carnality and passion—it was something palpable if not defined—even when she was asleep and clothed. That was what gave the work its tension. Puberty meant that Ann lost what she had and became frankly rather than implicitly sexual, which is not interesting, and so I cannot take any more good pictures. Re. the other work, the photographs you reviewed last weekend, I remain convinced that it is impossible to release such images. The legal problems alone would be insurmountable.

For now there are at least ten archived negatives for each that I have printed from, so the work will yet continue, even if I have no model. As I said, Harry, I did know always that this was coming to an end and prepared accordingly. Photography is such a mystery that even I am not sure what I have taken. And of course, we can't judge the value of those pictures which haven't been seen by anyone other than ourselves.

I'm in a period of depression, exacerbated by the discovery of fog in prints from several old negatives. Evidently, changes in humidity damaged the bellows of the Deardorff and caused light leaks. If the majority are not fine, then I suppose I will have to consider a new model. Well, this is one of the discoveries awaiting me.

I met with Monica, and you are right, she has an interesting head, but there's nothing there for me. I'm not going to choose another subject unless it is myself, assuming I can muster sufficient interest in autobiographical portraits. We'll see. Have you heard from Barnes re. the Linhoff? I want that lens.

Best,
Edgar

New York
August 24–25, 1992

A nn leans on a counter in Bloomingdale's, considering a display of umbrellas. She can't find anything to wear to the opening and she's given up for today, she'll just get Doris a present, something to say thank you for all the extra work the retrospective has caused her. Then she'll head up to Visage to pick up some blank tape for tonight's assignment.

But when the salesgirl leaves the register to okay an exchange with her supervisor, Ann drifts upstairs and ends up trying on jackets in the Donna Karan collection and then suddenly finds herself heading back down the escalator toward cosmetics with a jacket in her bag. *What the fuck are you doing?* the voice says as she fingers, then pockets a bracelet from accessories.

In the cosmetics department, her heart pounding, Ann examines lip pencils, tries an eye shadow. She has to get rid of the jacket. She's feeling off today, her timing isn't right, she could get into trouble, she just feels it. She keeps turning around, has someone called her name? All she needs in the world is one crummy formal dress, so why is there a blue silk jacket, one that she doesn't particularly like, in her camera bag?

Behind the salesgirl a television monitor plays a video loop of runway models in short plastic raincoats of all colors, bright and shiny. Close-ups of their freshly sprayed faces reveal perfectly waterproof makeup jobs. Their features have a hard-edged gleam, like the detailing on sports cars, precise and inhuman. The salesgirl bounces to the music from the video as she talks to a coworker. "So I said to him, no way. I mean has he never heard of safe sex or what?" She rolls her eyes in exaggerated disgust. "This is a guy I met like two minutes before."

Yes, definitely, she has a problem. Stalled at the makeup counter, eavesdropping on the salesgirls, she spots a security officer approaching heavily, silently. Most shoppers are women, most security personnel men: that's the first clue. His totally unhip civilian clothes and his pointedly engaged manner of examining hand lotions give him away.

She's still standing by the eye makeup, frozen by the thought of Carl picking up the phone in his office—one call, that's all people get, isn't it?—when the guard takes her by the arm. If she were at all herself, she'd have been gone by this time, out on the street, the jacket ditched in some corner, the bracelet rolling under a display of moisturizer. Instead, she's being led away from cosmetics by a detective; down the escalator from the main floor and through a door in the gifts department, a door covered with trompe l'oeil architectural detail. The fake mantelpiece gives way to a cement staircase painted with emergency yellow stripes. It's like a journey in a science-fiction movie, as if Ann has simply dropped out of the calming confusion of commerce onto some subterranean freeway. The officer and Ann navigate the stairs together, his hand on her arm. The jacket from designer sportswear is a dead loss, she knows that, but will they find the bracelet in her underpants?

Just outside the security office, a stainless steel rail is bolted to the wall. It looks as if it belongs in a nursing home corridor—a hand hold for the weak or disabled—except that hanging from it are two sets of handcuffs: one manacle locked to the pole, the other open, ready to receive a wrist.

The panic Ann feels is strangely muffled by the sense that she's being forced into some ridiculous charade. All the excitement of stealing evaporated at the touch of the guard, and she was left feeling exhausted more than anything else: how can she make it through the scene to come, how can she survive all this, such a complicated dance?

She wonders if it is legal to apprehend someone who hasn't actually quit the premises with stolen goods. But wouldn't mentioning this imply guilt? Should she insist she was going to pay? Maybe she should call Doris. God, how humiliating.

As she is mulling over her options, Ann hears someone saying that she will be released with a warning, that a second offense will result in prosecution. As dictated by store policy, the jacket alone isn't quite expensive enough to merit calling the police. The bracelet, a clunky thing with fake emeralds the size of almonds that are biting into her flesh, goes undetected. If only it stays where she put it until she gets outside. It does.

Three in the afternoon, and hot. Ann walks from Fifty-ninth and Third Avenue to the southeast corner of Central Park, sits on a splintery bench. Watches kids line up to buy hot dogs and pretzels from a man with a pushcart. She knows she should feel chastened by being caught and thrown out of Bloomingdale's, but now that she's escaped, she doesn't. You just can't go there again, that's all it means, she tells herself. Nothing else. She stands, somewhat weak under the weight of her camera bag, and walks to the vendor, thinking maybe she'll buy a Coke. But looking at the hot dogs, she thinks, how can they eat them? and backs away, shaking her head when the vendor asks what she wants.

What has happened to her today? When she woke up this morning, she kissed Carl awake. "I'll make you French toast," she offered. "Whole-grain bread."

He opened his eyes. "You're pretty chipper," he observed.

"Uh huh," she said, and she got up and pulled on a kimono.

"So, are you, uh, feeling more relaxed about things?" he asked, sitting up.

They had talked the night before about the show's being a couple of days away, and Carl had asked again if she didn't want to talk with a therapist. It seemed to Ann that someone suggested this about every other day now, and she had embarked on a course of wild cheerfulness to avert any concerns Carl might have. This morning she cooked while he showered, kept up a steady stream of conversation while they ate, and slipped her hand down his pants as she kissed him goodbye.

Then she went immediately to her camera bag. She did a quarter of a hit, another quarter twenty minutes after that, and rounded it up to a whole while watching a girl on a talk show explain how her mother always stole her boyfriends. On the night of the senior prom, the girl said, weeping, her mother had come downstairs in a bathing suit to wish them well; then she had kissed the boyfriend on the mouth. A man in the studio audience raised his hand. "You're just jealous," he said, "because at fifty your mother looks better than you do at nineteen." Ann turned the TV off and went to her closet, began double-hanging her clothes, old blouses over new, bought dresses over stolen ones. She'd been stealing again, but not every day. And not on drugs.

It's the opening of the retrospective that's done it. She's known all along that she'd never get through the opening without crystal; why postpone it? That's why she kept it, after all. Not that she planned to, but it's suddenly obvious why she never threw the drug away: she knew she would need it on Wednesday. And besides, she's been clean for thirty days, one whole month, and even so her blood pressure never came down. If speed makes her feel better, less anxious, maybe it actually improves her health. The fact that she has diarrhea of course demonstrates the fallacy of the argument, but, buoyed up by crystal, she is immune to reason.

This morning she shoved the garments she had yet to conceal back into her closet, slammed the door, and got ready to go out shopping for a dress. What a stupid idea double-hanging the graments was. As soon as she gets home, she'll have to put the clothes back the way they were. If Carl sees them like that, he'll be suspicious, and just when she's made progress convincing him that everything's fine. Maybe she should drag some of the stolen stuff into work, hide it in her empty file drawers. Carl never goes to Visage.

She heads down Fifth Avenue toward the spire of St. Patrick's Cathedral. In the next block is Saks, and inside the store's cool air conditioning Ann walks as though in a dream through the paneled perfume department, up and down the shining aisles. Her eyes ache, and that frightens her, but there's only, what?, two days until the opening. Then, she tells herself, she'll flush away whatever's left of the drug.

Circling the first floor's collections of handbags, makeup, scarves, and costume jewelry, she is approached by one and then another woman who tries to spray fragrance on her arm. The sun is bright outside but the women are dressed in evening gowns, and their hair is bright with glitter. Looking at them, Ann is reminded suddenly of the old angel Mariette used to put on the top of the Christmas tree. Its sparkling hair and gold wings above the dry branches that year they left the tree up. She backs away, shaking her head.

Ann goes to the rear of the store, past the mirrored doors of the old elevator. She stands before the escalator, letting shoppers wash around her, staring at the moving stairs. She can't think about an escalator without picturing herself falling, tumbling down, down, to the bottom where the silvery, meshing teeth slide into the belly of the building. Her body turning over and over, clothes torn off, undergarments gone, her flesh flayed. Finally, red and bloody and naked like a frankfurter, shoppers stepping discreetly around her.

When she isn't busy fleeing with stolen goods, Ann avoids escalators; she contemplates them, testing herself, her cowardice—she can't help it. She mentally times the placement of her feet: best foot forward, the left joining the right. How can she be afraid of a simple skill mastered by millions of idiots? When she's on the run she uses them readily enough, but with time to think, it's difficult. She gives power to her fears, granting them the status of premonitions. She thinks that because she is scared of escalators, there is some kind of warning in her fear.

In all probability, something much more easily predictable will kill her, her own traitorous flesh will give up, only a matter of time and probably less than she banks on. But by avoiding the moving staircase when she can, she feels that she is somehow forestalling the inevitable. She returns to the elevators, pushes UP. After what seems like a long time the old doors, covered in panes of mirrored glass, open and let her in.

On the third floor, in Oscar de la Renta, she fakes a dead faint just as she feels the approach of the guard. He doesn't speak, hasn't apprehended her, but she feels him closing in, knows she's caught; she pitches deliberately forward between two racks of short wool jackets trimmed with velvet collars. In her camera bag is a mink muff from Revillon and a tiny coin purse of gold mail that she tweaked off a manikin a couple of departments back. She opens her eyes to his face, round and red as he bends over her.

Saks's security office is remarkably like the one in Bloomingdale's, and again the passage from the world of shoppers to that of apprehension has been mysterious, via tunnels in the walls of the old building. After navigating a series of narrow staircases, both up and down, Ann cannot guess if she has gained or lost altitude in the journey. They pass a man in a room full of television monitors. It looks like Visage, but he is studying the bank of closed-circuit cameras, looking for thieves.

Sitting in the chair by the metal desk, she cries, allowing herself to slip into something that sounds like hysterics; but at the center of herself she is calm, calculating her moves. She says she can't remember her address, allows them to look for identification in her wallet where a clear plastic window prominently displays the little card whose message begins I AM NOT INTOXICATED.

When she asks to go to the bathroom, the officer walks her to the door of an unmarked personnel facility. At least there are stalls, privacy. The guard sits heavily in a chair by the sinks. She's pale, that horrible, sick pale that a Coke would have averted, and she is shocked by her reflection in the mirror.

"The light's not very good in here," she says faintly.

"Huh?" says the guard, as he rises out of the chair.

"Nothing. Nothing. I'm perfectly fine," says Ann. Inside the locked gray stall door, she forgets for a minute what her plan is. "Oh, right. Right. Right. I know. I know what to do," she says, out loud evidently, because the guard says again, "Huh?"

"Nothing." What's wrong with her? She can't tell inside from out. Ann puts her head on her knees for a minute before she gets her syringe of insulin out of her pocket, where she'd transferred it, deftly slipping it under her cuff as the detectives were engrossed in the contents of her wallet. *Okay now, no more talking, no more talking,* she says to herself, and her fingers are on her lips so she knows she's just thinking not saying the words. The syringe is filled—she'd done it that morning—and she thinks again, as she did while filling it, Why? Why did she prepare the shot ahead of time? Did she know even then she was going to do this today? Too much insulin, she thinks, too much, and she somehow stops herself at half the injection.

Never mind, never mind, they're professionals, they won't let her die or anything. Still, she hasn't eaten for hours, or has she? Did she eat a hot dog? Is she in a reaction already? She can't remember.

She took the alarm device off the fur muff. That's why she's been caught, she realizes, the only thought that resounds with any clarity. And the same thing with the jacket in Bloomingdale's. Not only did she take it off before she planned to leave—something she's never done before—but she did it while someone was watching. Either that, or the alarm device had a transmitter that told security it was being tampered with. She puts her head down between her knees. Last week, an article in *The Times* about manikins that have little cameras behind their eyes. New ways to catch thieves. God, she hopes she isn't going to be sick. But then, what has she eaten? "Not a hot dog," she says out loud. "Not a hot dog."

"Huh?" the guard says again.

It seems impossible, but she stands and flushes the toilet. The guard looks at her a little oddly as she exits the stall; she stumbles against the door and leans heavily on his arm as they walk the interminable distance back to the security office.

In the little metal folding chair by the security chief's desk, Ann faints, this time for real, that familiar feeling of losing altitude, going down too quickly in a glass elevator. The security chief is saying something, she has no idea what, but she leans forward as if to hear him more clearly and her head drops onto his desk.

When she comes to, in the emergency room of a hospital, Ann lies on the gurney without opening her eyes. In the dark, under her closed lids, she is at the mercy of the sound of her pulse, can feel it in her fingertips, her neck; her heart is the central drum in a sickening symphony of thuds and throbs. She listens to the voices around her, trying to discern if she's being treated for a simple insulin reaction or one complicated by illicit drug use. Carl is talking to the nurse; they discuss the insulin she typically uses, nothing more. She opens her eyes, struggles up on her elbows, and a blue plastic emesis basin falls off her chest onto the floor.

––––––––––

"You were stealing, weren't you?" Carl says when they're home, finally, after what seemed like hours of red tape at the hospital, after Doris's arrival, Carl's calling Benny to explain that Ann was ill, he'd have to get someone else for tonight. Fear ignites Carl's anger into rage and as they come in the door he holds the back of Ann's neck as if he'd like to snap it.

"Let me go," she says, and he pushes her into the couch. He paces in front of her, yelling.

"I'm not half as mad about the stealing as I am about the whole insulin thing. That is really sick. I've never known you to have a reaction this severe, to *lose consciousness*. You overdosed on purpose. I KNOW it, don't bother to lie to me."

"So why is this such a big fucking deal?" Ann screams. "It's easily treatable. I'm here, aren't I?" She feels worse than she can ever remember, bruised to the bone, scared and sick. All she wants to do is lie down. She gets up from the couch, moves toward the bedroom, and he follows her.

"*Why?* Why is this a big deal?" Carl shakes his head violently, as if trying to dislodge something from his ear. "Something's going on here and you're spinning totally out of control. You're like a different person. And until the real Ann comes back, I'm putting my foot down now when it comes to blatant acts of self-destruction.

"Irresponsibility is one thing, shoplifting is one thing. They're childish and embarrassing, but *nothing* compared to what happened today. Willful insulin shock is *insane*. JESUS, WHAT IS THE MATTER WITH YOU?"

Ann sits down on the bed, puts her hands up before her eyes. It's no use. He's not ill, he can yell at a paralyzing decibel level. Besides, she has nothing to say, she can't explain this; what can she possibly say? *I'm sorry, Carl, I'm feeling stressed out about what to wear to the opening.* She lies down, turns on her side and draws her knees up. When he tries to pull her toward him, she pushes his hand off her shoulder.

"Ann," he says. "We're going to have to work—"

"I AM NOT A FUCKING RENOVATION," she screams. "Don't touch me, just don't *touch* me."

He says nothing. She feels his shock, it's almost something animal, something she can smell. After a minute, he gets a blanket from the closet and covers her, turns out the light and leaves.

When she wakes up the next day, at four in the afternoon, she has trouble remembering the fight, distinguishing what was real from the bad dreams that followed. It's true that she often feels like a wonderful project for Carl, a once lovely house in total disrepair. And never more than today. She finds a note on the dining table, pinned under a glass of orange juice. There's a muffin on a plate next to it—he must have done the dishes since there wasn't a single one that was washed when they came in the previous evening—and her morning shot is there too. It reads, "Dinner reservation at eight. Hiroko's. Corner of 5th and 38th."

Ann looks at the clock on the kitchen wall; it's five-thirty. She has slept without waking for nearly twenty hours. It seems that such a profligate amount of sleep should make her feel better—it's about four times what she usually gets, a hundred times what she's gotten lately—but she feels awful. She takes her shot, makes some coffee, drinks it and eats her breakfast, then creeps geriatrically toward the bathroom and thanks God that she has two hours, anyway, to try to make herself look, if not beautiful, at least less like a ghost. Maybe dinner will be okay, Carl isn't the type to make scenes in restaurants.

She shouldn't have married him, she thinks, it wasn't fair. He should have married one of the other ones, the girlfriends, all disconcertingly beautiful, who turn up from time to time—at a restaurant, on the phone. Old snapshots reveal the kind of women who look as good without makeup as with. Healthy smiles, bright eyes, ponytails. They all looked like they should be featured in ads for sports equipment. Any of them would have made a better wife than Ann.

But everything was going so well for a while, wasn't it? After living a peculiar, itinerant life as a house sitter, half of her clothes in boxes filling the kneehole of her desk at work, she'd really settled down. And it seemed, for a while at least, that the past could be redeemed as well as forgotten.

At dinner at Hiroko's, her favorite restaurant, neither of them talk about what happened the day before. They talk about work: his, hers. It's the first time since dating that she can remember such a topic of conversation on a night out.

But at home, after dinner, Carl lifts his head off the mattress to look at her. "You used to be stronger than you are now. Physically stronger." He puts his hands behind his head and frowns. "Do you still have the runs?" he asks.

Ann sighs. "Jesus, what a romantic guy you are," she says. She tries to kiss him to make him shut up.

"Ann," he says. "What are you eating for lunch these days? I won't ask about breakfast."

"You know, Professor Graves," she says, "I resent my implied status as your biggest project: the perfectible, redeemable Ann." Carl opens his mouth to protest. "Don't talk," she says, struggling to keep her balance on him with one hand over his lips.

"I'm talking," Carl says through her hand, "I'm *talking* about having a functional relationship."

Ann lies with her head on his chest, touches his thigh, his testicles, strokes the fragile skin. Carl tips his head back and closes his eyes. It's a sure way to render him speechless, but she can't touch him there forever. When she lets go, she can feel his body tense again.

Carl sits up. "Maybe you overlook the astonishing possibility that my love isn't entirely selfless. That if you weren't squandering so much of your energy on your pathologies, I'd get to enjoy more of you. *Me.*" Carl points to himself as he says the word. "I feel disheartened, Ann." When she doesn't respond, he continues. "I know we've talked about this before. I know how sick we both are of talking about this. But I think you need to see someone—"

"Look, I've been to shrinks before."

"No," Carl says. "Once, in college, you were given the choice of mandatory counseling or expulsion. That was something forced on a child, years ago. It's not the same as going willingly into some kind of therapy to find out why, for example, you shoplift."

Ann heaves an exaggerated sigh. "If we're talking about *willingly*—"

"Don't do that," he says. "I hate it when you sigh like that. I'm not persecuting you, and I'm not suggesting you tell *me* why you think you steal. I'm not the person you should talk to about this and, and . . ."

"And what?"

"And whatever other issues there are to talk about."

"Like what, for example?"

"Like the whole forgetting thing. Don't you wonder why you do that? Or like the way you say you don't know about most of the pictures your father took. Pictures of *you.*"

"Well, don't let's make it all sound like I'm crazy or anything."

"*Like* you're crazy?" He stops. "Look, I'm sorry. I'm frustrated. I'm scared, for you, for me. For *us.*"

Ann picks at a thread in the border of the white sheet. "What do you mean, *us?*" she says quietly.

He says nothing, and then he says, "Yes, Ann. Us."

When she cries it's silent, tears running down over the bridge of her nose.

Looking at her husband sitting up against the pillows, arms crossed, she remembers suddenly their first real date, going together to the Metropolitan Museum and strolling through the period furnishings. The idea of it had sounded a little boring to her, but in fact she found it pleasant to look over the velvet rope into those long-ago rooms, perfect wax fruit on immaculate dining tables, a music book open on the stand of a gilded Italian piano. Carl studied things closely, the details of craftsmanship, sometimes leaning over the rope and nodding in admiration at an inlaid sideboard, a set of silver sconces.

Ann lingered, entranced by rooms that were so still, perfect, peaceful. No one ever yelled at one another in rooms like these. No one raised a hand, no one broke things or spilled wine on the Persian rug. No one lay weeping on the chintz divan. All that ever happened was that people wandered by, single and silent or murmuring to one another, gazing at bright, polished surfaces laid open for view.

Carl could easily live in such a room, looking up from his book as people filed by. His modest sins—sloppiness, harmless self-indulgences, occasional pedestrian selfishness—are nothing that would surprise or disgust anyone.

Now he looks at her expectantly. "He followed me," Ann says, looking away. "He spied on me."

"Your father?"

"Yes."

Carl nods slowly. "But he didn't do anything to you?" he says.

"No."

"So then, what he did is, he took pictures of what you thought you were doing in private."

"Yes."

He closes his eyes. "Why did you deliberately hurt yourself?" he asks finally.

Ann gets out of bed and stands by the headboard, tracing her finger along the inlay. It's an antique four-poster that they bought off the street a few months after they moved into the loft. Some woman was relocating to Los Angeles, leaving hurriedly for a television job she'd just landed. She'd had no time for the complications of packing, said she wanted to start her life over with new furniture. She sold the big bed to them for five hundred dollars. Ann touches a place where a piece of wood in the shape of a leaf is missing. Finally, she answers. "It made me feel better," she says.

Carl screws up his closed eyes as if a bright light has suddenly been shined in them. "How?" he says. "Why?" When he opens his eyes and looks at her, his expression is uncharacteristically hard. She doesn't answer, the expression fades.

"I'm not your father," he says. "I don't like what you're doing. I don't want to stick around and watch more of it." He takes her chin in his hand, holds it so that she must face him. "There is a point at which I can't sustain your self-destructiveness," he says. "I'm hoping you don't make us find out just where that point lies."

Ann pulls back, and he lets her chin go. "Me, too," she says quietly.

July 27, 1992

Mr. Carl Graves
Box 1598, General Post Office
James A. Farley Building
New York, New York 10116

RE: Merchandise Removal Payment Agreement

Dear Mr. Graves:

Thank you for arranging payment for your wife's outstanding charges of $11,965.12, the check for which has been forwarded to our billing department. As I noted to you, Bergdorf Goodman is able to accommodate certain patrons who choose not to pay for merchandise in the Store in the usual manner of using a Bergdorf card, personal cheque, American Express or cash. It has been our experience that in dealing with such customers it is advantageous to arrange a formal agreement between the Store and the spouse, legal counsel, or accountant of the patron in question.

If you agree to the terms outlined in this letter, we will mail to Ms. Rogers a new Bergdorf Goodman & Co. credit card for her use. A communication will accompany the card indicating that because of a computer records error, she is being issued a new card and should destroy her original card.

The new card, which is identical in all visible respects to the original one, will function as a regular credit card, but it will also trigger a silent security system that will alert the Security Department when Ms. Rogers is on Store premises. We ask that you provide Bergdorf Goodman with a photograph of Ms. Rogers so that Security Department personnel may familiarize themselves with her appearance, in the event that she enters Store premises without her card.

Security personnel will observe Ms. Rogers both by plainclothed detectives and by remote surveillance camera locations, and record which items she secretes on her person and removes from the Store. For items charged to her Bergdorf Goodman account, Ms. Rogers will be billed to her home address. For items removed from the Store without payment, she will be billed indirectly at Doris Ashton, Esq.'s address. To cover the additional expense of surveillance, all items removed from the Store without payment will be marked up fifty (50) percent in price. Items on sale will be calculated at their pre-sale prices. In the event that Ms. Rogers spends more than one hour in the Store during any one visit, she will be billed for surveillance at the cost of $175 an hour for each hour or fragment thereof above the one-hour limit. This charge will be in addition to any charges for merchandise. The Store will continue to provide the usual Store services, such as interpreters, personal shopping assistance, fur storage, bridal registry, complimentary gift wrap, alterations, etc.

We request that upon receipt of the Store bill, payment is remitted within ten business days. Interest charges will accrue after the fifteenth day of non-payment at an annual rate of 24 percent. Additionally, to cover merchandise that may be removed without our awareness, we require a deposit of $25,000, payment of which must accompany this agreement. Interest on this sum will be calculated at the prevailing three-month average federal funds discount rate, currently 6.56 percent, and will be credited to Ms. Rogers's account.

If you agree to the above-mentioned terms, the store will continue to serve Ms. Rogers as a valued patron and will not initiate any criminal or civil proceedings for shoplifting against her as long as this agreement is in force. This agreement may be canceled at any time by either party, upon written notice. Please sign each of the six copies here enclosed and return them to me. Countersigned copies will be returned to you and to Doris Ashton, Esq., once the deposit has been credited.

On behalf of Bergdorf Goodman & Co., may I say that we look forward to continuing to be of service to our valued patrons.

Cordially,
Ellis Fricker
Manager
Security Department

Accepted and agreed to:

Carl Graves

Carl Graves

Illinois, 1979

Outside, the night gave way to dawn, the black shapes of trees emerging from the deep blue sky, the dormitory's eaves etched against the silver of clouds. Ann put her suitcase in the trunk of her car, checked that she had all that she needed, keys and wallet and insulin, syringes. It was so cold outside that when she put her hand to her head she found that her wet hair had frozen stiff. Inside the car her breath fogged thickly.

She turned the key in the ignition, but the engine didn't start. Ann turned the key again, the ignition gave the same useless click. She got out of the car, slammed its door, and ran back toward the dorm. Slipping on ice on the cement stairs, she fell against the heavy fire doors. Once in her room, she checked the clock on her desk, turned and saw her roommate sitting up in her bed, obviously confused by the light and the noise.

"Hi," Marsha said, absurdly, her red lipstick smeared beyond the boundary of her prim mouth, remains of feverish bedtime necking with her boyfriend.

Five-thirty. Ann turned the light back off. Maybe it would work now, she'd try again, maybe it was just a little test of faith. Please make it be just a little test, she thought, running down the stairs three, four, at a time. She grazed her knuckle on the crash bar of the door as she ran outside.

Behind the wheel, nothing. The key was answered by the same useless click. Ann beat on the steering wheel in frustration. She'd miss her plane, she'd miss the connections. How would she get to Houston by noon, just seven hours away? Mariette had been so vague, so stupid, over the phone, as if she didn't actually know what was wrong, didn't know if Papi were dying or just sick. Couldn't tell her how much time she had.

Ann burst out of the car and slammed the door again. She started to run. It was snowing. She'd call a cab, she'd give him all her money, thank God she had some cash on her. Maybe he'd get here quickly, maybe, if she paid him enough, he'd speed all the way; if they took route 14 to 294, it might take only twenty-five minutes. But the snow, the snow, what if the plows hadn't come yet? Still, she might make it.

She was running in the near dark, planning the call, how she'd explain the situation to the dispatcher—"Look, my father is dying, I have to make this plane"—as she approached the fence at full speed.

How many times had she gone through the gate, lifted the temperamental latch, jiggled it open? How often had she avoided the wire that stuck out? How many times that very day had she closed the gate and walked the path to the dorm's west door? This winter morning the entire obstacle of the fence disappeared from Ann's memory. She was running quickly in her snow-filled shoes, unaware of anything but her goal of the door, the room, the phone, the cab.

Then, suddenly, she was airborne. The aluminum pole, joined at either end to a post planted in concrete, hit Ann at groin level, and her momentum carried her forward into the air, over the fence, and into the dark night sky. For a moment Ann was both nowhere and everywhere at once. She was right side up, then upside down: a complete flip. She hit the ground, spread-eagle like a snow angel in the untouched crust under the oak tree. Her back struck the packed surface and her breath was knocked completely out of her.

She lay there without memory, found herself looking up into the deep blue of the sky as it quickened with light from the east. The sky spun on its axis, and as if Ann's consciousness had been jolted from her body, she was briefly aware of all things: of the terrible slow turning of the earth, the melting and refreezing of the margins of the polar ice caps, the molten rock at the center of it all. As all the impossibly large and slow changes were manifest, so were the infinitesimally small; she could hear the ringing conversation of wood lice in the trees, the crack of a dying ember on a distant hearth. Finally, she inhaled, breathed, and the earth stopped turning, at least within her perception.

She struggled up out of her likeness in the snow, looked around her. The packed white mold of her arrested run from the car, the way she was caught in flight, reminded her of something, what? The freak storm in Jessup that had left enough snow to play in, of rolling in that snow with Mark. A long long time ago. Jessup. She had to get there.

Ann arrived at O'Hare just three minutes after her flight was scheduled to depart, ran through the terminal to the gate. Bad weather had bought her an extra twenty minutes; when she explained to the woman at the check-in counter that her father was dying, she picked up a receiver and asked the steward to reopen the door to the plane. The woman looked at her watch. "Good timing," she said to Ann, "half a minute to spare."

The plane wasn't full, Ann had her choice of seats and stepped over an elderly couple to get to a window.

Impossible that he might actually be seriously ill. Just the thought of his bathroom, all the hoarded supplies. The regimented rows of twenty bottles of aspirin, not a major brand name but bottles of one hundred–count regular aspirin from the drugstore, two thousand generic tablets adding up to one thousand doses of aspirin. Five eight-ounce bottles, seal unbroken, of Kaopectate. Four twelve-ounce blue glass bottles of Phillips' milk of magnesia. Ten dispensers of dental floss, two hundred yards each: white, unwaxed, unflavored floss, extrafine to slip between his tightly packed teeth. Ten tubes of toothpaste, Crest, stacked in their boxes, economy size. Eight toothbrushes sealed in blister packs, Extra Hard bristles. Two one-ounce bottles of Dr. Scholl's corn remover. Absorbine, Jr. antiseptic liniment for sore muscles. Soap: antibacterial; shampoo: antiseborrheal, antidandruff, non-supposedly-irritating, but how could that be true if it did all it claimed? Athlete's foot spray: antifungal. All of the bathroom cabinets were packed like a store's with stacked displays of supplies, neatly boxed and wrapped, unperishable, and the linen closet in the hallway off the bathroom was also given over to health care products, sheets and towels piled on the floor of the hall.

Her father had feared the body, its potential for illness and malodor, its consistent tendency to return to a state of unhygiene. The body was a betrayer. Traitorously, it expressed itself in undesirable ways.

Ann kept her syringes in a cookie tin, a hatbox, a ski boot, anywhere but a medicine cabinet; because each time she opened one's mirrored door she thought of her father, every private ritual of health or hygiene in some measure complicated, stolen by the memory of his medicine chest. Even when the memory was not fully formed but just a fledgling, passing vision, still it moved briefly through her consciousness.

Theirs had never been anything like other people's medicine cabinets. Ann had looked into her friends', never went to someone's home without looking through their bathroom cabinets and drawers. The one mysterious bottle with an unidentified pill of unknown vintage, packages of gummy, useless cough drops, a dark bottle with a crust of lotion dried in its deep well, a few dusty, unhygienic swabs. Contraceptive jelly in a rumpled, flattened tube. No one else so completely armed themselves against physical insurrection.

When Ann got to Jessup, when she opened the door of the third cab of the day and stepped out onto the concrete drive up to the house and her father's darkroom, she knew he was already dead. She could feel that he wasn't there any longer, an expansiveness that meant he was gone.

She paid the driver, and as he backed onto the quiet road, she walked toward the studio and darkroom, leaving her bag in the middle of the driveway. She opened the door, flipped on the light, and looked around the converted garage. The big white canvas backdrop had been used recently and was half bundled, half properly rolled into the far corner, very unlike her meticulous father. The director's chair she had given him, the first *P* of *Papi* slightly crooked where she had made a mistake with the stencil, was in the center of the cool cement floor, and in the seat was one of the white shirts her father wore every day, the sleeves stained yellow with chemicals. She picked it up, examined a small hole where a button had evidently been torn off, the rent where one sleeve had been cut. The paramedics must have ripped it, she thought. And then she thought, *That jerk, that fucker, he did it in here, in the chair I gave him.*

Ann looked around the room, at its tidy, spare quality. The lights were put away, only the rolled backdrops might indicate that the space had been used as a studio. The old banker's desk, usually stuffed with bills and inventories and letters from his dealer, all the detritus of an artist's business, was curiously empty. His props—a casket, gurney, hoods and masks—were all gone. He hadn't taken any new pictures for a long time, had spent the last few years printing from old negatives. The adjoining darkroom was similarly tidy, the smell of fixer not as strong as she remembered, dust in the developing trays.

She turned off the light and pulled the door shut behind her, walked under the carport to the unlocked kitchen door. Mariette was sitting at the breakfast table.

Ann sat down opposite her. "He's dead," she said. "You lied to me. Why did you lie to me?" Her aunt's fingers rested over a cup of something hot, tea perhaps. She often warmed them that way, without drinking the tea.

"I don't know," Mariette said. "I just couldn't say it. Not to you. Not over the phone." She stood up from the table and emptied her mug into the sink, poured hot water from the kettle into her cup, no pretense of drinking what it held. Leaning against the counter, she looked shorter than Ann remembered. "I'm sorry," she said. "I didn't know what to do."

She put her hand over her mouth for a moment, then removed it and went on. "I was out near where the trash cans are when I heard a crash from the studio. I knocked but there was just a noise, I don't know, like choking. I went in and he was on the floor." She looked at Ann, who said nothing. "I couldn't get in the ambulance with him. He didn't even make it to the hospital. When I called Dick Adams, he said your father had signed a new will last month. You're named executrix.

"We're to be at Dick's office tomorrow for the reading. There are three beneficiaries, evidently. You, me, and Diane Castleton."

"Diane Castleton?"

"He left money for her in a trust. Like he did for each of us."

"But why?" Ann said. Diane Castleton's was a name she remembered only vaguely, a woman who had worked, she thought, behind the desk of the Sunset Motel whose usually empty cottages were routinely broken into and used by high school students. Ann looked at Mariette in confusion. Why would her father have left Diane Castleton so much money?

"He had an affair with her, obviously," Mariette said.

"But Diane Castleton is ugly," Ann said. "And when? He was always here."

Mariette sighed. "Not always," she said, as she folded her arms. Ann thought of her father slipping away at night to one of those motel cottages. High school kids seeing him as they peered out from the dark rooms where they hid.

She looked at Mariette. "What about a funeral?" she said at last.

"What do you mean?"

"Are we having one?, I guess is what I mean." Ann put her head down on the kitchen table. She couldn't remember what she had eaten, when she had eaten, or if she'd taken her shot. She felt cold and wretched, her head ached. She thought she remembered injecting herself in the plane's lavatory, but she could as easily have contemplated it, pictured herself doing it, and not.

"No. He didn't want a funeral. And there will be enough trouble as it is, when everyone knows that he did it himself. And how he did it." Mariette's voice took on an uncharacteristic edge. "Harry's probably told everyone already," she said. "A handler came to pick up all the prints he had here last month. I knew something was up, but I didn't guess it was this. Harry must be sitting at his desk right now, with his calculator, trying to figure out just how much money he'll make."

"You don't mean that Harry knew he was planning this?"

"No." Mariette shook her head slowly. "Not really. I don't know."

"How long has he been dead, Mariette?"

Ann's aunt looked at her. "A day," she said. "I called you as soon as it happened."

———

At the reading of the will, in the lawyer's offices in Odessa, Ann looked over carefully at Diane Castleton. She was overweight, her hair was gray. Ann couldn't pay attention to the lawyer, she was so transfixed by the presence of this woman with whom her father had slept.

"My good friend for nine years," the will read. Good friend. Two hundred and fifty thousand dollars. Nine years. Since Ann was ten.

Her father, who could have had anyone. At every party or opening in Dallas, Harry introduced him to one lovely woman after another. Women propositioned him, Ann had watched them. Of all the arms she had ever pictured around her father's back, of all the fingers she imagined in his black hair, Diane Castleton's seemed the least likely. She was soft-spoken, when she spoke at all, and she seemed embarrassed to be present at a family tragedy. When she said hello, goodbye, she offered her broad, warm hand to Ann. During the reading, she indicated her attention by nods and whispers, and then she left.

On the drive home, Ann and Mariette stopped at the Wrangler Diner in downtown Jessup. One of the three restaurants in town, it sat across the street from the hospital with a view of the emergency entrance, the double doors that Ann could still see opening from a kick of her father's foot. Carrying her.

She picked distractedly at the menu's peeling laminate cover. "So now what?" she said.

"We need to meet with Harry. The photographs need to be looked at now, before they're sold." When the waitress, a thin girl with a cross around her neck, brought their food, Mariette began to take her lunch apart. She ate like someone who expected to be poisoned, opening sandwiches, surveying their contents, removing suspect veins of fat from meat, rejecting a slice of cheese, a lettuce leaf, then neatly reordering the elements.

Ann had ordered a tuna melt, and she bit carelessly into its greasy, sodden layers. "Why can't all that wait?" she said.

"Well, I guess because of what it said in the will—that certain photographs are to be sold and the money from the sale will go into probate or however it works. Others you inherit and are to take possession of immediately." Mariette replaced her sandwich in the center of her plate. She put her hand over Ann's. "Might as well get it over with, no? Then you can go back to school and not worry about anything."

Mariette stopped talking, picked up her sandwich, put it back down. "Ann," she said, "Harry told me on the phone that there are a number of prints that your father archived without ever showing to anyone. He said they were— He said—

"Evidently the subject is—Harry suggested they might be received as sort of obscene. Or something."

"Maybe they're of Diane Castleton," Ann said, and she pushed away her half eaten food, grease coagulating opaquely over the plate's picture of a rodeo rider.

———

"Ah, my dear," the dealer greeted Ann, "how lovely to see you. In the flesh, I mean." He laughed at his little joke; photographs of Ann lined the walls of his Dallas offices. He handed Ann and Mariette each a pair of thin, white cotton gloves and asked that they keep the gloves on while handling the prints, that they not touch their faces with the gloves. "Skin oils," he cautioned, "very destructive." His own face and hands were fastidiously dry and scented of aftershave, a sweet sandalwood fragrance that Ann could smell as he bent over the conference table to make six neat piles of the black acid-free paper envelopes that came from archive boxes lined up on the credenza.

"These are not all of the photographs," he said, his palms together reverently. "But I've selected these as representative of the content of the work as a whole. Of course, you're free to see whatever I have. I'm just the custodian, after all."

Ann's nose itched, she moved her hands quickly away from her face at a scolding look from Mr. Elliott. "Go ahead," he said, and he stood back against the wall. "The three piles on the right are from the body of work that you have inherited, those on the left are from the works to be sold. Go ahead," he said again, and he folded his arms in an attitude of resigned patience.

"You open them," Mariette said. "I'll look over your shoulder." Ann selected one of the largest of the envelopes from the right and pulled the print from its dark sleeve.

"*Ann CLXXX*, 1972," was printed in her father's neat hand on the white mat. In the photograph was a girl, herself, at approximately thirteen, lying on a bare mattress. Her body was slender, undeveloped, naked; she was curled tautly on her back, her knees up and her head lifted off the mattress. Her hair fell down over the side of the bed, her feet were on the headboard, and her right hand was between her legs. She was biting her lips and her eyes were squeezed shut. She was masturbating.

"That one has a mate," Mr. Elliott interjected. He stood and opened another of the largest envelopes. In the photograph the subject, still naked, lay on her side, her face turned toward the camera. Both her hands were tucked between her thighs, her eyes were closed, her lips looked puffy, bitten. In the foreground of both was the expectable clutter of an adolescent's bedroom, textbooks and sneakers, discarded gym shorts, magazines.

Mariette said nothing after a strangled "Oh."

Ann, too, was silent for a moment. Then, as if to herself, she said quietly, "This is me. Mine."

"You," Mariette said, her voice low as a whisper. She sat back in her chair as Ann continued to open envelopes. At first she was careful to replace photographs in their sleeves, or at least to stack them neatly with an envelope separating one from another, but as she gained momentum, she started tossing them aside. It was all before her, *she* was all before them: even the dirt under her fingernails exposed. Ann saw a child that she recognized as herself—undeniably that was the same face she found in the mirror. But when did all this happen?

"You," Mariette said more loudly, "you posed like, like that!" Her look was a struggle between pity and disgust.

"No," Ann said. "I didn't. I did not pose for these."

Mr. Elliott busily re-sleeved the prints. He had a handwritten list, many pages long, of all the photographs, each title painstakingly printed in her father's minuscule hand. The photographs to be sold were those that documented self-mutilation. Sexually explicit images were bequeathed to Ann.

Mr. Elliott looked at Mariette witheringly. "This is *art*," he said, uselessly. Photographs were spread over the long table, hundreds of images of Ann with Mark, of Ann masturbating. Of her injecting insulin into her thigh in the bathroom, wearing a training bra, underpants torn at the hip. Mariette had always been a poor housekeeper; discarded towels and dirty laundry surrounded Ann as she sat on the closed toilet lid. Her hair was tousled from sleep, marks of bedclothes wound around her limbs like lines left by the rope of a kidnapper. Her face was set in dull, early-morning concentration.

Ann stood. "I'm just going to the rest room," she said. Mariette looked up at her and then back into her lap.

The dealer's bathroom was well-lit and the mirror was one that flattered. Ann looked at herself for a minute before she reached under the cuff of her jeans and into her sock for her dental floss container. She squeezed the tiny white casket, and it popped open along the seam, revealing a spool of white filament and next to it a minuscule white envelope of cocaine. She held the envelope under her nose and inhaled, unfolded the little paper and licked it.

She leaned over the black marble counter surrounding the sink, looked closely at her reflection. She squeezed a pore on her chin, then stopped herself before she made a mess of her face. She washed with the new bar of fragrant soap, running it under the water until the sharp relief of the cameo pressed into the soap melted away, the little features lost under her hands.

Ann blotted her face on the hand towel and looked into the mirror. She pretended, as she had many times in the past few days, that she was old, thirty or forty, and that all this was behind her. "Oh, I was nineteen when my father died," she said to her reflection. "I can hardly remember him, actually. I must have been, what was it, nineteen. Can it have been that long ago?" She folded her arms, cocked her head on one side. "It was a hard thing for me," she said. "Of course it's a long time ago now."

Ann stopped talking. There was a small bottle of perfume on a shelf over the toilet tank and she picked it up, unscrewed the lid, smelled it. It was a one-half-ounce bottle of Chanel Number Nineteen, and suddenly she wanted it. Instead of replacing it on the shelf, she screwed the cap on tightly and put it into her pocket.

Ann returned to Mariette and the dealer, who, idle, both looked up guiltily as if caught in a shameful act.

"So, any business to take care of, papers to sign, anything?" Ann said brightly.

"Mr. Adams has taken care of everything," Mr. Elliott said. "I just need to know where to ship the photographs that are yours."

———

After returning from the dealer's office, Ann and Mariette cleaned out the whole house in preparation for selling it and leaving the town for good. On the way home from Dallas, Mariette had turned to her and said, "I don't want to talk about this again, but I'm asking you now, while we're alone. Did you pose for those pictures?"

Ann looked at her aunt. "No, Mariette," she said. "I didn't. I swear."

Mariette pulled the car off the road onto the shoulder. She stopped unevenly, and gravel sprayed, clattering, up into the car's wheel wells. She put her head down on the steering wheel. "Oh God," Mariette said after a minute. "Oh God, oh God, oh God."

Ann looked out the window. "You said you didn't want to talk about it," she said. "Please just keep driving. Or I will."

When they got back to Jessup, they began to pack. Mariette started with the house, Ann with the studio and darkroom. She felt on fire with, if not energy, something that did as well: an imperative to accomplish it all quickly and get away. The studio would be easy: the cameras were already packed in their velvet-lined cases and shelved, light umbrellas furled and sheathed, tripods folded. There was one camera that Ann didn't recognize, a Polaroid single-lens reflex, the SX-70. Her father had often used Polaroids to set up compositions, test the light. Evidently he had replaced the older Land camera that used pull-apart film with this newer one that produced instant pictures, pictures that materialized before his eyes. He would have liked the cheap, instant magic of it.

The Polaroid was wired to a heavy tripod usually reserved for the view camera and looked small and insignificant there. Ann saw that it was attached by a cable to a timing device, one of the pieces of supplemental gadgetry her father had tinkered with in his spare time.

Ann found a box for the camera and put it away. She wrapped the connecting cable around the timer and put that in a box with all the other devices that weren't strictly photographic. What could she do with the five backdrops? Rolled, they were at least fifteen feet long, too large to transport in her aunt's little car to the storage facility they'd rented in Odessa. Whoever put away the white one—it couldn't have been her father—did a poor job. It was rumpled and scuffed, the last five feet or so just bunched together instead of rolled, and Ann took the edge of the canvas and gave it a smart shake, intending to reroll the material properly.

A number of little colored cards—trash?—flew up as she shook it. She picked up one from the floor. It was, in fact, a Polaroid snapshot, a picture of her father's chair, the one she had given him, and something, legs—*his legs*—lying next to it, the rest of the body covered with the canvas she held. She dropped the material.

There were six of the Polaroids, and Ann took them to the drafting table, lay them under the high-intensity light her father had used for mounting prints. Together, the pictures told a story; arranging them in their probable order, she studied them.

Pictures of a middle-aged man, forty-nine, of medium build, with graying black hair, neatly combed. He was dressed in the habitual white shirt, black pants, and black wingtip shoes.

In the first the man—*her father*—was seated in the canvas director's chair against a white backdrop. On his lap was a white cloth on which rested a small white box. In his left hand, held toward the camera so that the arm was foreshortened, was a syringe. It was larger than a typical insulin syringe, its plunger extended.

In the second picture the man, still seated, had dropped his black pants around his ankles. At a point just below the hem of his shorts, he injected his right thigh with the contents of the syringe.

In the third, the man was again fully dressed. He remained seated as before, with his hands folded in his lap. He looked directly at the camera's lens, his expression betraying nothing beyond the determination to look into the very eye he was accustomed to peering out of. The syringe, white cloth, and box had been removed from the space framed by the photograph.

In the fourth, the man was in the throes of some violent physical contretemps, presumably a convulsion. His left arm moved at the instant of the exposure and created a ghostly blur, as if he were escaping already into the next life. His face was a rictus of pain, and his back unnaturally arched. One leg splayed awkwardly into the foreground; the other was bent crazily, its foot hooked around one of the chair legs.

The last two pictures were virtually identical. The chair was tipped over, turned upside down. Stenciled on its white canvas backrest was the word *Papi* upside down in block letters. The man lay inert on the floor. In so violently falling from the chair, he had apparently pulled the cloth backdrop down. His head was covered by the border of the white cloth, and his body curled tightly, knees drawn up to his chest in that position called fetal, its disposition echoed in the tight clench of his fists.

Ann put her head down on the table. Was it possible that her father had deliberately killed himself and recorded it? Left the pictures as a message? For her?

Could anyone, even her father, do anything so crazy and so, so hateful?

How was it that no one else had seen them? But then Ann hadn't thought of them as photographs. They were small and in color. All of her father's work was black and white and very large. She couldn't remember his having ever shot in color. And perhaps the ambulance crew had pushed the fallen backdrop out of the way. They wouldn't have been paying attention to anything beyond the emergency at hand.

Papi is dead, my father is dead, my Papi is dead, she said to herself. And then she tried to pretend she was much older. *My father, yes, he died two years ago. Five years ago. Ten. Fifteen years my father has been dead.* If she could only survive this part, this day, this night, tomorrow, next month, next spring, next year, it would get better.

Even as she sat quietly, it seemed to Ann that the appropriate response to the six pictures would have been violent: screaming or smashing the camera she had just laid in its box, rending her clothes, wrecking the tidy darkroom. Even something less purposeful would have sufficed, a physical seizure; if only her body, usually so willful, would have taken over. If only she would have lost consciousness, trembled, thrown up, anything. Just not this nothing.

Sitting on the stool, Ann gathered up the little snapshots, held them against her chest, and lay her head on the drafting table. After a while, she couldn't have said how long, she quit the studio, took the six photographs back to her old room. She cut a slit in the lining of her suitcase and dropped them in, sewed the little rent closed.

It was eight o'clock. She hadn't had dinner, hadn't taken her shot. She lay down on her bed and went to sleep.

The next morning she returned to the darkroom, packed all the equipment into cartons and taped them shut, labeled them. She swept the floor, checked that the water taps were tightly twisted shut, and, finished, locked the door behind her. When she came back into the house, Mariette was still mired in the kitchen. Like the bathroom, it was stocked with supplies: canned goods, dried food in plastic bags, instant rice, macaroni—products that would last indefinitely. A few years before her father had turned Mariette out of the kitchen, started cooking for himself.

"Why don't you leave?" Ann had said to her aunt the day before she went to Illinois for her first semester of college. "What's the point of staying here?"

"Oh, I don't know," Mariette answered. "I have my master's. I just have to take the board exams and apply for a position. As soon as I know where I'm going, I'll go there."

Ann shook her head. "It's nice for me to see you when I come back, but I think you should get out of here. Look at this place." She opened a cabinet packed with cans of tuna.

He had first started to hoard food when Ann was in high school, and she used to come home after track practice and open the kitchen closets and stare inside, wondering how many meals were planned, how many plates of macaroni with reconstituted powdered cheese, how many bowls of tuna with two spoons of sweet pickle relish added? How many days exactly could he last in the house when he closed it up?

For that was what was implied by such careful gathering and stacking and inventorying of the right number of aspirins and toothpastes—had he counted how many squeezes he got from each tube?—the necessary servings of canned beans, of precooked, parboiled rice. Her father could close up the house, take that final step and lock the shutters which remained closed all day anyway, nail them shut, bright cracks of light outlining each panel, sunlight outside and the living room thrust into a constant gloom of twilight. He could survive for how long, a year? two years?

The last month of his life, Mariette said, as she packed food into boxes to leave at the church, he hadn't gone outside in daylight, had spent almost all his time in the studio or darkroom, had even slept there. His life became one of intense scrutiny under artificial light, peering at negatives under a bright fluorescent bulb. He wandered through the house during the day with the camera around his neck, the sun blocked out by black shades. He went outside only at night, to smoke on the back porch. "I was thinking of writing you, calling," Mariette said. "But then I thought, no, let the poor girl be. What can she do?"

Once, Ann had tried to estimate just how long he could last were he to lock himself in once and for all. She opened the pantry, stood looking at all the supplies. Impossible to say. How many bowls of cooked macaroni are represented by a case of one-pound boxes? All the food looked like at least enough for a year. On the other hand, what if it were supplies for two people?

He could force her to stay, too.

One day Mariette would go out to a store, come home and find herself locked out. She would try her key and find that it no longer fit the lock to the front door. She'd stand there, puzzled for a moment perhaps, her dark hair falling across her pale forehead, her eyes wide and worried, but she'd know, really, what had happened. She wouldn't be surprised. And then what? Would she knock? Probably not. She'd sit on the steps—there would be no point in climbing the gate and trying the back door because she'd know what had happened, what he'd done. She'd smoke a cigarette, a Virginia Slim, take the time to dig between the bricks with her now useless key, uproot the little weeds that sprang up between them. She'd sit there for perhaps a half hour in the afternoon's vanishing light. Were Ann, trapped inside, to peek through the crack in the shutters, she would see the familiar dejected slump of her aunt's narrow back, the white slice of her flesh visible where her shirt always came untucked from her waistband. Mariette would stand up—would she look back at the house? Possibly not, and Ann wouldn't have the chance of seeing her one more time, the crookedness of her wide mouth, the one generous portion of flesh about her, the way she chewed her lip when she was anxious. Knowing Mariette, she would have been absolutely fatalistic, passive about it. She wouldn't have tried the key again. What they'd all been waiting for would have finally happened.

Mariette would walk down the four brick stairs, step over the coiled hose that perpetually blocked the path, and get back into her car. She'd roll down the window just a few inches, as she always did, no matter the weather, so that the cigarette smoke would escape without the wind blowing her hair in her eyes; she'd slip the key on its Allstate "you're in good hands" key chain into the ignition, depress the accelerator twice, quickly, two instant clouds of poisonous fumes coming from the old Toyota's engine, always out of tune, and then she'd be gone. She would have left, finally, and Ann would have been locked in the house with her father forever.

But Ann had applied only to out-of-state schools, places so far that she could visit only infrequently, and it had been Mariette, after all, who found herself trapped in that house with the closed shutters, the cracks of light seeping into the living room. Not Ann but Mariette who never had the chance to leave.

As they cleaned out the closets filled with toothpaste and dried beans and aspirins, Mariette wept. "It'll be better for you," Ann said. "You'll see." She sealed a box of dishes with tape. She moved quickly, hurrying, hurrying through the work of cleaning out and closing up the house. She sorted and packed, slept and ate, walked and talked, breathed and laughed and even cried without feeling anything. She listened with interest to the words that came out of her mouth, listened to hear what she was saying.

"I know," Mariette said. "It's just that I should have left, I don't know why I didn't leave. I should have left and you should never have come back here from school. It wasn't safe for anyone. He could have done it to us instead of to himself."

"Why didn't you? Why didn't you go?" Ann said.

But Mariette just shook her head, tears falling down her nose. She was no help with the packing, she stumbled ineffectually from room to room, trailing bags, tissue paper, laundry.

When Ann hugged her goodbye, she was standing by her packed car at the local airport. Having dropped Ann off for her flight back to Chicago, Mariette was pointed east, back toward San Antonio. The house was empty and in the care of a real estate office. Ann would be contacted by the lawyer when it was sold.

W hat went wrong went wrong so long before, we never had a chance to make it right. I wish I remembered a time that we were happy, longer than a few hours I mean, like a happy season. The only vacation I do remember was that time on the gulf when we went to Padre Island. Mostly it was just Mariette and I, you stayed behind the closed curtains of the hotel room. We were fogged in that vacation, but Mariette and I were on the beach every day. She with her bird books, the fog so thick some mornings that the horizon was lost, waves delineated only by silver lines of foam approaching. She bought bags of popcorn, and seagulls appeared out of the mist, their gullets open in a scream, their eyes rimmed in red. "Laughing gulls" was the common name of the species, she said, and she threw the popcorn up into the air, into their open beaks. Their black legs hung down from their bodies, their wings beat to hold them in the sky above her head. The noise they made did sound like laughing, high and hysterical, the kind of laughter that accompanies tears.

The one sunny day I squandered on the swing set, so much bigger than any back home. I was eleven. Back and forth like a pendulum over the sand, I looked out over the gulf, the waves wrinkled and green, and pumped my legs until the swing arced to its limit, until my head swung up, even with the bar. And then I let go. From that highest point I let myself fall through the air into the hot sand. Over and over. I didn't stop until I could hardly walk, my bare feet blistered from the friction. When we left the beach the ocean was bright green, as it is before a storm. Sitting on the orange bedspread in the hotel room, swinging my leg, I broke one of the blisters and began to cry. "It serves you right," you said, my heel in your hand. The next day, as we were leaving, we passed the housekeeper's cart in the hall, and I hung behind, filled my pockets with tiny soaps.

But it wasn't until after you died that I really began to take things, when I was in college. A plastic barrette, a tube of lip balm, nothing big: just flotsam from the drawers of people whose lives seemed charmed, things I thought would protect me. I carried them in my bag, didn't use them, took them out to look at sometimes.

At first, I wasn't careful enough, and I became known as a thief. I wasn't despised for it, because nothing I took was of much value. When my roommate couldn't find her pen, her mascara, we didn't talk about it, she simply searched my bag.

Even now I prowl through people's houses. Arriving for a party, I hang my coat in the closet and glance at the shelf above the pole, wondering: what's in those boxes? Upstairs to wash my hands and look in the medicine cabinet. Dental floss and Jolen cream bleach for facial hair. A prescription for tetracycline, one for antifungal ointment. Nothing shameful—no Valium, Xanax, or worse, Prozac. These people aren't anxious or depressed. They have sinus infections and athlete's foot. They don't spend the minutes between waking and showering reciting reasons not to kill themselves.

I suspect that people from unhappy families are always searching the cupboards and drawers of happy people. Sliding a hand between the neat stacks of towels in the linen closet, slipping a finger under the hinged lid of a jewel box, flipping furtively through the pages of a book. They are looking everywhere. As if, perhaps, out might fall a list, an outline, the formula for how they do it.

On the morning of the opening, Ann goes to Bergdorf's. She *buys* a dress. It takes her twenty-five minutes to find it, try it on, charge it on her card, and arrange to have it delivered to her building. At eleven-thirty, she meets Doris at the coffee shop around the corner from Visage. She sits down across from her, sighing heavily. "This feels like the day I smashed into your car," she says. "I feel just about that strung out." She sees the pack of Camels lying on Doris's attaché. "Can I have a hit?" she asks.

"You don't smoke," Doris says. "Remember?"

"I know. That's why the occasional cigarette has such a profoundly calming effect on me. Especially these. You should at least try ones with a filter, for Christ's sake." Ann reaches for the pack and Doris snatches it out of her hand.

"I don't think so," she says. "Conflict of interest. Your existence is the foundation of my career, so I have to look out for your welfare. Personal affection aside." Doris studies Ann. "You're not looking especially well as it is," she says.

Ann makes a face. She enjoys Doris's concern so much that she finds herself pretending that she doesn't, an act for her own benefit, not Doris's.

"What's wrong?" Doris says. "Nervous?"

"Yeah, I guess."

"Anything else?"

"No, nothing, really. Some condition too embarrassing to mention."

"Too embarrassing to tell *me?*" Doris says, and because she looks genuinely insulted, Ann relents. Between doctors, Carl, and Doris, she's always being asked for some private information: it's like she's inside out.

"It's nothing, really," Ann says. "I have the runs. But I'm dealing with it, I'm coping, I'm addressing the situation. It's about to go away."

Doris squints through the smoke. She's one of the few women Ann knows who can leave a cigarette between her lips while it burns. "You're pale," she observes.

"Yeah, well," Ann dismisses the subject.

Doris conscientiously blows the smoke over her left shoulder and away from Ann. "So, here's the guest list for tonight."

Ann looks at the envelope, doesn't take it.

"Aren't you going to open it?" Doris asks. "I thought that's why we were meeting here."

"Sorry," Ann says. "I mean thanks." She takes the envelope, opens it. "Jesus, how many people R.S.V.P.'d yes?"

"They all did, practically. Three hundred and sixty nine. There will be press there, but no photographs at the reception, and no interviews."

"You're sure?" Ann scans the list, sees a few familiar names—people from work, art world personalities to whom she's been introduced recently—but for the most part, it's just words.

"I'm sure," Doris says. "You're tired. Why don't you go home, take a nap? Imagine how delighted your husband would be to find you asleep, chamomile dregs in your mug."

"Can't," Ann says. "I've got some stuff to do at the office. This summer has been enough to pretty much convince my partners that I ought to become a full-time invalid and nut."

Doris looks at her with concern. "Well," she says, "maybe just lie down for half an hour before the reception, huh? You're about as white as a fish belly."

"Thanks," Ann says. "I guess I'll hit the rouge hard tonight." She *is* tired. All last night she lay awake next to Carl, trying to hold still.

Ann says goodbye to Doris, collects a kiss, and then hurries off to Visage to edit tape from a wedding she recorded the previous weekend. It should be an easy job—attractive couple, cooperative family, outdoor ceremony with plenty of light—but even so she's having trouble finishing up. She keeps forgetting where certain switches are, it's as if she's never seen all this equipment before: malevolent snarls of cable and little blinking lights. Her eyes ache, but she tells herself it's tension, not crystal.

At one point, someone comes into the editing room. She turns around to find Benny staring at her. "So," he says, "how are you?"

"Okay," Ann says.

"That's good." He looks at her. "Big night, tonight," he says.

"Uh huh." Unable to sort out genuine innuendo from hypersensitivity on her part, Ann sticks to the briefest possible answers, trying to abort the conversation.

Benny says nothing else to her; at one-thirty he leaves for lunch with two of the other partners and doesn't even ask if Ann wants to join them.

She's sure they're talking about her, maybe even planning how to cut her out.

She works until she senses that she's making the video worse instead of better, and then gives up, ejects the unfinished tape and drops it into her bag. En route to the bathroom she trips over the rug in the reception area for the third time.

"Care for a Xanax?" Theo says.

Is he being nasty? She can't tell. "It's four-thirty," she says. "I think I'll just go home."

The black-tie reception at the museum doesn't begin until eight. When she walks into the loft she sees Carl's new tuxedo hanging in a clear plastic bag on the back of the bedroom door, but no Carl. He's probably on his way home, she thinks. She leans over the bar and gets a syringe from the ice bucket, her insulin from the fridge. Going through the familiar motions of pricking her finger, staining a test strip with her blood, and inserting the strip into the tiny monitor that reads her glucose level, she pays no attention to what she's doing and has already thrown away the strip and put the monitor back in its case by the time she realizes she didn't even take note of the readout. She pulls the needle from the stopper of the insulin vial and caps it, leaves the half-filled syringe and the insulin on the bar. She'll wait for the shot until just before she leaves, skip dinner and eat hors d'oeuvres at the reception. She's too nervous to eat now anyway.

In the bathroom Ann strips and stands on the scale. She is told by an automated female voice, which implies neither congratulation nor recrimination, that she weighs one hundred and six pounds. If she were to flip a switch on the bottom of the slender, lightweight gadget, the report would be made in kilograms: forty-eight.

Ann feels herself, runs her hands critically over her ribs, her chest. She feels her bones under her hands, even the knob at the end of that bone that knits her ribs together and the two crests of her pelvis that stick out over her buttocks. She inspects herself in the full-length mirror on the back of her bathroom door. There are a lot of mirrors in Ann's bathroom, including the hand mirror that she holds up to see the reflection of her back in the long one behind the door. She's too thin, she knows it, and she thinks of Doris's scrutiny this morning, her diagnostic embrace. Maybe she looks worse than she thinks, maybe she's just used to herself. Still, so many men say sly and brutal things to her on the street that she knows she looks good enough, at least in that way.

Ann removes herself from her body; its demands are constant and aggravating: she is forever trying to ignore or silence them. Carl, who wants to see the breasts that he believes Ann would have were she heavier, bargains with her. "Five pounds," he says. "Just five." She looks at herself now, tries to *see* herself. It's almost impossible: her defection has its price. All the reflections she seeks in the course of a day are not so much to ascertain how she looks, but that she is *there.*

Not only in her bathroom, undressed, dressing, applying makeup, does Ann look at herself. She doesn't resist the temptation of any shiny surface: even the bloated image in the kettle's metal sides, the seemingly incidental glimpses offered by shop windows, the shivering, shimmering face in a November puddle. Between the loft and the best corner from which to hail a cab—two blocks east to Fifth Avenue—Ann knows and anticipates each reflection. Needs them to tell her that whatever has happened in her life, it hasn't erased her.

When Carl comes in, she's standing in her bra and slip admiring her new dress. It's black silk velvet, fitted and short—a fabric that looks almost as good as it feels and sets off her hair nicely. "What do you think, up or down?" she says to Carl. Loose, her hair hangs past her waist, countless red-gold ringlets.

"Down," he says, "definitely down." He gives her a kiss, looking past her shoulder into her closet. "Hey," he says. "I was thinking on the way home how great you look in that blue dress—you know, the dark one with the sort of square neckline." He starts rooting among the clothes in her crammed closet. "Why don't you wear that one?" he says.

Ann doesn't answer for a moment, transfixed as he searches. Wondering if she's left any double-hung garments, remembering the fate of that particular dress. "I threw it out," she says finally.

"You did? Why?"

Because I was changing in a cab. "I don't know," she lies. "It sort of itched. It had this label in back, stitched into a seam at the neck, you know, and when I tried to rip it out, I sort of opened the seam. And, well, I just threw the dress in the trash." She pauses, avoiding his eyes. "I'm wearing this black one—you'll love it. The blue wasn't dressy enough anyway." When she looks at Carl, he returns her gaze as if in that moment he can see what she's seeing: the blue dress crumpled on the floor of a cab as she pulled another garment over her head. He opens his mouth as if to speak, but then closes it, just nods.

When he goes into the bedroom, she can hear the squeaking of the bedsprings as he sits, the thud of his shoes hitting the floor. "I'm going to take a nap before I shower," he says. "Call me when I have to get up."

Ann kisses his forehead at six-thirty, and when he doesn't stir, shakes his shoulder a little. In the hour he's been asleep she has done her makeup twice, with no palpable difference in the end product.

"Jesus," he says, looking up at her from their bed. "Too bad we have to go to this party."

"Yeah," she laughs nervously. "Come on, get up."

While Carl showers and dresses, Ann paces. At seven-thirty, she measures her blood glucose again. It's up, way up, she doesn't even know how high because with any reading over four hundred and seventy-five the monitor just flashes the word *High High High*. She thought she felt light-headed from nerves, but obviously her chemistry has its effects. Or vice versa. She puts her hands over her aching eyes. Just one more night, just one more, she promises. She draws a few extra units into the prepared syringe and injects herself in the thigh. At seven forty-five, they leave.

The Museum of Modern Art is on Fifty-third Street, just west of Fifth Avenue. Carl and Ann meet Doris at the Waldorf, where she's staying tonight, and together they walk the few blocks to the museum. They fall in with the crowd at the one unlocked door. Just inside, all the invitations are checked against a master list kept by a woman standing at a lectern. Behind her is a security guard with a gun on his hip, and another guard ushers the line of verified guests through the portal of a metal detector. Everyone must leave their outerwear and all parcels aside from evening bags with the coat check in the main lobby.

The museum looks odd without its daily tide of students, tourists bearing shopping bags, cameras, and maps. Tonight's well-dressed crowd seems excited by the novelty of such tight security measures; pleased by their inclusion in a select, scrutinized group, they laugh and talk animatedly as if expecting a good party. Ann sees Theo hand his bag to the coat check. He catches her eye and waves.

On the east wall of the lobby is a huge promotional poster for the retrospective: her father's name, dates, and a photograph of herself at thirteen, nude from the waist up. Her chest is flat and a gag of white tape forces her lips apart. "Speak No Evil" say the words under the picture. Underneath, a table bears a display of big books bearing the same photograph and title: the show's catalog; three hundred twenty-two duotones, seventy-five dollars for the hardcover, forty dollars for the paperbound. The photographs themselves are hung in the Steichen Photography Center on the second level of the museum, which, along with the lobby and rest rooms on the ground floor, is open to guests; guards prevent entry to other floors and galleries. The elevators are turned off and only the two escalators carry people between the ground and second levels.

Elsin waves at her from where he's standing next to Herbert Gravenstein, the director of the museum's photography department, and she signals that she's just going to get a drink before joining them. A wet bar is set up between the escalators, and behind it a plate-glass window reveals the sculpture garden, dramatically lit with floodlights. "That's where that girl burned herself," Ann hears a woman say, words so faint that Ann wonders if she imagined them. There is no evidence of the event, now almost two months past, and Ann still doesn't know whether the young woman is dead or alive. Her hand shakes as she reaches to take a glass of seltzer from the bartender. In the sculpture garden there is a statue of a woman lying on her back as if she has fallen into the water of the fountain, her torso is twisted, her hands held up in surrender. Ann moves away.

It's a youthful crowd for an art opening, few gray heads, but photography tends to draw younger enthusiasts than painting or sculpture. There's the usual cadre of art press, a lot of rich people that Ann might better be able to identify if she read the society columns, rich people's grown-up children being initiated into the world of patronage, art groupies, a few people from Visage, and the unavoidable minority of peculiar and underdressed, actually indigent-looking people who, on questioning, turn out to be genuine artists or photographers. Everyone mills around and rubs elbows determinedly in the lobby space, drinking with equal resolve, and then leaves their empty glasses to stroll through the exhibit where no beverages are allowed.

Ann knows she should eat something, but there is no food to be found. For the first hour they stand in a clot of people that includes museum officials, the big donors, and the curator. Elsin steadily introduces her to a bewildering stream of faces; most of the people who come forward wring her hands warmly and seem genuinely delighted to meet her. A few squint as if trying to remember who Ann is exactly, and why they should care.

She trades in her seltzer for a plastic cup of Coke, Carl hovering at her side. He is clearly not comfortable in such a setting and has little interest in talking to most of these people, but he is determinedly friendly. She resists adjusting his tie as if he were the tuxedoed groom in a wedding. Having expected something dramatic to happen, she couldn't have guessed what—a real rather than a threatened bomb?—Ann feels a little surprised by the decorous, pleasant tone of the whole affair. She's both relieved and disappointed, realizing as she has so often while working that one person's climactic moment is rarely shared by anyone else. Actually, she would have been having more fun if she were taping the whole thing for Visage, hiding behind the camera and figuring the best angles, grabbing good shots.

After the informal receiving line disintegrates and she's murmured some greeting to every last guest, Ann breaks free from Carl and the garrulous museum people and heads upstairs to look at the photographs. She holds her breath as she steps on the smooth escalator that bears her upward, offering a better view of the sculpture garden en route. On the landing at the top is a Brancusi, like a huge gold knife balanced on end. The wall at the entrance to the retrospective bears her father's name and the dates of his birth and death: 1929–1978. Seeing them is like looking at the gravestone he never had, the one she wouldn't give him.

The show looks good. All the photographs are presented in identical silver frames with white mats; placards under each bear the work's name and date of execution. Separate cases in the middle of the rooms hold smaller items—the ferrotypes taken by her great-grandfather, the Polaroids of her father's suicide.

Ann found those photographs just last winter. Considering throwing away an old suitcase, she opened its latch to check that it was empty and discovered a repair made to the lining, a rent closed with black thread. The stitches were untidy, but the fabric appeared to have been slit intentionally. She opened the stitches, slipped her hand behind the lining, and drew out a photograph. Standing quite still, she considered it.

Was this picture of a dead man one she remembered? She owned a Polaroid camera; the picture came from her suitcase. The man was her father.

At the time Ann experienced a sensation not unlike that associated with phantom limbs: she felt pain where there could be no pain; what had been amputated began to throb. Reaching behind the lining, she retrieved five more photographs of her father's body. She placed all of them between two sheets of cardboard and sealed them into a manila envelope with a note to Doris that read simply, "Please arrange meeting with Elsin." She mailed the package insured and registered.

Even displayed under glass, the Polaroids have a terribly casual quality, perhaps because they were taken with the same model camera people bring to parties, point at birthday cakes.

The galleries are very quiet, the only noise that of people's feet on the gray carpet, the hum of climate control. Viewers enter the gallery singly or in small, tight groups as if huddled for safety. Many do not look at every photograph, but select one or two per room, their eyes passing summarily over the others. Some of the viewers frown, but most move impassively through, their faces set in closed-mouth concentration. No one speaks, but some of the couples hold hands. In front of the pictures of her father as he died, a woman hides her face in the long hair of her companion.

Ann stops in front of a monumental picture of her mother's hand, a galaxy of wrinkles over one knuckle. Next to it is a photograph of herself, posed as if dead. Like those saints exhumed centuries after their martyrdom, she looks more beautiful dead than alive, as if her flesh had been preserved in a state of grace. The red exit light from over the gallery door is reflected backward on the frame's glass, and under it she sees Benny's reflection as he enters the exhibit. She moves hurriedly through the final room, large photographs exclusively of herself—naked, alone—and goes into the women's rest room on the other side of the hall.

She's had three Cokes, no dinner, taken her shot two hours ago. Where does that leave her? Hard to guess. She sits on a bench opposite the mirror. She's pale, a little shaky. The bathroom is empty but for one woman in the far stall. Still sitting, Ann fusses with her hair, combing it with her fingers.

This is not a good idea, says the voice as she closes the door of the middle stall and takes off her black suede pump. Just one more quarter hit to get me through this, she answers, retrieving the tiny bag of crystal from the toe of her shoe. My sugar was so high, it won't drop. She uses her fingernail to serve herself a tiny portion of the drug, waits behind the locked door to feel it kick in.

The occupant of the neighboring stall lies a beaded jet bag on the floor next to her feet. Ann looks at it. When she hears the rustling of involvement with undergarments, she snatches it.

She clutches the purse for a moment before opening it silently. Inside: a lipstick, two aspirins, a Kleenex, four hairpins, sixteen dollars. She stares at the contents of the little purse: a survival kit, two aspirin. Oh, she thinks, stricken, what is between this woman and the world? Only lipstick and aspirin. Sixteen dollars.

Nothing between you and the world, nothing at all. She doubles over suddenly, hugging the little evening bag.

What is the point? What is the point? What does it mean, any of it? Oh God, God, God.

A sudden vision of herself, fourteen years old, lying on the studio floor as if dead. Her father's stained finger tips, nails pitted from chemicals. The way he touched his neck as he was thinking, considering the shot. In her closed hand, a talisman, the little diamond ring she found in one of the suitcases in the attic. Eyes closed, holding the ring. The snap of the shutter.

I had that ring in my hand when I woke up in the hospital in Jessup, so long ago. Where is it now?

Where is the ring, where is any of it? She doesn't know what or how much she's lost.

She tries to think. She *can't* start to cry. She can't. The door to the neighboring stall opens, and Ann hears its occupant's high-heeled shoes on the tile floor. The heels stop at the stall on the opposite side, pause, and then walk back and hesitate in front of the door to Ann's stall. A knock.

Ann doesn't reply. What should she do? She'll just open the door and hand the woman the bag. *Sorry. I've made a mistake.* Oh God, no. She can't do that. She'll wait her out and then, after she's gone, throw the bag in the trash can. But she wants it, she realizes. What should she do? As she sits, thinking, the little evening bag hidden in her lap, the woman quits the bathroom, leaving only Ann inside.

Ann jumps off the toilet and bursts out of the stall. She has one of the four hairpins from the woman's evening bag ready in her hand and within seconds has unlocked the simple catch on the paper towel dispenser. She lies the bag on the stack of fresh towels in the stainless-steel box, then recloses it. Her heart pounding, she checks her lipstick in the mirror.

Measuring her steps, Ann leaves the rest room unhurriedly. A blond woman outside the door, the owner of the heels, looks at her carefully as she walks past. The woman opens her mouth, but, undoubtedly recognizing Ann, says nothing. She goes back into the ladies' room. Watching from an unobtrusive spot across the hall, Ann sees her exit again, frowning.

She waits a few minutes before following the woman down the escalator and rejoins Carl and Doris in the main lobby. Doris is drinking wine, talking loudly. When she sees Ann, she squeezes her hand. "Not so bad, huh? Almost fun, don't you think?" Ann nods. The noise level has climbed until even in such a large space—the atrium ceiling at least a hundred feet above the crowd—one voice is barely distinguishable from another.

The crystal, instead of having the desired elevating effect, seems to inhibit Ann's senses until everything, all the people, clothes, and conversation, is reduced to a bland gruel of sensation. She breaks away from Carl and Doris to get another cup of Coke, but it doesn't really help. She feels confused and, still separated from her husband, by ten o'clock she is recycling a rehearsed line that makes more sense in response to some salutations than others.

A man introduces himself as the editor of *American Photographer.* "Pretty wild," he says. "This is . . . well, it makes Mapplethorpe look a little tame."

"Thank you," she says, absurdly.

"Just, I don't know . . . an astonishing candor, I guess. You must have had a very special and trusting relationship with your father."

Ann laughs, not the sound of amusement but a thin, keening noise that cuts through the suffocating babble around them. She puts her hand over her mouth, and the editor steps back. "Of course it's very exciting for us at *American Photographer*," he says hurriedly, looking over his shoulder as he speaks, "just the fact that we published that first photograph almost twenty-five years ago." He looks at her, hand still covering her mouth. "You did see the August issue, didn't you?" he says and he hands her his card. "Let me know if you'd like extra copies." At the first opportunity, he slips sideways into the crowd.

Miraculously, Ann finds Carl among all the tirelessly milling and talking and laughing people. She takes his hand, puts her mouth to his ear, and whispers, "I don't feel well, I want to get out of here." She looks down at the gray and white marble floor beneath them, and it looks like an overcast sky, as if they are all standing on air. If she were at home, she'd put her head down between her knees.

Doris is just helping her into her coat, looking anxiously at her pallor, when Ann remembers the little bag. "Wait," she says, "I think I better go to the bathroom before we leave."

"I'll come with you," Doris says.

"No!" At such abrupt rejection, Doris steps back in surprise, almost as if Ann has struck her. Carl starts after Ann, but she shakes his hand off her shoulder and runs into the crowd toward the up escalator and the second-floor ladies' room. When she gets there, she feels sick, from the exertion, the crystal, something; she's sweating and her head aches ominously. There are two women chatting by the sink, and Ann passes them hurriedly and shuts herself in the stall. She puts her cheek against the cold metal door.

When she throws up, it's just clear, brown. Coca-Cola. The noise isn't that bad, but it empties the bathroom. The bag, she thinks, on her knees, the bag. She rests her forehead on the cold lip of the toilet bowl, and as soon as she can stand, she gets up and retrieves the hairpin from where she'd hidden it in the cup of her bra. Moving as quickly as she can, she gets the little purse from the paper towel dispenser. By the time Doris comes, tentatively, into the rest room, she has it in her pocket.

"You okay?" Doris says. "Why'd you come all the way up here? I went to the first-floor bathroom."

Ann shakes her head. "I didn't know there was another bathroom," she says. "I'm sorry I snapped at you. You know how I am about people watching me puke."

"No dinner," she admits, "and four Cokes. Maybe five."

"Jesus," Doris says. She looks hard at Ann. "Are you having an insulin reaction?" she says loudly, as if deafness might be a symptom.

"No. I don't know. Just not built for stress," Ann says, shaking her head. "I'm sorry. Stupid to skip dinner."

Doris sighs. "Let's get out of here," she says. "Let's just go." Ann follows her, the little bag hidden under her hand in her pocket.

As the three of them, Carl, Doris, and Ann, are getting into a taxi, they turn at the sound of high heels on concrete, a woman running. Doris is already in the cab, but Carl takes Ann's elbow protectively as the tall, blond woman reaches them, panting. She says nothing, but she holds her hand out toward Ann. Palm up, fingers extended, even the undersides of her very long nails are painted red.

"What is this?" Carl says.

"My bag," says the women, looking at Ann, and then Carl looks at her, too. For a moment no one moves, then Ann takes her hand from her pocket. She places the evening bag in the woman's hand. It glints prettily in the streetlight. The woman opens it, checks the contents. "Thank you," she says, sharply, like a slap, and then she walks away.

"What was that about?" Carl says as they get into the cab. "Who was that?"

Ann doesn't answer, and Doris says finally, "That was Priscilla Avery. She owns the Avery Gallery. And about half of downtown."

———

"I don't believe you," Carl says in the bedroom.

"Well, why do *you* think I threw it out?" Ann says. They're sitting on the end of the bed and Carl has a toothbrush in one hand, paste in the other. They are arguing about the blue dress.

"I think," says Carl slowly, looking at his toothbrush, "that you're stealing so many clothes that you have to get rid of some of them to prevent the glut that would inevitably build up. And that's why you got rid of the blue dress that I liked." He walks over to her closet. "Practically everything in here is brand-new," he says, pointing.

"I've bought a lot of clothes lately. I threw some stuff out," Ann says, her voice unconvincing even to herself.

"It's not just the stealing," Carl says slowly. "It's the betrayal—the fact that you lie all the time. If I can't trust you about this, then I can't trust you about anything." Carl slams the closet door, which makes a disappointing little noise in the big loft. "I don't want to share my life with someone who lies to me," he says.

"Oh God," Ann says. "Why do we have to go through this tonight of all times? If you don't trust me—"

"Ann, there's no reason why I *should* trust you." He sits down in the rocking chair. After a short silence he says, "I love you, Ann, and generally

I think that my love is enough to make everything all right. I'm stupid that way. Egotistical maybe. I have this dumb chivalry complex that says if my heart is pure, my mere presence will make everything turn out okay, undo all the bad things that ever happened, or at least heal them. In other words," he concludes, "I'm a fool."

Oh, but I believe those things, too, Ann thinks. She lies on the bed and looks up at the skylight, clouds reflecting the city's nonstop light. The heavens are pink, as though the city burns beneath them. "You help," she says, beginning to cry. Tears run from her eyes into her ears. "I know lately has been bad, this summer has been very bad, but in general don't things seem okay? I mean, for someone who never even had a permanent address for years, I've come around, haven't I?" She sits up, looks at him.

He rocks slowly for a while before speaking again. "I've had a detective follow you," he says finally. "I know how much you're stealing. And I'm guessing—"

"You *what?*"

"—that you're doing drugs and all the things that go along with them. That you're sick half the time and that your eyes are deteriorating because you're taking speed." Carl sits back in the rocker, arms crossed. "I think you were doing drugs tonight," he says.

Ann looks at him. "I can't believe that you'd have me *followed*. When? When?"

"Three days. Thursday the thirteenth of August through Saturday the fifteenth."

"So why didn't you talk to me about it then? Why did you wait until tonight to pounce on me?"

"Because *tonight* was what I was waiting to get through. Because you've obviously been so terrorized by this show that I figured if we just got past it, then we could talk about what it's all meant to you. And all the other things you've avoided discussing for the past five years."

"Well, you certainly didn't waste any time bringing this up." She looks at her watch. "It's what, two hours since we were standing in the museum? And anyway, Jesus, a detective. It's not like I was cheating on you for Christ's sake."

"Oh, but it *is*," Carl says. "That's *exactly* what you're doing." He picks up his toothbrush from the floor beside the rocker where it has fallen, looks around for the paste. "There's other kinds of infidelity besides sexual—"

"But if I've been dishonest, so have you," Ann protests, weeping.

"Yes, but you *started* the dishonesty. I'm trying to prevent us, you, from real trouble. From going to jail. Have you ever thought about that?"

She jumps to her feet. "Preventing *us*," she cries. "That's what it comes down to, doesn't it? The fact that you can't deal with any embarrassment, isn't that it?"

"What's so evil about wanting to avoid public humiliation?" he says. "Haven't you had enough of that? Isn't it enough that strangers have seen your cunt revealed under brighter lights than I have?" His voice trails off after the word *cunt*. The only other time she's ever heard him use it was when referring to the radicals who threatened the museum.

She looks away, says nothing, sits back down on the bed.

"Listen," Carl says, "that isn't what I wanted to say. Let's agree that we've both been dishonest. The fact remains that I cannot take any more of what our life has been like lately. I didn't want to talk about any of this tonight. I had planned to wait until you saw that this whole thing was survivable. What I didn't figure on was your little *problem* in the powder room. When that Priscilla-whoever-she-is demanded her purse back, it seemed a little absurd to go on pretending that nothing is going on."

"Doris did very well," Ann says, not really intending to be flippant; it just comes out that way under fire. But when Carl looks at her she knows she's made him angry enough for him to have pictured himself hitting her. His expression is complicated, his cheek twitches as if he recoils under his own imagined blow.

"I want a separation, Ann," he says.

"No!" Ann scrambles off the bed and onto Carl's lap. The rocker groans under the two of them as they lurch crazily backward, almost tipping over. "Please, no, don't even say that word. Don't give up on me, on us! I'm just what—I don't know. I promise everything will be better now that the show is over. I'll be okay and you'll be okay. The stealing thing is just something I do because, I don't know. Because it's the only thing that helps me not be scared. I just—life seems so *impossible*, all of it. But I promise, I promise, I'll be good. *Please*." She presses her face into his neck so hard that she feels his shaved skin burn her lips. Her tears are wet on his chest. They remain bound tightly together for some minutes until, finally, the chair stops moving.

He pries her off, takes her by the shoulders and sits her on the bed. On his knees, he starts to speak. "If you can convince me that you're trying," he says. "If you go into detox or get a shrink or do anything, *anything* that says you're really trying. But unless that happens, I want a separation. I can't take any more shit." He gets up from the floor. "Everything you do mocks me," he says, "mocks us."

"But that's not what I mean to do," she cries. "I'm just trying to cope, too. It may not look like it, but I'm trying just as hard as, no, *harder* than anyone else." She follows him into the bathroom.

He picks up his work shirt and pants from the floor where he left them earlier that evening, an eon before. He takes off his pajama bottoms and puts the clothes on. "But that's what it adds up to," he says. "Anyway, it's not a matter of pride, it's a question of how much pain someone can take." He walks into the living area, puts on his coat, pushes the button for the elevator. He turns and faces her. "If this is how you end up when you're trying really hard, you're in big trouble," he says.

"Where are you going?" Ann asks.

"Out. For a drink."

She says nothing as he closes the gate behind him. "Great," she yells after him as the elevator descends. "I thought you were supposed to be the big role model around here." No answer. The elevator creaks as it carries Carl down to the street.

Ann sits down heavily onto the couch. She's too tired to cry anymore, and at least he hasn't walked out. And if she manages to pull herself together, he won't.

A detective. She'll never be able to go into a store again. Maybe she'll just have to buy everything from catalogs. Can you get decent underwear through the mail? How can she be thinking about something so stupid when her life is in a shambles?

Ann stands and retrieves her black pump from the closet. She takes the little bag of crystal from the toe, does a hit without bothering to measure, and digs the yellow pages out from under the piles of magazines on the floor near the bar. She flips through the directory until she finds the listings for drug-rehab programs.

Your ashes were returned to me in a heavy-gauge black plastic box whose lid would not yield to the pressure of fingers but had to be pried open with a knife. Inside: a plastic bag bearing a few pounds of dust and grit and a little metal coin with the number 7759D stamped on it. The number corresponded to the one on official crematory documents, so I would be assured of having received the correct remains.

I poured the ashes out into a bowl and looked at them. Dug my hand into what was left of you. It came out gray. I licked my palm, and then I had taken some of you inside me.

What I wanted was to sit with my bowl and a spoon and eat you up, grind what was left between my teeth.

What I did was I borrowed Mariette's car, put the bowl in the passenger seat, and drove to the reservoir where we used to feed the ducks. I stood for a while on the bank and then tipped the bowl into the dark water. The ducks, expecting bread, plunged after the sinking crumbs. They surfaced, disappointed, but dove again and again.

Back home, I threw out the box, but I kept the little coin. Currency minted for the dead, the words Rockwood Cemetery in raised letters in a circle around the number. When I went back to college I had it in my pocket and I would take it out sometimes and look at it. There was a little hole punched in the coin, as if it were a charm, part of a necklace.

Yesterday when I went to return a bracelet to my jewelry box, I saw it there, 7759D. I picked it up, looked at it for the first time in years. Touched my tongue to it, taste of metal. I thought of that time I looked up from the breakfast table and saw you through the window, walking toward the darkroom. It was February and the night's rain had frozen, covering the driveway with ice. You slipped just outside the door to the studio, you slipped and hit your head on the corner of the cement steps. I could see, as you stood, the blood on your temple. It was the only bright color in the gray winter sun.

You put up your hand and touched your head and then you looked at it, so red on your fingers, as if you also were surprised by such frank evidence of your vulnerability.

I used to think I wanted you to die, but after that morning, as I stood up from the table, my throat closing with fear, I realized that nothing frightened me more than the idea of losing you.

Illinois, 1979

On a Saturday evening, the first of spring break of her junior year and just a day after her roommate had left for home, Ann, who would spend the break on campus and who had made an elaborate list for herself of "Things To Do," was sitting on her bed in her underwear. She planned to fill the unstructured hours of the coming week writing a term paper for a course, American Art: 1945 to the Present, in which she had taken an incomplete the previous semester. But as she read through her notes she found she had nothing to say on her proposed topic. And now it was the break, her professor was away, she couldn't get another subject approved.

Perhaps she just wouldn't do it, she thought, perhaps she wouldn't do anything. She was aware of a brief elated feeling, one that went beyond the childish thrill of rebellion; she felt as if she were contemplating a new clean world of possibility, as if, unfettered, she were filled with strength and freedom. She had just performed a urinalysis in the unusual privacy of the abandoned dorm bathroom, whose stall she hadn't even bothered to lock but sat on one of the six toilets in nothing but a bra, her underpants around her ankles. She dipped the pH strip into the glass of urine she had collected; the imprecise measure revealed her sugar level as quite high. She was supposed to do this at least once a day, but it had been weeks since she'd checked it.

Back in her room, rubbing her thigh in preparation for the insulin she had already drawn into the syringe, Ann placed the needle on her desk. She kept rubbing her leg, feeling the slightly thickened quality of the skin where she habitually injected herself, and then she stood, pulled back the bedspread, and slipped under the covers. It was early evening, an hour before sunset and just the time when she was supposed to take her evening injection. Her doctor asked at each checkup if Ann took her shots the ideal half hour before meals, and she always answered yes, but that was untrue. Sometimes she didn't bother to eat. Sometimes she didn't bother with the shot. Sometimes, like that afternoon, she ate candy.

Her dorm was quiet; there wasn't anyone on her floor. Out of loneliness rather than hunger, she had passed through food service an hour ago and, once in line, requested a take-out meal. The attendant at the register checked that her photo ID was appropriately stickered for the break, entitling Ann to eat on campus between semesters, and handed it back to her. There was no one she knew in the dining hall, just a handful of graduate students eating alone, books open before their trays, and Ann took her paper plate filled with cold cuts and salad back to her room. It was sitting next to the unused syringe of insulin on her desk, round slices of turkey, salami, a dollop of cold slaw still shaped by the scoop that had served it.

Ann got out from under the covers. She placed the syringe in the center of the plate, rolled the limp paper disk up around the food and the needle, and secured the package with a rubber band. Then she walked down the hall, still wearing only her underwear—but no matter, the place was deserted—and threw the little missile down the garbage chute. She heard it clatter distantly against the metal sides of the chute where it took a slight turn before emptying into the Dumpster in the basement. Then she went quickly, almost running, back to her room and put all the diabetic paraphernalia away: the test strips, the cup in which she collected her urine, the syringes she kept hidden in her ski boot. She put the insulin in the compact refrigerator, hid it in a Chinese take-out box that had been there since the beginning of the year and which untidy, scatterbrained Marsha had never opened. Then she got back into bed.

At first she thought she was just skipping dinner since she hadn't taken her insulin. Uncharacteristically, she fell asleep on her back while looking at the ceiling, her head exactly in the middle of her pillow, her hands at her sides.

The next morning, Ann woke at the summons of her clock radio. She sat up. She felt hungry or sick, one or the other. "Sunday," she said to herself out loud. She lay back down. The clock read 8:45. The cafeteria opened at seven for breakfast and closed two hours later. She had plenty of time for her shot and breakfast, she noted to herself with distant interest, as if cataloging a stranger's health. She got up, went to the bathroom. She felt dizzy and frail as she walked down the hall, which seemed immensely long, the cold tiles of the bathroom floor rebuking her. Shivering, she lay back down in her bed and pulled the quilt up to her chin, fell asleep before she had a chance to turn the radio off.

When she woke, she was thirsty and sweating profusely. She knew she was ill, but she didn't want to take her shot, didn't want to eat anything. Wanted to be empty, go away, disappear somehow. She struggled out from under the quilt, went to the bathroom, and returned to bed.

Finally, before losing consciousness completely sometime on Sunday afternoon, Ann dreamed of herself as a younger girl peeling her strangely two-dimensional, flat form up off her father's cold darkroom floor and slipping like a vapor out under the tight crack of the door. She floated off, and the image of herself lingered on the periphery of her consciousness like a kite, blown first here, then there, and finally a speck, disappearing.

On Monday afternoon, the woman from the campus cleaning service, hearing the radio playing all day but getting no answer to her persistent banging on the locked door, called the security guard, who opened the lock with a skeleton key and then called an ambulance.

"How do you like that," the guard said to the ambulance attendants, shaking his head. A young woman, nineteen, in her bed, the cover drawn neatly up to her chin. She was breathing shallowly, her skin pale and covered with a film of perspiration. When they lifted her onto the gurney, they found the sheet beneath her soaked with urine. "Isn't that a shame?" the guard said, still shaking his head. "A pretty girl like that."

The attendants made a cursory check of the tidy room, looking for evidence of substance abuse, but found nothing. No one reached into the toe of the ski boot, the unused dose of insulin on its way to the dump. The girl wore no diabetic identification.

At the emergency room, Ann's stomach was routinely pumped, lavaged, its meager contents examined, revealing nothing, telling the doctors as little as the ambulance man's inspection of her room had done. Her breath, the way her body reeked of sweetness, was the giveaway, confirmed by the lab's quick response. She remained a mysterious empty vessel only briefly, until the blood work came back from the emergency lab: diabetic coma.

Dutifully every day, and then after two months on Mondays, Wednesdays, and Fridays, and then finally after a year only once a week on Wednesdays, Ann showed up for her afternoon counseling session. If she didn't, she would be expelled. As it was, she had already lost a semester, incarcerated in the university hospital during registration, transferred to a psychiatric facility for a month after that. The days that she was denied her freedom passed slowly, one barely distinguishable from another, and when she returned to school for the summer session she had a new roommate in a new dorm. If anyone knew what had happened, they never let on.

Her new dorm was nine blocks from Dr. Alda's office and she always felt a brief panic as she entered the sunny room and sat in a chair facing the kind woman. She knew she was supposed to speak, but she couldn't. How could she explain why, after being revived, she had sobbed with disappointment? Or worse, that she'd later become violent and tried to kick a nurse who came into her room to administer insulin?

After five minutes or so elapsed, and perhaps anticipating that Ann would rather flee than initiate any conversation, Dr. Alda asked a question, always the same one:

"How are you feeling?"

"In general? Or right now?"

"Either. Whichever is easier to answer."

Ann had learned in the psychiatric ward, muzzled by the artificial calm of Lithium, that freedom lay in figuring out what was expected of her and behaving accordingly. Since she could not bring herself to think or feel in ways deemed acceptable, she kept such insurrection to herself. That was in the beginning, when her defenses were rudimentary. Over the course of therapy, she evolved.

Because Dr. Alda's questions, to the extent that she thought about them, intensified the urge to respond in ways she had learned were unacceptable, Ann made herself into someone with a sort of two-way mirror in her head. All the things that frightened her—the memory of the pictures she saw at the dealer's, the Polaroids of her father, and older memories, too, the trial over whether her father was a fit parent, the time the science teacher kidnapped her—they all simply disappeared through the trick mirror. She became so adept at this that even as she uttered words that made sense to Dr. Alda—after all, the woman always nodded and asked another question—Ann couldn't have said what they were talking about. It all went into the little dark room behind the mirror, and even if Ann were to look for it, all she would find would be a reflection of her own puzzled countenance.

After each session, a tortured fifty minutes of no progress that Ann could discern, she walked immediately from the Student Mental Health building, which was not on campus but, perhaps out of sensitivity to the feelings of those who used its services, on a side street in the small university town, to the public library across the street. She went into the children's room, where she sat on an undersized chair painted a bright primary color, her knees bent up awkwardly, higher than the top of the matching round table.

She read Nancy Drew mysteries, one each afternoon she saw the counselor. Motherless Nancy Drew had the solace of Hannah Gruen's faithful, generous bosom; Carson Drew, her handsome attorney father, was well-respected in Riverdale. Nancy had good friends who routinely risked their lives for her, athletic George Fayne and George's pretty, plump cousin Bess Marvin. Nancy was an amateur sleuth who figured everything out with ease. Kidnapped by thugs, beaten unconscious, bound, gagged, drugged, she was always returned to her father's side without any real harm done to her. Clues dropped into her lap: the secrets of old clocks and staircases and Larkspur Lanes, the mysteries of old trees and bookcases. The endless hoaxes and pranks and capers all gave themselves up to titian-haired Nancy, who carried a picture of Ned Nickerson, her handsome boyfriend, in her wallet.

Show Poses Questions It Cannot Answer

Fifteen years ago the art world was shocked by the sudden release of hundreds of previously concealed photographs by Edgar Rogers. Monumental images that detailed masochistic practices, most remained in private collections and were never seen by the public. Now these and others newly released by the photographer's estate are displayed for the first time by the Museum of Modern Art.

Bitter protests over the planned retrospective threatened the safety of both the works and viewers, but the museum remained adamant in its support of Rogers's work and freedom of expression. Added security forces and metal detectors at the entrance to the galleries were installed.

Such measures, together with media attention to the protests, raise the expectations for Edgar Evans Rogers, 1929–1978. Can the photographs live up to the controversy they have spawned? The answer is a resounding yes. The same question dogged the photographer even before his death, and before the release of those images he chose to hide.

Rogers's career was always one in which notoriety eclipsed craft, and his refusal to grant interviews or make any clarifying statements about his work has forced curator Eric Elsin into a detective's rather than enthusiast's role.

Elsin's rule of thumb seems to have been to exclude nothing, and the current show at the Modern suffers from the collective weight of its images in that the majority of the photographs are oppressive in content. Arranged chronologically, the show begins with eight ferrotypes taken by the photographer's grandfather, elegant memorial portraits taken in Mexico in the last century. It then moves through the familiar early series of his wife Virginia and of his daughter Ann posed as if dead.

One regrets that Elsin's desire for unedited revelation led him so far as to include the tasteless final self-portraits: color Polaroids of the photographer's suicide at forty-seven. But only these are to be regretted. The newly released works make it clear that if Rogers understood anything as an artist, it is the profound and ironical effect of offensive subject matter exquisitely crafted. His photographs of his daughter, most enigmatically titled with only her name and a numeral, are technically unsurpassed; even the darkest is evoked in worshipful detail. The light in these life-size prints is elegiac, and the viewer finds himself shocked by the beauty of composition, of texture, especially when the subject is a graceful limb traced with blood.

It will be a surprise to many that it is the newly released photographs that offer relief, in that they are the most lighthearted of the works. A sort of peeping Tom's record of adolescent sexual experimentation, they are nudes of Ann either alone or with a male companion: happy photographs, even though their bewitching lack of self-consciousness leads the viewer to wonder if they weren't taken without the subjects' awareness.

Scandal has unfortunately conspired to obscure

the real seductiveness of Rogers's photographs, a quality which derives from their mystery. Fifteen years after his death, all that remains clear is the intensity of Rogers's feeling for his subject, Ann. One could not define that emotion as either love or hate, pride or pity. In view of the photographs' power other questions recede, especially those seeking to define and thus limit art.

This is a show not to be missed. Sprawling, poorly organized, unedited, it offers a remarkable experience, a revelation not only of one artist's work but of our culture which both reveres and rejects death and sexuality; which encourages exploitation even as it punishes those who chronicle it. Never before has the gallery goer been forced so emphatically into the position of voyeur, and for that experience alone, the current show at the Museum of Modern Art is worthy of support.

A nn is on her knees when she finds the letter. She's trying to retrieve an earring from under Carl's bureau. The gold hoop emerges festooned with dust and hair, and with it a piece of official-looking correspondence, a piece of rich, creamy stationery decorated with the letterhead of Bergdorf Goodman and Company.

Ann reads the words on the page twice before she refolds it; the letter must have slipped out of Carl's satchel, which he leaves on the bureau, and down behind the tall chest of drawers. It's not like him to be careless; perhaps it's something he wanted her to find. She puts the letter into her camera bag.

For a few minutes Ann sits at the bar, one earring on, the other in her hand, chin propped on the ice bucket. She isn't thinking at all, at least not in a coherent, one-thought-following-another pattern, and it isn't until she's in the bathroom, agitated—she's just done one little hit for coping purposes—that it occurs to her that she must clean out her closet. She has an eleven-thirty appointment with a Ms. Caroline Waldhausen of the Cornerstone Chemical Dependency Treatment Program; it's Tuesday, her day to hold the babies at Bellevue; and Benny's called her in for a meeting at work. But she's not going to make it to any of her appointments now.

She empties her entire walk-in closet of its contents—shirts and skirts and dresses, sweaters and slacks all heaped around her ankles in a growing pile. With strength she wouldn't have imagined she had, she pulls one of the shoe racks off the back of the door, popping it effortlessly from its bracket and turning it upside down. The creations of Frizon, Blahnik, Jourdan, and Chanel drop to the floor like heavy exotic fruit. A decorative rhinestone clip breaks off a black calfskin high-heeled pump and releases several stones that wink like tears from the floor. On her knees, Ann tries to sort the stolen from the purchased, but gives up when she comes upon a skirt she doesn't recognize, let alone remember how she came to own it.

She walks through the pile of expensive fabrics, stepping squarely on a silk suit that must have cost her well over two thousand dollars with the usurious surcharge described in Bergdorf's letter.

How could Doris have deceived her, too? She hadn't figured on her involvement. If Ann didn't trust Doris so completely that she never kept up with how much money she had, then she might have realized how much was going to Bergdorf's every month, not to mention any other store with which Carl might have made similar arrangements. A whole twenty-five thousand security deposit.

Ann takes the big janitorial broom and sweeps the pile, piecemeal, toward the window behind the couch. None of the tall windows open, and Ann tries but can't get the clothes through the transoms above; even with the aid of a stepladder they're too high. She retrieves a screwdriver from the studio's junk drawer and goes to work on the window frame. When it won't yield, she ends up repeatedly shoving the legs of the stepladder into the heavy pane. The greenish glass is reinforced with chicken wire; and after she breaks the window Ann still has to use her wirecutters to make a real opening through the pane. As she pushes the clothes out of the ragged hole, she cuts herself, and her hands bleed onto the silk shirts and suede shoes, the white wool trousers that she's worn only once. But then, few of these garments have been worn more than once.

Gingerly, she brushes a few needle-like splinters of glass from her fore-arm. The noise of glass breaking is one that Ann heard only days before while she was taping a wedding: a wine glass under the heel of the groom, the shatter muffled to a crunch by a napkin wrapped around it. Ritual glass whose fragility represents that of love itself. Ann presses her finger over one of the places where she is cut. The wound is small but bleeds extrava-gantly if she does not hold it closed.

After a minute she shoves the last of her clothes out the window and watches as the clot of fabric falls to the crowded pavement below; she sticks her head carefully out of the broken window. Pedestrians dodge the stuff which falls mostly in a heavy mass, legs and sleeves tangled, embracing. A camisole catches the wind like a sail and travels across the street. One blouse falls like a shroud over a traffic light, the red stop sign burning like an ember through the material, reminding Ann of a picture Mariette had of the Mother of God with her heart on fire under her robes. Pedestrians look up and then away. Caught in the observance of some indiscretion, they display that particular politeness of humans forced into uncomfort-able proximity to a stranger's passions; either that, or they simply don't care.

Ann is finished—hours, days, weeks of her life out the window in less than a few minutes. She pokes her head through the hole one more time and looks at the pavement below. Already two street people are scavenging, collecting her clothes into stolen supermarket carts. Ann looks around the loft. One shoe is left under the coffee table, and she retrieves it and throws it out the window without pausing to check its descent. Already the air conditioning has leaked out and the warm breath of the city is blowing in.

She steps out of the dress she is wearing, a blue linen sheath with a new collar of blood, and throws it with her bra and underpants out the window. There's a cut on her left arm, two on her right hand, and one on her neck. When she takes off the single earring, she's wearing nothing but her own blood. She goes back to the bathroom and sponges the cuts with a wet washcloth, but they still leak a little, spreading pink on her damp skin.

She dries her hands, does just a little more crystal for energy, then starts looking through Carl's closet for something to wear. Luckily he's not a very large man, not much taller than she, but still it's a challenge to dress herself in his clothes without looking odd. She cinches his best belt to the tightest notch but it's still too big to keep the olive pants she's chosen over her hips. At the bar she makes another hole with the ice pick.

With the long black tuxedo jacket, sleeves rolled to expose the satin lining and a new white tank top underneath, she'll pass. Shoes are the problem—she'll have to buy some en route. She gets cash from Carl's sock drawer and puts it, with her key and a compact, into her pocket. She applies a discreet amount of makeup to compensate for the crystal pallor and, barefoot, leaves the loft.

W hat gets me is that all the time I've been a hopeful person. I really thought it would add up differently, that something would happen to change it all. I always wanted one shining perfect thing in my life, the one thing no one can have, I suppose.

I hate the thought of my not being there when you died, like I was cheated. Would I have seen you then, Papi, the real you? I remember fantasizing about it, I was waiting for that last minute with you as if it would have explained it all. So much I counted on in that last moment of consciousness, before the last breath. What would you have said to me? Something that was magic like a spell, something that would have made everything different. I was waiting for your words, or even some sign, your squeezing my hand. It was going to be the last chance, and I saw myself with my head on your chest, and we spoke truthfully to one another at the end. I pictured it like that.

Probably I didn't miss anything by not being there, probably it's like everything else, death, you wait for transcendence and there isn't any anywhere, it's all just chemicals in the brain.

Long after you died, Papi, I persisted in this foolishness, seeking the answer, the magic answer. Searching through correspondence, reading other people's reviews of your work, looking at the old movies; the more I forgot, the more desperately I searched through whatever was left—as if somehow I'd find something that would have made it all make sense. But it wasn't there, no critic knew, no one could tell me what I couldn't remember. Maybe that's why Mariette's death was so hard. She was the only one who might have helped to solve the puzzle. And as long as she was alive, I didn't have to own my memory.

After she died, it was just me looking. Looking without knowing what I was looking for. Sifting through the artifacts like an emotional archaeologist. One tooth, one rib, one knuckle bone from which to reconstruct a life.

Because we all try to make sense of it somehow, don't we? We have to. That was what the cameras were all about, wasn't it? Your trying to understand the world. Because there is no sense that isn't fabricated, no inherent meaning. Life has no meaning other than what we give it.

When Doris and I talked late that autumn night—my thirtieth birthday and she had toasted me to the point of philosophy—we talked about existentialism. I could tell she disapproved, she said the names Sartre and Camus as if she felt a little sorry for them, their loneliness. I was scared listening to her, frightened by evidence of her faith, because what they said has always made sense to me.

I've always wanted so much to believe and when I don't and look back on my periods of faith as delusions—necessary delusions, but still—I see that they were a gift to me, maybe from myself, but a needed gift, and who knew better than I what I needed? Who cares if God exists? The people who believe it are better off for doing so. Einstein said his sense of God was his sense of wonder at the universe. You'd think he, anyway, would have been smart enough to figure it out. But perhaps from where he was looking everything was orderly and beautiful, like seeing farms and fields from the window of a plane.

I don't wish I had a chance to do it all over with you, Papi, but I wish we had been different people who would have done it right. Some people's lives seem better than others, they live them more cleanly or something. And if life only has the meaning one gives it, then I've made a mess of it all, haven't I? The love that I have, Carl's, Doris's, I've wasted while trying to figure out what happened with you. Just as other years were wasted trying to trick you into loving me.

I tried to make it up to you, but I never could have been good enough to make up for killing Mother. That's what you blamed me for, isn't it? Merely by existing, I stole her and ruined your happiness.

Another man, more generous, would have reacted differently; another man, a man like Carl, would have become devoted to his daughter because she preserved her mother's essence. But you couldn't do that; you were lacking one necessary talent; you were unable to translate suffering into love.

W hen Ann gets out of the cab in Carl's tuxedo jacket, she does not immediately enter Tiffany and Company; she reconnoiters in Trump Tower next door where she wanders seemingly without purpose through the lofty pink lobby suffused with yellow light, stopping to watch the water fall down the golden wall of the atrium to the feet of the bistro diners below. It drops sonorously into a shallow pool bright with quarters and dimes, pennies being now insufficient to buy wishes. In all the glistening, opulent surfaces Ann is offered endless reflections of herself, she sees herself even in the sheen of the floor and in the polished sides of the escalator whose stairs revolve endlessly under a cage of bars that buttresses the skylight. The stairs make a chewing sound like teeth grinding and gnashing, and Ann hesitates before traveling below ground level to the rest rooms.

Behind the stall door she stands in the cool metal sanctuary and inhales deeply, taking a moment of privacy. She doesn't have her camera bag with her, but she doesn't need it. The new shoes, which she bought at Barney's, running quickly through the departments so no one would notice her bare feet, are rubbing savagely, already making a blister on her left heel. She bought the first pair she slipped on her dirty feet; she should also have taken the bewildered salesman's suggestion that she make a stop in the hosiery department, but she just pressed the money into his hand and left, not waiting for change.

Watching herself walk now from the bathroom, she considers her reflection in the mirror at the end of the corridor. The new shoes' black patent leather shine and gold buckles do somehow complete her eccentric outfit of Carl's clothing and make it all work. But heading upstairs on the escalator, she catches one of the narrow heels in the metal tread of a rising stair. Panicking, she twists her ankle as she frees her foot. The shoe is stuck for a moment as the stair flattens and disappears at the top, and then pops free.

A man bends down to pick up the shoe, holding it out to Ann. Thank you, she thinks to say, but only manages to accept it silently from his hand. She limps to a bench. The leather is torn on the heel, but that is all. She eases the pump back over the blister. *It doesn't mean anything, it doesn't mean anything,* she says to herself over and over; still, it takes some moments to pull herself together.

Ann limps through the tower's atrium, looking at the contents of display cases, reading a framed menu for a restaurant somewhere above. She touches one of the trees that springs from the holes cut in the stone floor and is surprised by the feel of life in its leaves and bark. The plants are flawless specimens, so perfect she assumed they must be artificial, and the atrium itself is a pleasant place, one where she could linger for some time, watching as the shining brass doors of the elevator part and disgorge passengers, close again on another load. But Ann has no business here other than to collect herself, and so she walks, finally, out of the glass doors.

The few steps of sidewalk between the exit from Trump Tower and the entrance to Tiffany's are bright, the late summer sun bouncing harshly up from the cement to her eyes. A fur activist wearing a sandwich board with the words "Prisoner of Greed" and a photograph of a bloodied lynx caught in a trap tries to thrust a pamphlet into Ann's hands but she turns away, feigning interest in Tiffany's window dressing.

Ann has gazed into the store's windows many times. En route to Bergdorf's, just across the intersection of Fifth Avenue and Fifty-seventh, she has hesitated before the squat temple of jewels. Like miniature stages, Tiffany's marble-framed windows are outfitted with gold curtains which, when parted, reveal a ring, a bracelet, a diamond. The whole commerce of sex, all the frank and brutal equations of desirability, is distilled in a diamond; just as surely as coal is squashed by the weight of centuries until its black mud yields what will be a glistening, many-faceted stone.

The store's glass portal revolves heavily under the statue of a man who bears a great clock on his shoulders, as if to allude to Atlas and his burden of the world, and to make the further, more important connection between time and money. As Ann enters Tiffany's, she pictures herself caught in the door, trapped like an insect by its thick panels of glass; but she is urged in by the insistence of another customer who pushes at the partition behind her.

The jewelry showroom is a square box, high ceilings supported by cliffs of dark wood paneling and deep green marble. No column or corner blocks the vision of one end of the salon from another. Tiffany and Company is a store without whimsy; its purpose is unneedful of decoration, the merchandise itself sufficient to seduce. And despite the inclusion of chairs for the consideration of a ring or a watch or a choker of fat pearls, a place to sit while awaiting credit clearance, the room offers no comfort other than the implied protection of wealth. Even the floral arrangements, a garden's worth of flowers and leaves crammed into each great urn, are ponderous, stressing mass over beauty.

Just ahead of Ann at the diamond counter, stands a middle-aged businessman and a girl whose scant clothes and obviously bleached hair declare her his mistress. They consider a wide gold bracelet with a modest garnish of diamonds. "I'm afraid that only stones weighing a carat or more are certified by Tiffany's," the salesman replies to a murmured question. "But, as you can see, these diamonds are of superb clarity." As he speaks, turning the bracelet under the lights, the woman's hand strays to the back of her thigh where a little sliver of tanned flesh and a lace panty border are revealed by the artfully torn denim of her tight jeans.

Tiffany's seems populated by tourists, people traveling, yet always in the country of wealth. A store directory is provided in five languages, and the blue brochure is considered by the weary eyes of a group of French women and clutched in the earnest hands of Japanese wives resplendent in clashing designer initials. Their teenaged daughters lean over the counters, glassy-eyed in their tee-shirts and blue jeans, their white canvas sneakers. A faded debutante, wrapped in an Hermes scarf and sniffing in boredom, passes by a silent group of Arabs wearing djellabas and Nikes, passes by as ephemerally as the wafting scent of her perfume, a dab of Chanel. Just behind her a pregnant woman, perspiring gravidly, makes her way to the elevators, no doubt en route to the second floor to register for its selection of silver rattles and cups.

Ann is wearing no jewelry; she feels naked. There seem to be as many security personnel as patrons; and, unlike detectives in a department store, theirs is an announced presence. Like Secret Service agents, their ears are stoppered with tiny earphones whose wires disappear down the necks of their jackets. Tall and solid and devoid of any expression beyond the occasional frown of attention paid to a remote message, they look powerfully lithe, like animals in clothing. For those brief moments of a transaction that leave a ring untended on its velvet pad between the busy tallying hands of a salesman and the eager fingers of a purchaser, a guard steps forward unabashedly, his eyes trained on the gem.

Ann should be browsing, feigning nonchalance, but she can't stop herself from staring at the people around her. The salesman waiting on the businessman and his mistress calls softly over his shoulder to one of the guards. "Will you stand over to Susan?" he says. His diction is of no discernible origin, a false British affectation: the dialect of imagined privilege. The guard closes in obediently as the indicated saleswoman draws a pair of earrings from a display case.

A customer takes one from where the saleswoman lays it on a velvet pad. "Oh, these are clip-ons," she says.

"Yes," the saleswoman says. "But they can be converted for pierced ears, of course."

"Oh no," says the woman. "I've let my holes close. I deeply regret having had my ears pierced. It destroys the integrity of the body." Ann stares at the woman whose flesh, tanned to leather, doesn't exactly look like a temple to the Holy Ghost.

At a signal from the salesman—he raps his keyes to the jewel case on its thick glass counter—a guard comes forward to collect the businessman's credit card and take it to the rear of the store where its validity will be assessed. Ann hears this occasional rapping throughout the store. A communication that all the employees use, it is the only discordant note from a vast organ in which every stop slips with the great lubricant of money.

A videocamera in each of the square ceiling's corners silently records the activity in the room. Ann walks among the various cases, estate jewelry and band rings, pearls and watches; finally she gravitates toward the case bearing the largest of the diamonds.

Five rings rest on a central brown velvet dais, each on a tiny pedestal. Ann kneels to look through the glass. Behind her, the pressure of scrutiny—the eyes of the guards and of the sales personnel and of the cameras—is a familiar weight. Intended to awe and frighten, instead it excites her, making her feel, in this moment, more fully alive.

She beckons to a salesman, who leans languidly against a cabinet enclosed by the counters. "I'd like to see the ring on the far left, please, the, what is it, a round-cut solitaire?"

"Yes, that would be the larger of the two brilliants." The salesman's tongue lingers on his teeth at each t.

With the sensual acuity of arousal, Ann hears the passage of the key into the showcase's lock and even the tumbling of the lock's chambers behind the man's modulated voice. His hand slips into the back of the case and withdraws the ring. "Four carats and one point," he says. "That's four and one one-hundredth of a carat." He does not slip the ring on Ann's waiting finger or even offer it to her hand, but polishes the stone against a velvet pad the color of chocolate and, after holding it aloft for her appreciation, places it just so on a ring mount in the center of the pad.

The ring is not pretty, one stone of vulgar size set in a platinum band, but Ann feels her mouth go dry with desire for it. The largest facet on the diamond is so big that it makes a tiny, perfect mirror which, she is sure, would give back a miniature likeness of her face. The salesman turns the ring's tag over with his index finger and reports a few statistics from the minuscule legend inscribed there; he neglects to mention the price. Is this because he assumes she cannot afford such a ring or because when contemplating a stone of such magnitude, the cost is entirely beside the point? As she looks at the ring, she feels the salesman's eyes move over her unadorned hands, wrists, and ears; her throat without the choker of gold or pearls.

The pressure of surveillance settles on her shoulders like a shroud, and with a rush of pulse in her ears Ann understands suddenly that she is standing somewhere she shouldn't be. Like an open window on the fiftieth floor, a razor blade on the bathroom counter, the glowing electric heater within reach of the bath, her position offers the collusion of longing and repulsion. Only in Ann's case the balance is tipped, undone. She should never have entered this store.

As her hand closes over the ring, Ann hears the rapping of the salesman's keys on the thick glass counter. She turns away and takes two quick steps toward the door behind her, and before she can take another, she is stopped by the painfully firm grip of a guard above either elbow. She says nothing. Like a perfectly choreographed dance, her disposal is quiet and dignified, and most of the shoppers are sufficiently engrossed by the merchandise that they do not see that Ann is being led away by security to the back of the store.

There are no alarms, no accusations. By the time she is seated in a tastefully nondescript office, her hands are empty. She remembers holding the ring—like a bullet, it weighed more than its size would suggest—but she cannot remember how it was taken from her. When she closes her fingers and makes a fist, she feels it still, the small, sharp presence in her hand.

A phone call, the arrival of an unmarked car to the rear door: Ann's exit from Tiffany and Company is swifter and less dramatic than her arrival. Had a photographer been present to capture her expression, had her crime been attended by closer consideration than that of a

ceiling-mounted surveillance camera, her departure, "strangely exultant" as the manager will later note to the police, would have been recorded, the wet rapture of her eyes like the bright hungry hope of prayer.
But, as it was, the abbreviated story in the *New York Post* ran without a
photograph.

Carl, pick up. It's Doris. Pick up. Pick up. Where are you? This is the fifth time I've called. It's, uh, Christ, it's four-thirty on Tuesday. Which means I've been at Riker's for six hours. I dropped off the insulin and had Ettinger call the prison doctor. Just to emphasize the situation. I told him to say she'd practically go blind if they were even a goddamn minute late with a shot. I don't know if he'll get through, they only have one doctor for all the people here. She's all right, though, considering. If the women here have any teeth, they're capped in gold, did you notice that? This machine is making weird noises, I hope the blasted thing isn't running out of tape. I've contacted this psychiatrist I know to do an evaluation. He's good and he's done them before to, uh, effect. I mean it will be messy but it might be okay. I'm figuring we should be able to get her out of here by tomorrow, the day after at the latest. First the bail hearing, then the bank for a certified check, and then straight into New York Hospital. Sanders wants her admitted—if yesterday's any indication, her sugar's totally out of control, probably because of the drugs, stress. They wouldn't let me bring the monitor in, so I don't know what it's like today. They said don't worry they knew what they were doing. Uh, what else?, oh—I talked to this criminal lawyer, and he's going to handle the bail hearing, but we're not going to get away with less than two hundred and fifty thousand. He's pretty sure. Did you *tell* her about the thing with Bergdorf's? She's been talking about it nonstop. Well, whatever. Listen, I'm leaving now, I have to lie down. I don't know where I'm staying, some place in Queens I guess, one of the dives on whatever that road is that takes you into La Guardia—I'll call when I get there, leave you the number. So . . . Carl, I know we've talked a little about this and I know you're feeling at the end of your rope, but maybe this will be the end of it all. Maybe this is what it takes to get her to the point where she can take a look at this whole thing. You know, I never really agreed with you about the arrangement—I thought it was irresponsible. Not that I didn't make a mistake, too, in letting her get so involved with the show, I really didn't understand what was going on with her about all this—I mean, she said something this afternoon, that at least no one here recognized her, and she seemed almost comfortable in this awful place. She even laughed about the mug shot. I guess it never occurred to me—well, I'm just sorry I didn't get it, that she felt so looked at. Judged. Anyway. Take care. Uh, something else—one other thing, I called your doorman to ask when you'd left, at, uh, oh maybe an hour ago, and he said he hadn't seen you since Sunday so I guess he didn't tell you what he told me, that yesterday Ann had gone on a tear around noon, broke a window and threw all sorts of stuff out. He's keeping it for you—oh there's that funny beeping, is my time up?— he's keeping it for you when you come back and—"

The night after I was arrested, I had a dream. I shared a cell with five other women. All of us were thieves or prostitutes or both. Four of us were drug addicts. We didn't speak beyond these introductions, we were all tired, we lay on the dirty bunks and slept.

I dreamed I was on an autopsy table, that I was dead. When the coroner cut into me he saw that I was empty, I didn't take a thing. It sounds grisly, but it was a happy dream. When I saw the knife slip in, my entrails revealed with nothing inside them, I was so relieved, I felt pure and exultant. Like an angel, I had lived on air.

Suddenly it seems to me that I dreamed this once before, in college, yes, and I told the psychiatrist about it.

This is what they want to hear, they want to know where you go in the privacy of your dreams, they want the few things that are genuinely yours and that no one can take from you. They tell you to give away what you've guarded so carefully, that then you'll be happier.

It's the kind of thing that you demanded. You'd take me apart, unpack me to get what you wanted. Watching you at dinner sometimes as you were eating without paying attention to what Mariette cooked, I wished you'd choke sometimes, I wish once you would have said thanks it was good or thanks, Ann, you were good.

Years ago, I used to fantasize about my own wedding. About the minister asking who gives this woman? And you stepping forward to entrust me to hands more kind than your own. It was impossible to please you, it should have felt better when you were finally gone, maybe it will someday.

I am so very tired sometimes of trying. I'm trying all the time, I don't know how to do anything else. It looks like I'm breezing through, it looks like I couldn't care less, it looks that way because I intend for it to look that way. And that person, the one underground, buried deep, a spadeful of earth insufficient to gag her, she's not even someone you could talk to, I'm afraid she won't stop screaming to listen even.

Confidential Psychological Evaluation

NAME:	Ann Elizabeth Rogers
DATE OF BIRTH:	November 8, 1959
DATE OF EVALUATION:	September 7, 1992
AGE:	33 years
CONSULTANT:	Jonathan S. Miller, Ph.D.
SUPERIOR COURT #:	1283747
EVALUATION PROCEDURE:	Review of Available Records
	Consultation to Thomas Sanders, M.D.
	Clinical Interview
TESTS ADMINISTERED:	Incomplete Sentences Blank
	16 Personality Factor Inventory
	MMPI
	Rorschach

Reason for Referral:

Ann Rogers was referred for psychological evaluation by her attorney, Doris Ashton. Ms. Rogers is currently charged with grand larceny. She is free on bail pending a hearing. Ms. Rogers was arrested on the afternoon of August 28, 1992, after store security of Tiffany and Co. apprehended her in the attempt to steal a diamond solitaire ring valued at $78,000. Ms. Rogers was described by responding officers as cooperative. Subsequent blood tests revealed a level of .0013 of methamphetamine and of Humulin NR, a synthetic insulin product. Ms. Rogers is diabetic (Type A, onset at 12 years).

Counselor Ashton informed me that Ms. Rogers has a psychiatric history which includes one hospitalization at the age of 19 when she was placed on Lithium (LiCO$_3$), suggesting that she may have been suffering from a major disturbance of mood. Ms. Rogers has had no formal psychiatric history during the past fourteen years, although information provided by both the defendant and her husband suggests that there may have been one episode of serious depression during that time. In making the present referral, Counselor Ashton stated that Ms. Rogers did not have any prior criminal history, per se. Previous offenses, when they occurred, were negotiated through private arrangements. It appears that Ms. Rogers does have a recent history of compulsive shoplifting.

Ms. Rogers is married to Mr. Carl Graves, who renovates landmark buildings in New York. She has functioned professionally as a videographer for the past eight years and is a partner in Visage Video, a successful company. A large portion of her income supports legal aid for destitute immigrants, and Ms. Rogers donates her own time each week to charitable causes. Given these facts, Counselor Ashton was hopeful that a psychiatric disposition could be rendered as regards the immediate offense. Results of this evaluation are to be made available to Counselor Ashton prior to an arraignment scheduled for November 27, 1992.

Pertinent Social History:

Inasmuch as the immediate offense does constitute Ms. Rogers's first criminal-justice contact, there is no written history available on this case. And, while Ms. Rogers appears to have been hospitalized in the past, there has not been time to gain access to out-of-state medical records as of this dictation.

However, Counselor Ashton did provide some historical information. Ann Rogers was born in Jessup, Texas, the only child of Edgar Rogers and Virginia Crane, who died in childbirth. A maternal aunt, Mariette Crane, cared for Ann as Edgar Rogers grew to become a nationally prominent art photographer. He committed suicide in 1978.

Ann Rogers attended public schools in Jessup. Her childhood was unusual in that she served as the model for her father's work, an occupation that robbed her of recreational time and alienated her from her peers. An accident of severe insulin shock when she was fourteen resulted in the discovery of the family's chronic mishandling of Ann's diabetes and the subsequent intervention of Child Protection Services. Two years later social services again interviewed Ms. Rogers in regard to an accusation of rape made against a schoolteacher. There was no evidence of sexual assault, however, and Ms. Rogers retracted her statement, which she said had been made in a confused state. I am apprised of these details by a social worker currently employed by Child Protection Services, but was unable to obtain actual records on such short notice.

Ms. Rogers graduated from high school at 17 and moved to Evanston, Illinois, where she attended Northwestern University, graduating in 1981. Ms. Rogers's only clinically documented breakdown occurred during her junior year of college, following the 1978 suicide of her father. As per my phone conversation with Dr. Irene Alda of Northwestern's Student Mental Health Services, Ms. Rogers's failure to take the insulin upon which she is completely dependent resulted in hospitalization and was interpreted as a passive suicide attempt. When her health was secured, Ms. Rogers was transferred to Rush-St. Luke's Hospital in Chicago for further observation and testing. After one month she was returned to school on a mandatory program of counseling. Ms. Rogers recalls with considerable sarcasm that "their [Rush-St. Luke's] idea of treatment was to sit me in a circle of depressive losers and drop buttons into a coffee can, saying, 'These are my anxieties over which I have control.' " The Lithium therapy initiated in the clinical environment was terminated on her discharge from Rush-St. Luke's.

According to transcripts and individual reports, Ms. Rogers was a gifted student and, after recovering from her collapse, graduated from Northwestern summa cum laude in 1981.

Counselor Ashton disclosed that there had been an extensive psychiatric history on the father's side of Ms. Rogers's family in that the elder of the defendant's paternal aunts was hospitalized for many years in Ector County, Texas, while the younger's clinical depression was managed with electroshock therapy. Ms. Rogers's father, although never formally diagnosed, appears to have suffered cyclical depressions that ranged from mild to incapacitating. In Ms. Rogers's words, "There were months when it was pretty much just Mariette and me because my father stayed in his room all the time with the shutters closed."

Counselor Ashton informs me that Ms. Rogers has had no formal psychiatric contacts since the 1979 hospitalization. It would appear that Ms. Rogers began slowly to lose her grip around last June, becoming increasingly restless and excitable.

The defendant herself made reference to anxieties relating to a show of her father's photographs, which I gather revived latent fears and hostilities in reference to her father. Apparently, her discovery of a document alluding to a legal arrangement between her husband and Bergdorf Goodman, one drawn up to address the likelihood of her shoplifting, provided the final push into hysteria and poor judgment. In response to feelings of betrayal and loss of control, Ms. Rogers found herself irresistibly drawn to Tiffany & Co., where the capture of a diamond ring presented itself as the solution to all her fears.

Throughout the interviewing and testing procedures, Ms. Rogers made a transparent attempt to positize all aspects of her background as well as her present levels of functioning and future aspirations. As such, she is a difficult person to read emotionally, but I would guess that her present adjustment is not markedly different than the way her adjustment has been for the past years, that it is only her ability to control her behavior which has deteriorated significantly.

Mental Status and Interview:

Ann Rogers is a 33-year-old white woman, attractive if underweight, with red hair and a pale but arresting face. She is well-groomed, articulate, and responsive and entered our initial interview in a cooperative manner, but soon became distraught about "this letter thing" and overly concerned about her clothing, asking repeatedly if anyone had left a suitcase for her. For the past week Ms. Rogers has been detained in New York Hospital for purposes of observation, detoxification, and diabetic treatment stabilization. Although her thinking was generally clear, there was some loosening of associations at the introduction of any stressful topic.

With respect to issues of procedural competence, Ms. Rogers was oriented as to time, place, person, and situation. She understood why she had been arrested and was able to discuss the immediate offense with clarity and to relate effectively with counsel. Ms. Rogers was difficult to evaluate because, despite evidence of exceptional intelligence, she was a poor historian, sometimes describing events without respect to any coherent chronology or appreciation of casual relations. Often I was forced to extrapolate from her narrative and to reconstruct the probable order of what she considered the significant events of her life.

In discussing her history, Ms. Rogers described her childhood as unremarkable up until the time that she began to pose for her father's photographs, when she was seven or eight. She remembers little of her childhood, and most of her comments were preceded by the disclaimer that she "guessed" things were as she described them. When I asked what she meant by "guessed," she said that she had had some trouble remembering her past, and that only in the last months had certain episodes been restored to her memory.

Her aunt, Marietta Crane, deceased as of 1989, did evidently suggest some psychiatric evaluation of Ann at the age of fifteen when, as Ms. Rogers said, "I was doing things to myself, making little cuts and things. Nothing dangerous. It was all in the pictures. You remember." Such remarks were typical of Ms. Rogers's delusional sense that the details of her life were apprehended by everyone. I did not of course remember any such

Kathryn Harrison

210

details, but thought to obtain a copy of *Speak No Evil: Edgar Rogers, 1929–1978* to study the photographs featured in the current retrospective. While such a document would not usually be pertinent, it seemed that in consideration of Ms. Rogers's apparent lacunas in memory, the pictures might prove illuminating. Those to which she alluded are, in fact, profoundly disturbing documentary photographs of self-mutilation, indicating some trauma of early development that was, I assume, never addressed.

Ms. Rogers was reluctant to comment on her feelings in relation to her father, and when I asked her about the crisis that followed his suicide, she became distraught and requested a short break. When we resumed she said that the discovery of photographs that her father had surreptitiously taken of her was as shocking to her as his suicide, and that while she might have been able to handle one or the other of these traumas, the two together were defeating. In her own words: "I was so tired of the whole thing. It's not really like me to give up but I just went to bed and didn't get up for anything, not the shots, not food, nothing. I thought I could just disappear. That it would all be over. I was so very tired."

It would appear that Ms. Rogers spent much of her adolescence defending herself against her father's abusive nature; and while it is hard to imagine that photographs such as those taken of Ms. Rogers by her father could have been taken surreptitiously, her defenses are so evolved that it is not inconceivable that she was able to maintain something of a fugue state while they were taken and remember nothing of it afterward. After Edgar Rogers's death, what crisis intervention Ms. Rogers received in the wake of her own suicide attempt proved inadequate to help her resolve the issues that precipitated it, and her current dilemma is not new but one which was forestalled until now.

Ms. Rogers stated that she met her husband in 1986 and that they were married in 1987. She feels that their relationship is a good one and that it has provided a great deal of stability. She attributed her current dilemma to her having been dishonest with her husband "about the drugs, about myself, what I was feeling. I wasn't able to be as honest as I wanted. I don't know why. I have this privacy thing. It isn't good, I know."

I asked Ms. Rogers about her attempt to steal the ring from Tiffany's and she attributed the decompensation to "being stupid. I was not taking care of myself, you know, skipping the insulin, doing some crystal. I guess I just did too much. Something. It's hard to be sure about these things. I was upset about a quarrel I was having with Carl." Ms. Rogers's husband described the event as an inevitable result of too many stresses, both physical and emotional, the greatest of which he judged to be the retrospective, which naturally brought issues relating to her father into the open. When she contacted me, Counselor Ashton claimed responsibility for Ms. Rogers's involvement in the show, saying that she had encouraged her in what she now believes was a misguided attempt to give her some sense of control over her life. It was as the opening approached that Ms. Rogers found herself increasingly troubled by compulsive behaviors.

When I pressed the subject of the ring, Ms. Rogers gave a somewhat unclear account of her husband's disloyalty in arranging with Bergdorf Goodman & Co. for her to be billed for items she believed she had stolen. Her conversation, which until that point had been terse and clear, was rambling, pressured at times, and had a delusional quality.

In her own words, "I had this disagreement with Carl when he found out about the shoplifting, and I planned to get a hold of the speed problem, figuring that then I'd be able to control the stealing. But I was pretty upset anyway about his having me followed by detectives, and the letter was just the last straw. I just felt, I don't know. The clothes. You know, I put them on in the cabs and it was like, I don't know, just this thing I had, protection. A secret, sort of. It was dumb, but in that moment, when I found the letter, I mean, it seemed like the stealing was the only thing that made my life even bearable. And even though I didn't plan to do it, exactly, I just ended up at Tiffany's."

Comments and Conclusions

Attached to this report are Ms. Rogers's Rorschach sequence of scores, structural summary, and constellation table results. The revealed personality instrument data is that associated with individuals who experienced anger or resentment in early childhood, traumas which caused the child to self-protect by shutting down. During problem solving or decision making, Ms. Rogers's thoughts merge with feeling, and ironically, this woman who has gone to such great lengths not to feel cannot make decisions that are not undermined by emotional vicissitudes.

The device of compulsive shoplifting is a sophisticated psychological apparatus by which Ms. Rogers arms herself against her fears, each offense providing her with a new amulet. The discovery of the letter about the arrangement her husband had made with Bergdorf Goodman & Co., allowing her to pay for items she believed she had stolen, was not unlike a revelation that the power had been stripped from her totemic devices, and of course echoed the traumatic discovery that her father had invaded her privacy. Ms. Rogers, perceiving herself in danger, sought to re-protect herself with the capture of a prize of some value.

I think it unlikely that Ms. Rogers will stop stealing until she discovers and addresses the fears that drive her to shoplift. More optimistically, I would guess that the immediate crisis makes usually latent issues of hostility and despair relating to the father ascendant and accessible.

Family history and results of psychological profiling suggest that Ms. Rogers may be afflicted with bipolar disorder, depressive type. She should be considered significantly disturbed at the present time, and I would judge her to be an individual whose psychologic adaptation has been marginal since adolescence, possibly earlier. Her current decompensation is, in my opinion, less surprising than the years of apparent health that preceded it. Based on that same history of superficial normalcy, I would judge Ms. Rogers to be a woman of exceptionally strong will, and I anticipate that when she faces those issues that have conspired to create this crisis she will make good progress in resolving them.

Withdrawal from methamphetamine abuse does complicate diagnosis, but the facts remain that Ms. Rogers is at the present time suffering from disordered thinking, impaired judgment, and tenuous impulse control. I would not advise release into a nonclinical setting.

Treatment Recommendation:

Given the preceding discussion, it is felt that Ms. Rogers's condition most closely approximates the following diagnoses:

Bipolar Disorder, Depressive. (DSM III-R 296.44)

Methamphetamine Abuse, (DSM III-R 689.20)

With respect to the recommendations in this case, it is my firm clinical opinion that Ms. Rogers should be placed under psychiatric care. Should the above diagnosis prove correct, the Court should be advised that the standard treatment for Bipolar disorder is Lithium therapy. Lithium is a drug which requires regular blood serum testing to determine proper therapeutic level and to eliminate toxic side effects.

New York
October 10, 1992

Two privileges have been restored to Ann in acknowledgment of satisfactory progress. Saturdays she may spend with Carl, provided he signs her out of the hospital and has her signed back in by eight, and Wednesdays she is permitted to leave from two until six to resume her volunteer work.

On this, their first Saturday, Carl and Ann eat lunch at a Chinese place around the corner from the hospital and then take a cab home to their loft. When she walks in with him, the place looks dusty, as if no one has lived there in the past weeks. A piece of plastic is taped over the hole she made in the window. Dark green plastic: a garbage bag. Her closet stands open, empty, the shoe rack replaced on the bracket behind the door. All the clothes salvaged by the doorman have been given away.

Ann walks around the bedroom, pausing at objects she has missed. She picks up a bird's nest from the windowsill—an abandoned nest they found on Carl's birthday picnic, can it have been just last June? There is an egg in it, one that never hatched, and when she holds it up to the light, she can see the dead yolk through the shell, dried and clotted on one side. It seems to Ann that she has been away for ages, as if, in the meantime, all the reclaimed past has intervened, separating fall from summer with a chasm of years.

On the bureau are a few scattered Polaroids: a door, a section of molding, an elaborate cornice—pieces of a house. "New project?" she asks.

"We'll see," Carl says. "I haven't gotten an engineer's report yet."

Ann nods. She runs her hand over their bed, smooths the blanket, sits down.

Carl sits on the other side. Their conversations in the hospital have been abbreviated and upbeat; now, in their bedroom, words are difficult, and when Carl removes his clothes, it is a gesture of vulnerability more than desire. She unbuttons her shirt.

"You've gained a little weight," he says and she nods again. "It looks good," he says. "I like it." But when they lie down together under the sheet, Ann finds herself holding her breath, waiting for whatever recriminations he has saved until they had this measure of privacy.

What he does say is "I'm sorry," and she begins to cry silently. "It was a mistake to have you followed," he says. "When I caught on to the thing with the clothes, I stopped thinking clearly."

He takes his glasses off, puts them on the table by the bed, turns toward her. Bed is the only place Ann ever sees Carl with his glasses off—he is nearsighted enough that without them his expression is slightly puzzled. "I checked with Doris," he goes on, "and once I was certain you weren't spending any money on them, once I knew you had to be stealing them, I . . . Well, I took your secrecy as license to be secretive myself." He puts a hand on her arm tentatively, withdraws it. "I had to do something, Ann," he says. "You were so—so weird, I was afraid to confront you. But it was wrong. Especially considering what happened with your father, it was a mistake." He pauses but she says nothing. She wants to touch him, she wants him to hold her, but she cannot move, it's as if she's paralyzed.

She and Carl are lying on their sides, facing the same direction; whenever he moves, the mattress creaks under them. From the bed Ann can see the plastic taped over the broken window: it shudders as air moves over it. "I guess you have to trust that my motivation was different," he says finally. He pauses, clearly waiting for her to respond.

"Tell me you love me," she says. It is not what she intended to say.

"Ann," he says, "I think I do love you. But I don't know what that means—what it's worth—when you've hidden yourself from me. I don't know what it can mean to either of us." He turns on his back, faces the ceiling. "Do you realize we've never really talked about your father, your childhood, any of it? I mean, I knew that in college you had some sort of collapse after your father died, but nothing else." He looks back at her.

Ann nods against the pillow, saying nothing, and he grabs her shoulders. "Talk! Talk!" he says. "Please."

"I know," she says, "I know. I know. I know you didn't know." She can't stop crying, she can't stand to explain one more thing to one more person, not even to Carl. What she wants is to ask him what's left of it all, their marriage, but first she has to talk and talk until he understands everything—she owes that to him. It's just that she's too tired, she can't do it, not yet.

Ann looks at her closet, three shoe trees on the shelf, nothing more.

To leave the hospital, all she must know is that she is no longer a thief. She hasn't stolen anything since the Tiffany's fiasco, not that there's been an opportunity; and she won't be out in the world for a while, not unsuper-vised, at least not until the hearing. Oddly, the idea of staying in the hospital indefinitely isn't so bad. Of course, it's a voluntary commitment, and it won't be forever, not more than another month or two.

Ann closes her eyes. She actually likes the hospital, the yellow walls in her room, the insipid watercolors in the hall. She likes the too-green artificial plants that need no care, she enjoys being handled by people who expect so little of her. She isn't ready to be returned to her life, or to her husband, if he'll have her. Carl won't leave her when she's weak, he is too kind. And, secure in the reprieve of that thought, she falls asleep.

When she wakes up, Carl is asleep, and they are facing one another. Her hand is under his cheek, as if she has reached out to comfort him. Damp with perspiration, his hair falls straight back from his forehead, revealing an old scar, a souvenir of a boating accident with his brother. White and raised, with suture marks that disrupt the otherwise even arc of his hair-line, it's ugly, but like his maimed finger, she had found it erotic when they made love for the first time. A little reminder that everyone has a past, everyone got hurt. Ann pulls her hand carefully out from under Carl's cheek, but he opens his eyes with a start. It's five.

When he showers, Carl doesn't invite her in with him, as he usually would when they have the time. After the bathroom door closes she sits on the bed by herself, listening to the water, the sound of a bar of soap being dropped, a dull thud. When he gets out they dress silently and return to the hospital early.

She kisses him goodbye at the desk, and when she draws back she sees how dark the circles under his eyes are. "More wheat germ," she says, attempting a joke, but his expression registers enough appreciation of her concern that she realizes how long it has been since she's paid any atten-tion, really, to how he is.

She waits with him until the elevator doors open, then walks to her room alone, feeling ashamed for having fallen asleep while Carl was wait-ing for some answer, something to explain it all—the very thing she has always wanted.

When Ann gets to her room, Doris is there, and when she hears Ann enter she startles and stubs out her forbidden cigarette in the little portable ashtray she keeps in her briefcase. "Oh, hi," she says. "It's you."

On the floor at her feet is a shopping bag. "Just a couple of things you need, now that you're venturing out in the world," Doris says. The bag is stapled shut with the receipt, and when Ann looks up, she and Doris smile at one another in acknowledgment of the message, but then Ann sits on the bed and begins to cry.

"Come on," Doris says. "I know our taste isn't exactly the same, but you haven't even looked at the stuff. How far wrong could I go buying a black skirt?"

"I'm sorry, I just—" Ann shakes her head. "I spent the afternoon with Carl, and I—" She stops, licks the tears falling over her lips. "We were talking," she says, "and I fell asleep when it was my turn to say something. I don't know what's the matter with me. I've been sleeping about fourteen hours a day as it is."

"Maybe you're tired," Doris says.

"I guess." Ann puts her hands over her face, lets herself fall back on the yellow spread. Next to the bed is a shriveled flower arrangement, bearing a card that reads simply, *Get Better*. More a directive than a wish, it is signed "Visage," with none of the partners' names included, and Ann is not sure how to interpret this first communication from her office.

"Let's see," Doris says after a moment, and she takes out her pen. "June, July, August," she counts on her tan fingers. "That's say, ninety days of sleeping, what? maybe four hours a night on the outside. Take four away from the standard eight, leaves you four, right? Four times ninety gives you three hundred and sixty hours to make up." Doris's pen moves in time with her words.

"So, say you've been sleeping six more than you ordinarily need every night for the past month, that's six times thirty nights, or one hundred and eighty hours used up." A pink-smocked woman comes in with a fresh pitcher of ice water. She removes the old one and closes the door softly behind her. Ann looks back at Doris.

"Three sixty take away one eighty," Doris says and stops writing, hands the little paper with the calculations on it to Ann. "You have another month of fourteen-hour nights before you're even," she says.

The days are growing shorter. By six, the sun begins to set. Ann looks out the window at the East River. The light glitters on its surface, a fireboat travels slowly upstream. She shifts the baby from her right to her left shoulder.

When she walked into Bellevue's pediatric unit today, the duty nurse tried to help her off with her sweater, her unusual kindness implying that she had been warned of Ann's return. Perhaps the hospital is being paid to allow Ann to volunteer, just as Bergdorf's was paid to allow her to steal. It doesn't matter.

She is happy to be here, although no one would guess so from her face. She cannot keep from crying. Having not taken speed for weeks, it's as if all the drug did was prevent the tears that now flow unchecked.

The water of the East River looks unnaturally green through the hospital's tinted window, and the direction of the tide, the river's inexorable passage toward the ocean, is discernible only from the struggle of vessels moving upstream. When Ann tries to think of what she's supposed to do, of what is required to repair her marriage, her job, herself, she cannot think, her mind goes blank. That's why the routine of the pediatric ward is so soothing: she knows that here, in these hours that have been given back to her, all that is required of her is to hold these children.

As Ann walks around the nursery, tears fall down her cheeks onto the baby, plastering the downy, sparse hair to her head. Angela, the name given by the staff to the child she holds, has also been through withdrawal, from heroin her mother took while she was pregnant. Her mother died, and Angela arrived early and unprepared for life, snatched from her stuporous sleep in a place that was warm and close and dark. She goes rigid sometimes, stiff with what feels to Ann's arms like panic. Still, the baby is a miracle of sorts. She does not have AIDS or brain damage; she has gained weight, she is alert. At three months, the child has a lifetime of tests yet to pass, but so far she checks out as perfectly normal.

When it's time to settle Angela back into her crib, Ann lifts her gently from her shoulder but the baby starts awake and cries, and she holds her a little longer, brushes her lips against her warm head as she walks with her. The regulation mask has slipped down around Ann's neck, but the duty nurse hasn't asked that she put it back on.

With her mouth just touching the soft spot where the child's skull hasn't yet closed over her brain, Ann begins to sing a song, something Mariette used to sing. She gets a few of the words—something, something at twilight when the lights are low, and the something shadows softly come and go—and then she gives up and just hums the melody. She can feel the baby's heart against her chest.

Ann's voice is not loud enough to be heard by anyone else, but the baby takes note. Ann can feel her awareness: she draws in a deep breath and her head bumps up against Ann's nose. Surprised by the soft buzzing of a song against her scalp, the baby has stopped crying to listen.

D oris's little sheet of calculations is in the drawer of my bedside table. I know I cannot sleep like this forever. But for now, each night is like a deep black pool. I slip under the water's surface without disturbing its calm.

My dreams, too, are submarine, and when I look up to where the sky should be, I see the quicksilver surface of water, like an endless mirror through which I have passed.

I meet Angela's mother. She walks toward me with slow deliberation, her hair flows behind her. She is someone I have never seen before, but when her hand touches mine, I know who she is.

"Are you holding her?" she asks. I nod.

"Is she all right?" she says. I nod again.

ABOUT THE AUTHOR

KATHRYN HARRISON was educated at Stanford University and the University of Iowa Writers' Workshop. In 1989, she was awarded a James Michener fellowship. Her first novel, *Thicker Than Water*, was published in 1991. She and her husband, novelist Colin Harrison, live in Brooklyn, New York, with their two children.

A B O U T T H E T Y P E

This book was set in Photina, a typeface designed by José Mendoza in 1971. It is a very elegant design with high legibility, and its close character fit has made it a popular choice for use in quality magazines and art gallery publications.